TEMPER

Very best wishes
Bill Queen

BILL QUEEN

333 QUEENS DRIVE
NEWARK, OHIO 43055
(740) 344-1580
JQPQ@ROADRUNNER.COM

TEMPER

Temper -- Mold, Shape or Fashion,
Make stronger through hardship,
Impart toughness.

Temper -- Mood, Anger, Fury or Rage.

Cover and Book Design
Printing Arts Press Design Team

Printing
Printing Arts Press
8028 Newark Road
Box 431
Mount Vernon, Ohio
740-397-6106
www.printingartspress.com

Request for information should be addressed to:
Bill Queen
Newark, Ohio 43055
740-344-1580
JQPQ@roadrunner.com

Books by Bill Queen
The Escarpment
Valley of the Shadow
Death Follows
A Year of Fear

Printed in the United States 2009

PROLOGUE

Howie walked beside his mother, satisfied as always to be with her. The boy could feel the eyes on them as they entered the bank and approached the first teller's window. His mother was impeccably dressed and stunningly beautiful. Her hair was white blond and her skin pale and clear. Her seven-year-old son had the same hair, eyes and complexion. She was medium height and had a figure that caught the attention of every man who saw her. As the men noticed the woman, the women in the bank appraised her clothing. She wore a high collared pale blue dress that could have been silk or a similar expensive fabric. Her high-heeled shoes matched the color of her dress perfectly. Her only jewelry was a gold wedding band and a gold chain that held a sheer, white lace sweater that was draped across her shoulders. Her make-up, if she wore any, was so perfect as to be invisible.

Her son was holding his mother's hand. His attire suited an average child, horizontal striped tee shirt, Levis, and high-topped black tennis shoes.

Howie listened as she was directed by a teller to go to the desk of one of the men sitting off to one side of the lobby, a Mr. Wilson.

Howie and his mother walked to the man's desk, still hand-in-hand.

"Yes ma'am," Howie heard the man say as he stood up and came around the desk and pulled up two chairs so he and his mother could be seated. "How may I help you?"

She answered in a soft and cultured voice saying, "My name is Cornelia Lawson and I'm new in town. I'd like to make a deposit and arrange for the bank to help me with some business I will be transacting here in Newton."

As she finished speaking she placed a small suitcase on the desk, opened the snaps and lifted the lid so the man could see inside.

On the top of the contents was a plain white envelope, legal size.

The rest of the contents were bundles of cash made up in packets of bills according to different denominations. Wilson had never seen packets of five hundred and one thousand-dollar bills before, not even in the bank's own vault. The smallest bill size was fifty and there were bunches of them in the case. The woman opened the envelope on top and removed fourteen ten thousand-dollar bills. These would be the first anyone in the bank had ever seen.

Mr. Wilson closed the suitcase gently but firmly and said to the woman, "We will need to fill out some papers and this should be done in private. If you'll just come with me Mrs. Lawson, we'll go to that office up front and finish our business. Of course, bring the boy."

Without bothering to fasten the snaps, Wilson picked up the suitcase flatways, a hand under each end and headed towards the bank president's office. He walked in and placed the case on the desk of an older man.

"Mr. Allen," Wilson said, "I'd like to use your office for a few minutes to help Mrs. Lawson open an account with us." As he said this he lifted the lid on the suitcase and nodded with his head for the bank president to look inside.

If eyes could click the president's would have sounded like pool balls bumping together as his gaze snapped from the money to the woman, to the money, to the boy, to the bank officer, to the woman and finally back to the money. It was the most money he had ever seen in his life outside of his own bank vault.

"Yes, of course, William," Mr. Allen said. "That would be most appropriate." As he was speaking the bank president walked to a glass partition that separated his office from the rest of the bank and pulled a cord closing the drapes. "And who is this lovely woman and handsome young man that is going to open such a substantial account with us?"

"Excuse me," Wilson said turning to the woman. "Mrs. Lawson, this is Mr. Allen, the president of our bank. Mr. Allen, this is Mrs.

Lawson and her son, I'm sorry, I don't know his name"

"Howie," Cornelia Lawson volunteered quickly.

"How do you do, young man," Mr. Allen said, shaking hands with the lad. "Now William?" Allen continued looking at his employee.

"We are just getting ready to start the paper work on her account,"

Mr. Allen kept looking from the money to the woman as he straightened the lapels on his coat. "Yes, yes, Mrs. Lawson. I'm very pleased to meet you. Is young William here taking good care of you?" Allen said. "Business such as you are conducting is not to be taken lightly."

The woman flashed her most engaging smile at the two men and said, "Everything is just fine, so far. I would prefer to keep my business as private as possible. I would not care to have your employees making public speculations about my finances."

Wilson spoke up and said, "You can be sure all of your dealings with us will be absolutely confidential."

"That's fine," Lawson replied. "Now shall we get down to business?"

"While you two do the paperwork," Allen said, "I'll send in our most senior teller to verify the figures on Mrs. Lawson's paper in the case. Also, William, before you allow her to leave, I'd like to speak to you in private."

Allen walked out the door of the office but was soon replaced by an older, taciturn, bespectacled man who was every inch the senior bank teller. He showed no surprise at the contents of the suitcase, simply busying himself with the count and marking the figures by hand on a sheet of paper.

The paperwork on the deposit quickly completed, Wilson leaned back in the president's chair and looked at the woman and boy across from him. The papers showed her to be thirty-nine years old; although he would have guessed her to be ten years younger. She had stated that her husband had been killed two years earlier in 1944 in Europe. Now with the war over she had decided to leave New York

City and raise her son in the tranquil environment of Newton here in central Ohio. She had offered no explanation of the huge deposit of cash and Wilson had not felt it discreet to ask questions. Privately he speculated that she might have been in some type of show business. Her looks and dress made that guess more than possible.

Excusing himself, Wilson left the office and spoke briefly to Mr. Allen. Upon his return, the teller was done with the count and had found Mrs. Lawson's count to be absolutely accurate.

Now that they were alone, Wilson told Mrs. Lawson what the president had wanted. "Your deposit is the largest ever made in this bank at one time by a private individual and, as of now, you have the third largest private account in the bank," Wilson said. "Mr. Allen would like for me to offer you every assistance in getting settled here in Newton."

"Thank you very much, Mr. Wilson," Lawson said. "You see, I came here for the quiet and privacy of the small town and I wish to keep to myself and raise my son as best I can. If the bank would help me with my business affairs, I would be eternally grateful," and she rewarded young Mr. Wilson with a smile that he would remember for the rest of his life.

****

As they walked from the bank, Cornelia Lawson wondered at her ability to adjust to this new situation. It had certainly been easy to mislead the people in the bank in order to start a new life. She looked around at her new town and prayed she was doing the right thing. Her whole new life now hinged on the happiness of her son, Howie.

CHAPTER ONE

Howie, his mother and her maid had changed trains in Pittsburgh and were now almost to Columbus where they would either depart the train or purchase more tickets. This would be their last stop before arriving and Howie watched his mother looking out the window in the late afternoon sunlight. A sign in front of a large rooming house across from the depot caught her eye and she said, "Look Howie, this could be just what we're looking for," and she read it to the boy. It said 'FOR SALE by owner—Inquire Within'. She grabbed Howie's hand, her purse and a small suitcase from the seat beside her.

The large middle-aged black woman who had been sitting at her side reading a bible was startled by the sudden activity. "What is it, Miz Corny," she asked.

Cornelia grabbed a handful of paper money from her purse and thrust it at the woman and said, "Rosie, find the conductor and get them to unload our bags. Pay them whatever they want but have our luggage put in storage in the depot."

Accompanied by Howie, Cornelia got off the train. She walked directly to the rooming house and there she started another new life, her third one.

****

Cornelia sat in the front room of the apartment she had taken for herself, smoking a cigarette and reading a new novel, 'All the King's Men'. She was trying to relax and keep her mind on the book. This last month had been hectic and things were just starting to settle down. When they had left the train she had gone directly to the apartment house and inquired about a room for the three of them only to find that no children were allowed. The woman who was in charge of renting the rooms and apartments wasn't the owner so Cornelia had been unable to negotiate. They had instead left their luggage at the depot and walked two blocks up the street to the

Wilmar Hotel. There they took two connecting rooms and Cornelia started making moves that would lead to her ownership of the apartment house she had seen from the train window. It took longer than she thought and it was over two weeks before they moved in.

The house had already been furnished but she was not satisfied with used furniture so she had ordered all new accessories from a local store. It had all been delivered and now it was only a matter of arranging it to make this into their new home. She even had one of the new model television sets installed and an antenna mounted on the chimney.

Howie had started school and seemed to be getting along except for the fact he didn't like being away from his mother for hours at a time. Cornelia felt that, given a little time, he would adjust just fine.

Rosey, the housekeeper, was busy setting up the house and getting used to the trains that went past every ten minutes. At first Rosey had drawn some unfriendly looks from the other tenants because she was a black woman but when they discovered she was the maid and housekeeper for the new owner, that made her acceptable.

Cornelia had dealt through the bank in the purchase of the apartment house and everything had gone most satisfactorily. Mr. Wilson, the young vice-president, and Mr. Allen had been most helpful in assisting her with the details of the purchase. They had recommended a local attorney, Mr. Hughes, and she was well satisfied with the agreeable young man. In fact all the men she had met so far were more than a little taken with her looks and charming manner and had gone far beyond the usual in providing service. Cornelia, of course, was well aware of how to deal with men and make them feel special in her company.

There were four apartments on the first floor of the house and Cornelia had combined the two on one end for her own living quarters. The others were rented to older couples and the second floor was divided into one room sleeping apartments that were mostly rented by single men who worked for the railroad. There were bathrooms at each end of the upstairs hall for communal use. Keeping everything clean and tidy was more work than Rosey could handle on her own. Cornelia had arranged for a second woman to come in during the day, six days a week, to help out. Rosey had picked her own helper and had come up with a young black woman who could work rings around the rest of the world.

****

CHAPTER TWO

Clara Bailey had always sworn she had never seen a really bad child, believing that any student would be good with the proper motivation and guidance. Now she was not so sure. She had been teaching the first grade for more than ten years and had never run across a child like Howard Martin Lawson. He was the most repulsive child that had ever been placed in her care. When he had first been brought to her room she was taken with his physical appearance, slender and fair with blondish white hair, a boy beautiful enough to be a girl. This impression soon paled as she got to know the boy. He was selfish, mean and worst of all, demanding. He wanted his own way in every activity. She had been forced to remove him from the classroom twice in the first week because of his temper tantrums. She had to watch him every minute because he was capable of doing anything at anytime. Clara had a child of her own in the sixth grade and if he had ever behaved as Howie Lawson did, she would not have spared the rod. Clara had sent a note home with the boy two days ago requesting a meeting with his parents but she had received no response. She had assumed that the note had not been delivered. Now a trip to the boy's home would be necessary and she was not looking forward to it.

When she had arrived at the Lawson home, Clara Bailey asked that the boy be sent from the room so that she and the mother could talk more freely. Clara was surprised when the black housekeeper was summoned to take the boy into the kitchen.

The mother's name was Cornelia Lawson according to school records and she sat in a large chair with an ashtray in close attendance. She had been smoking steadily since Clara had been conducted into the room.

"Mrs. Lawson," Clara started out, "we are having a problem with your boy at school. He won't mind or follow instructions and becomes unruly every time he is corrected. We were hoping you might be able to help us control his behavior."

Cornelia studied the teacher intently and tried to get an idea of how to handle this situation. She had very little experience in dealing with women other than ordering them around and she was certain that ordering Mrs. Bailey would not be the tact to take. She proceeded cautiously.

"As you know," Cornelia said, "we are new in town and Howie is having a little trouble adjusting to Newton after living in New York City. As a matter of fact I'm having trouble of my own with the sudden change of pace. We have always lived in the middle of the city and all of this open space is unusual to us."

Cornelia paused after saying this and watched the teacher carefully to see if her opening statement was acceptable.

Mrs. Bailey knew they were new in town and was studying Cornelia just as intently as she knew she was being apprised. Without a doubt Howie's mother was the most beautiful woman Clara Bailey had ever seen and she, like many others, wondered if Cornelia had ever been in show business, maybe even the movies. Her clothing and make-up were absolutely perfect and so far, except for smoking, her manners were impeccable. Even as Clara thought this, Cornelia asked her if she would care for something cold to drink and when Clara replied in the affirmative, Cornelia called to the housekeeper to bring them lemonade. Almost immediately a tray with a large pitcher and two glasses full of ice was placed on a table between them. Cornelia poured and they continued to talk.

"I wouldn't have come to your home if I hadn't been really concerned for young Howie," Clara said. "I'm sure you want your son to get off on the right track and I want you to know I am willing to work with you in any way I can."

Cornelia leaned forward in her chair, her deep blue eyes shining as she answered. "I certainly appreciate that Mrs. Bailey. Just what do you suggest?"

Through the open kitchen door Clara Bailey could see the

subject of their conversation was sitting calmly at the kitchen table eating a devil dog cake and drinking a Nehi cream soda, his favorite snack. He seemed oblivious to the woman in the front room but the housekeeper, standing close behind the kitchen door, was hanging onto every word. As the teacher continued talking, Rosey turned from the doorway and looked curiously at the boy as he ate his snack.

Soon the conversation between Cornelia and Mrs. Bailey was finished and the teacher left with the assurance that Cornelia would do all she could to help with the boy's discipline problem. It was only after Clara had gotten into her car and was driving away that she noticed that no mention had been made of any Mr. Lawson. She made a mental note to check the school records to get more information on this gentleman.

****

After the teacher departed, Cornelia went into the kitchen and sat down at the table with Howie and said, "How do you like your teacher?"

He looked up with chocolate cake around his mouth and said, "She's okay but she makes me do things that I don't want to do. She makes me stay in my seat and not walk around and she won't let me talk when I want to and lots of things."

His speech became more rapid the longer he talked.

"Well, son, you're just going to have to start doing what Mrs. Bailey says when you're in school. If you don't, you are going to get in trouble with your teacher and she will be even harder on you. Will you try to be good and do as she says, just for me?"

Howie looked at her and smiled such a beautiful smile that she could almost feel her heart melt as he said, "Sure, mama, I'll try and be better. Now can I go and play?"

When she consented, he was out the door in a flash.

Rosey sat down at the table and started sweeping up cake crumbs with her hands. "Is there anything I can do, Miz Corny?" she asked.

"I don't know," Cornelia replied. "I guess I'm going to have to take more time for the boy and help him adjust. That's probably all it is with him, adjusting to the move and the new house and all. He'll be okay after he gets used to being here." At this point she gave Rosey a look that was almost pleading as she said, "and until then we'll just have to look after him as best we can."

Rosey, being a long way from New York where she had been given some good advice, got up from the table and started fixing supper. She didn't believe a little extra attention for the boy would solve the problem but kept her opinion to herself.

****

Howie, after escaping from the house, headed into the downtown area of Newton, Ohio. Howie had never known such freedom. In the city when he had gone outside, he had always stayed close around the house because he had been shy of the other children and not really interested in associating with them. Being alone in the carriage house out back and playing private games had been enough for him. Now, as he became more familiar with the area, he was going further out on every excursion.

He had found the railroad tracks to be a fascinating place and by following them had discovered rivers and forests. He had a child's natural curiosity and was not afraid to be alone; in fact he preferred being alone.

One thing he had not come to terms with as yet was darkness. He made it a point to be within sight of home before the streetlights came on.

For his age and experience he was remarkably self-reliant. Because of the time of year, numerous gardens were available to be raided for a quick snack and apple trees were everywhere. Not that he was particularly fond of fruits and vegetables, it was just that they were there for the taking and he helped himself. The fact that they might belong to someone who would object to his pillage never crossed his mind.

The downtown area of Newton also held a fascination and he was learning his way around all the streets and alley in the center of town. There were different kinds of treasures to be found in this area but so far he had only been looking without touching any of them. The entire town and its' surroundings had become his giant playground and he was not a bit interested in swings and merry-go-rounds that so interested his peers.

Howie discovered that railroads went everywhere in Newton and every major business in every area of town had its' own spur line. By following the tracks there was no limit to where he could go.

Howie scampered up a fire escape at the rear of the five and ten-cent store in the middle of downtown and walked across the roof to a spot where he could look down on the street. He watched the people, still surprised at how few ever looked up and saw him staring down at them. Those that did see him always ignored his presence. The act of seeing without being seen satisfied him in a way he could never explain. Although the building was only three stories high, it was still higher than most of the surrounding structures and it made Howie feel important.

From the top of the building Howie could see that the city was completely surrounded by hills. He could also see the routes of the rivers and railroads through town by following the tree lines near the rivers and the telephone poles along the railroads.

The relatively slow pace of the town and traffic allowed Howie to study everything in detail. He knew when the busses came and went, where they stopped and what one to use to go to the edge of town. When he did this it was always with the intention of walking home, learning more about the city every step of the way.

After half an hour on the roof, Howie came down and ran south to the railroad tracks that led to a trestle not far from town. Few trains ran along this spur line and Howie liked to sit on the huge blocks of stone that supported each end of the railroad bridge. From this vantage point he watched the fish swimming in the water of the river that ran beneath the bridge and he could also relax and think.

Today, as he leaned back against the cool stones, he allowed his mind to skip back to what his mother had said about the teacher. He understood he could not avoid school and there were some things about it he even liked. Learning to read fascinated him and he did enjoy books. His mother had read to him ever since he could remember and now he was going to be able to do it for himself. Although he didn't look forward to it, maybe he was going to need to go along with what that old Miss Bailey wanted him to do.

Howie looked at the sun starting to dip towards the treetops and started his walk for home. Ah well, he thought, it might not be so bad. With all the other freedoms he had school was just a minor inconvenience.

While walking along the tracks it had become his habit to pick up the fist sized pieces of limestone ripp-rapp that supported the railroad ties and throw them at whatever targets he could see. Today he could find nothing more interesting than tree trunks or cans to practice throwing at.

Thirty minutes later just as the shadows started to get long, Howie arrived at home and settled down in front of the television set.

Cornelia came into the room, sat down next to her son and put her arm around his shoulders.

"Did you think anymore about what your teacher said when she was here today?" Cornelia asked Howie.

"Yeah," Howie answered. "I thought about it while I was walking and I'm gonna' try harder to get along with old lady Bailey."

"Oh Howie," Cornelia said, "you don't know how happy that makes me. It's good to see you act so grown up. I know it's been hard on you coming to a new town surrounded by strangers except for Rosey and me."

"It's okay, mother," he said. "I like it here pretty good and I'm getting so I can find my way around to the stores and all. It's just that when I'm at school they make me do so many things that I don't want to do."

"Well, tomorrow is Saturday and there won't be any school so you can go shopping with me, how about that?"

"What will we be shopping for?" Howie asked.

"Do you remember that little car we had back in the city?" When Howie nodded his assent his mother went on. "Here in Newton we really need a car more than we did in the city so I'm going to go buy one. What kind do you think we ought to get?"

Howie never hesitated as he said, "Get a Buick, mama. Get the biggest one they got in this whole town. Will you, mama, will you?"

"If that's what you want, that's what we'll get," Cornelia said. "Anything to make my baby happy," and they hugged each other and laughed.

CHAPTER THREE

When Cornelia had bought her first car in Newton she needed a place to keep it so she had built a row of connected garages at the rear of the apartment house. She had one for her car, one for storage and had rented out the others so they could pay for themselves.

She had so enjoyed driving a new car that she had continued to get a new model every year and now, in the middle of summer in 1948, her new Buick Roadmaster had just been delivered. It had cost nearly three thousand dollars.

Howie was now going into the third grade and had been getting along with his teachers the past year better than he had with Clara Bailey. Cornelia believed it had been the transition of moving that had caused the problem but now Howie was getting along just fine.

Howie was nine years old and his joy in life was wandering the town of Newton and the surrounding countryside with one slight change.

Early in the summer, Howie had started out early one morning picking up his breakfast as he walked. He had grabbed a quart of milk from the porch of a house partially hidden by high hedges and a box of donuts pilfered from the back of an Omar delivery truck while the driver was in a nearby house.

He ate the donuts and drank the milk in the shade of a large poplar tree along the creek bank. He had three new comic books in his pocket and it was an hour before he finished them and started to wander. Walking along the railroad tracks he gathered up about twenty chunks of limestone and put them in his pockets, ammunition to be used on any animals he might encounter. Coming down from the tracks, Howie entered an alley that led back towards the downtown.

A dog that peeked around the corner of the garage looked like a good target for Howie's rocks but almost as soon as he had thrown the first one, he discovered it was a mistake. The dog was considerable larger than Howie had first supposed and instead of running away began barking, growling and then came charging at its' tormentor. Howie had no recourse but to retreat to the top of a nearby car, an old Model-A Ford. The commotion drew the attention of an old man who came out of a nearby garage and after chasing off the dog with his cane; he noticed Howie on top of the car and chased him away also.

Seeing the cane had given Howie the idea of carrying a stick of his own while on his travels around town. Now he had an accumulation standing in the corner of his back porch to choose from whenever he went out.

Howie had found the sticks to be good for other things besides the persecution of animals. Glass railroad signals, lights on autos, front or rear, and the windows in abandoned buildings were fair game. Fences, shrubs and trash cans had to take their licks and woe be to any cat that was not quick enough to avoid the first strike for it would surely be beaten to death. Other children were immune from his predatory actions as they tended to be in groups and he avoided them as much as possible.

Howie had learned the downtown as well as the fields and forests surrounding Newton. He could go over rooftops, into basements or through abandoned buildings as quick as an animal. He went almost anywhere he pleased except after dark.

Saturdays were always good for Howie. He was up and moving long before his mother was out of bed. He started roaming the downtown business area, watching and waiting for something of interest to occur and it always did. Accidents, fights, fires, flat tires were all the same to him. He wandered in and out of the stores, up and down alleys and over rooftops and into basements, always on the prowl, looking and listening. He had learned that drunks slept in unlocked cars on the car lots and under the locked ones. The lofts of most empty buildings were havens for pigeons and when he struck one with a stick, it would virtually explode into a cloud of feathers and blood.

Every theatre in town had loose fire escape doors and Howie went in and out at will. Magazine stands that displayed their wares on the sidewalks were at his mercy and he helped himself. The milk, bread and pastries that were left on the front porches of homes served as his source for snacks. Candy was available at the grocery stores and drug stores but he was less apt to go to the drug stores because there were fewer customers and the clerks offered individual service and watched the customers much closer. Sporting events were less attractive because they generally took place after dark.

In the woods he was equally at home and would sit quietly under a tree not really looking, just waiting for some movement to catch his eye. He often saw other children playing and sometimes followed at a distance, once again satisfied with the sensation of seeing without being seen. He walked as far out of town as the drive-in theatres but never stayed for the shows. They began after dark.

If he was unable to find any snacks he could steal, he would go to a bakery and buy day old cookies and sweet rolls for just a few cents. His mother always made sure he had money in his pockets. After making a purchase, he would continue to roam eating from his sack of goodies. But even at this young age he went alone, always alone.

Howie had discovered a new use for the stick he carried. Most of the traffic lights away from the downtown had a switch box on a nearby power pole and he found that by reaching up and hooking the lever he could turn the lights off. This would sometimes cause an accident but generally just a traffic jam would develop that would require the police to come and straighten it out. He enjoyed this diversion when there was nothing better to do. If there was anything to get into, Howie would find it.

Now, in the mid-morning, Howie stood on the railroad trestle looking down through the ties at the water. There was another boy about his own age sitting at the river's edge, fishing. The fact that the boy was black didn't really register with Howie because race had never been a factor in his environment. He had a box of powered sugar donuts under his arm that he had stolen from the front porch of a house on a side street. The Omar man would have difficulties collecting from the resident who would swear he had never received them.

The boy had looked up at Howie and had then gone back to his fishing. It was a beautiful summer day with a soft breeze blowing out of the south and making a gentle ripple on the water's surface. Howie crossed the trestle to the fisherman's side and, using his stick as a staff walked down the steep bank to the water's edge. The two boys just looked at each other for a few minutes without speaking.

Howie broke the silence by saying, "You want a donut?" and held out the box. There were eight left out of the original baker's dozen.

The other boy got up from the ground and took one and began eating. He didn't say anything and sat back down next to where his fishing pole was propped up on a forked stick. Howie sat down on the ground with the pole between them.

"What are you doing?" Howie asked.

"Fishin'", the boy said watching his pole and not looking at Howie.

"What's that?" Howie asked.

"Trying to catch fish," the boy said. "Ain't you never gone fishing?"

Howie shook his head solemnly and slowly before answering. "No, I never did."

"You want me to show you how?" the boy asked.

"Have another donut," Howie said as he thought about the proposition. He wasn't going to rush into anything but he was curious. After a few more minutes of thought he said, "Okay, I guess you can show me about it."

The boy picked up his rod and started to reel in his line as he looked over at Howie. Then he began explaining about hooks and sinkers and worms and fish and all the things he knew about fishing.

Howie was intrigued mostly because it was the first time in his life he ever had a conversation with a child of his own age.

The bait was cast back into the water and the boys sat quietly finishing off the donuts. A train passed overhead and Howie asked if it scared off the fish and the other boy said, "I don't think so. The fish get used to it just like people do."

About this time the rod started to twitch and the boy picked it up and started the procedure that would soon have a fat catfish flopping on the bank. He showed Howie about the spines on the fins and how to hold the fish to take it off the hook. Then he pulled a cord up out of the water and Howie was surprised to see several other catfish stacked on this second line.

"What are you gonna' do with those?" Howie asked indicating the fish.

"I take them home and my mama cleans them up and we eat them for supper," the boy said.

It took Howie a few more minutes to have the boy explain how they turned these slippery flopping creatures into food. The only food Howie had ever seen in his whole life came in a sack from the grocery store.

"If I get a fishin' pole, could I come and fish with you?" Howie asked.

"Sure," the boy said. "Anybody can fish anytime they want. I come here when schools out and sometimes I fish all day and all night."

This gave Howie something new to think about. The all night part would take a lot of thought and his first impression was that he could get by just fine without that.

"Are you gonna' be here tomorrow?" Howie asked.

"Yeah," was the reply.

"So if I get a fishing pole and the other stuff and come back tomorrow, we can fish?" Howie said.

"Yeah," the boy said, "and you can bring some more donuts if you want'a."

"Okay, I'll be here in the morning," Howie said as he jumped to his feet and headed up the riverbank headed for home.

Cornelia accepted his request with the usual equanimity that she applied to life in general. She assented to buy him some fishing equipment and they walked the short distance to the downtown stores and was mildly surprised when he could lead her to exactly the right department in the correct store to find what they were looking for. A small metal box with a latch on the front and the accessories to go in it were purchased along with a decent rod and reel. When he had explained how he had come to be interested in fishing, Cornelia was encouraged that this would help with the boy's usually sullen disposition. The idea of Howie making a friend was comforting.

The next morning Howie was on the go even earlier than usual and he left home with his hands full. Along with his fishing tackle he had a large sack of food for the boys to enjoy. He also carried his usual stick and, along the way, he added two pints of milk to the sack of food.

As early as he was, the other boy was already there and had two fish on his stringer. The boys set about putting Howie's equipment together and soon they relaxed in the morning sun and waited for the fish to come.

"What's your name?" Howie asked.

"Jess," the boy said. "What's yours?"

"Mine's Howie and there's lots of food in that sack and you can have some if you want."

Jess looked into the sack and found a regular feast, two apples, two oranges, a dozen chocolate cookies and a half dozen pieces of cold fried chicken. Rosey had fixed it up just fine knowing well what boys liked. They ate the cookies and drank the milk first and then Howie got a bite on his line and he caught his first fish. At that particular moment he was as happy as he had ever been in his whole life.

As they sat and continued to fish, Jess asked, "What for you carry that stick with you all the time?"

"Oh, just to whack things with," Howie replied.

"What do you whack?" Jess asked.

"Just things like dogs and cats and bottles and cars and stuff," Howie answered. "Things I wanta' whack, I whack."

The stick in question was Howie's best. He had found it along the riverbank earlier that summer. It had been rolled in the water and bleached by the sun and was about four feet long. It was as strong as a piece of pipe and not as heavy. The stick was as smooth as marble along its' entire length and was the best whacking stick Howie had ever found. Two cats, one dog and innumerable pigeons had succumbed to its' strength. Howie picked it up and swung it hard down on the ground once, twice, three times with a force that startled Jess.

"Whack, Whack," Howie said as he swung his stick. "I like to whack things with it."

CHAPTER FOUR

The two boys began prowling the streets together when they didn't feel like fishing and the way Jess had taught Howie to fish, now Howie instructed his new friend. Jess was sometimes frightened by the things he saw Howie do but in time had learned to accept the behavior and even started to participate in most of the escapades. One thing Jess would not do was whack things and when Howie caught a cat or dog where it was at his mercy, Jess backed away. Killing helpless animals didn't seem right to him.

Howie also found a drawback. When he went into stores and Jess was with him the clerks always watched them closer than when Howie went in alone. Howie had made it a practice of getting money from his mother whenever he went out so that if they couldn't steal something they wanted they could always break down and pay for it.

Howie was never selfish towards Jess and shared everything he had with his first and only friend. Another thing was Howie's complete lack of prejudice. He had never been exposed to such emotions in his life and did not even realize that he and Jess were different in any way. When he had brought Jess home with him for the first time, the only person who was surprised that Howie's friend was black was Rosey and she felt inside that Jess was running in bad company.

This year Howie would be going into the fourth grade and Jess into the third, but the one year difference in their ages didn't matter to the boys. They spent most of their time together, fishing and fooling around.

****

It was about six o'clock in the evening and Howie and Jess sat at their usual spot under the trestle. The fishing rods rested on the obligatory forked sticks with the lines running out towards midstream. They had not had much luck and Jess had only two catfish on his stringer and Howie had not caught anything. They leaned back on their elbows so they could relax but still see the tips on their fishing poles waiting for some type of action. They heard a rattle of gravel behind them and looked back to see an old man descending towards them.

He was wearing stained and dirty pants that were at least two sizes to big and an equally mussed and dirty dress shirt buttoned right to the top. He had on a blue pinstriped double-breasted suit coat that was frayed and torn on a number of places. His hair was shaggy and he badly needed a shave. Medium height and skinny, his tanned, craggy face never the less exuded a sense of danger.

Both boys knew that a regular hobo camp existed over near the edge of town not far from the main line of the railroad but neither boy had seen any of the bums over here along the small branch line. They got to their feet as the old man approached.

"I seen you boys fishing," the old man said in a raspy voice. "You catchin' anything?"

Jess replied reluctantly, looking down as he said, "We caught a couple small ones but there's not much happening today."

"How about you, boy?" the man said directing this last question to Howie.

Howie just looked defiantly at the old man but didn't answer. He recognized this type of individual from growing up in the city and he wanted nothing to do with a conversation. He knew it could only lead to trouble.

"You boys got anything to eat with you?" the man asked. "I ain't 'et all day and I'm getting' kind of hungry."

Howie stared at the man and said, "No, we don't. We had some sandwiches but we ate them a while ago. There ain't nothing left."

The man took a couple of steps forward and stared down at Howie's fair features, his face turning mean. "You boys got any money," he demanded.

When he said this Howie backed up a few steps but Jess held his ground looking down at the fishing poles that lay near his feet. He could not bring himself to abandon the equipment.

The old man immediately spotted the reason for his concern and bent down to pick up Jess's pole and reeled in the line. "Com'mere boy," he said to Jess, "and I'll show you how to catch some fish."

Jess reached out for his pole and suddenly found his arm caught in a painful grasp close to his shoulder. "You too, boy," the bum said to Howie. "I want to talk to both of you."

Jess was jerking around trying to get loose but his struggles were ineffective. "RUN HOWIE!" Jess yelled waving his free arm and kicking his feet. When one of his toes connected with the old man's shinbone he received a smashing blow along the side of the face and he was stunned to immobility.

Seeing the blow struck, Howie turned and fled along the creek bank. When he made it to the tracks he kept going without a backward glance.

Howie heard the old man yell after him, "Go ahead and run. I was gonna' have me a sweet little chicken but now I guess I'll just have some dark meat." Then the old hobo laughed loud and long and the sound almost covered Jess's screaming.

Howie ran all the way home and came crashing in the back door so out of breath it took Rosey and his mother several minutes to get the story out of him. It took another ten minutes before the police responded and picked up Cornelia and Howie on their way to the trestle. As they approached, driving along a street that paralleled the railroad they saw Jess walking along the tracks and called him over to the police cruiser.

"What happened?" the older policeman who was not driving asked Jess.

"Nothin' happened, he let me go," Jess replied, his face streaked with tears and his left eye starting to swell.

"It's okay kid," the other policeman said, "you can tell us."

"Nothin' happened, I just wanna' go home." Jess said looking at the ground as he talked. Then he turned and started back for the tracks and his route to home. Howie ran after him, caught up and walked at his side.

The two policemen looked at each other and shrugged, the driver saying to Cornelia, "We'll be glad to give you a ride back home. It looks like the boys just got scared and they're okay now."

"No thanks, officer," Cornelia said. "I'll just catch the boys and walk back with them," and she headed for the tracks and the two small retreating figures.

****

As the policemen got back in the car, the driver looked at his partner and said, "Man, did you see that? She's got to be the best looking woman I ever seen."

The second officer agreed adding a ribald remark and watched her catch the two boys and start walking between them, her arms around the small sets of shoulders.

Neither officer gave a second thought to the story about the boys and the old hobo.

****

All the way home Howie kept asking Jess what had happened but Jess wouldn't say a word. He kept walking with his head down and ignoring all of Howie's questions and when they reached the apartment house he kept right on walking and would not even come in for a snack.

It wasn't until he was in bed that night that Howie remembered his fishing pole. He decided to go look for it in the morning but he would take either his mother or Rosey with him.

After eating breakfast the next morning, Howie decided to go back to the riverbank alone. He knew the area well enough to be able to sneak up and see if the poles were still there without anyone seeing him. If the poles were there, he would just grab them and run.

All of Howie's senses were on full alert as he walked the mile and a half to the scene of yesterday's disaster. When he was sure that the area was deserted, Howie walked to the middle of the trestle and looked down through the ties to see if the poles were where he and

Jess had left them.

The only thing that appeared to remain was his walking stick, its' white outline clearly visible from a distance. After a few minutes hesitation to get up his courage, Howie dashed down the bank, grabbed his stick and then ran back to the middle of the trestle. Looking both ways, he saw a figure approaching from the direction of town and in another few minutes saw that it was Jess.

As soon as they were close enough to speak, Jess said, "I was at your house and Rosey told me you were gone. I came to see if the poles were still there."

"They're not," Howie said. "I got my stick back but the poles are gone. You suppose the old bum stole them?"

"I don't know," Jess answered. "When he let me go I just ran as fast as I could and I didn't look back for no fishin' poles."

"What did the old man do?" Howie asked. "Did he hurt you?"

Jess looked down for a second before turning and starting back for town as he said, "Nothin', he didn't do nothin' to me," but once again his eyes got large and tears appeared in them.

Howie was hitting weeds along the tracks as they walked and wishing it was the old hobo he was whacking. Whack, whack, the leaves and dust flew from the foliage. WHACK, he wished he had a dog or cat to hit. WHACK, he wished he could hit the old man over his dirty head and see how he would like it. WHACK, WHACK, WHACK, every swing becoming more intense until Howie was sweat covered and nearing exhaustion. Jess watched in awe until Howie finally slowed back to normal.

As Howie paused, Jess said, "I'm gonna' tell my mama that I left my fishing pole at your house last night and somebody stole it. I ain't gonna' tell her anything about the old bum."

"Let's go talk to my mother first," Howie said. "She might have a way to get things straightened out."

Cornelia solved the problem immediately. She took the two boys straight to the place where she had originally bought Howie's equipment and bought the boys new fishing outfits with all of the accessories. Jess wasn't sure it was right for him to receive such an expensive gift but it did solve a number of problems so he humbly accepted.

That same afternoon Jess and Howie sat on the back steps of the apartment house and tried to decide what to do. They didn't want to go fishing for fear that the old hobo might show up. Howie was sitting on the bottom step tapping his stick on the ground and Jess was on the top step.

"I'd like to find that old man," Howie said. "I'd whack him one he never would forget," and he brought his stick full force down on the ground, Whack.

Howie studied Jess for a few more seconds before his face broke into a grin and he said, "We could sneak up on him the same way he sneaked up on us and then we could whack him before he even knew what was happening."

"I don't wanna'," Jess said.

Howie stood up and walked to the corner of the porch where he kept his accumulation of sticks and picked out a good one. He handed it to Jess and said, "Here, take this and if we see him again we can both give him a good whack and make him leave us alone."

Jess reluctantly accepted the stick, got up and followed Howie out of the yard.

Howie knew exactly where he was going, the hobo campsite over near the main railroad line. He had crept up on this place many times, seeing without being seen and watching the bums sleeping and cooking around a small fire that was always burning in the clearing. It wasn't long before he had led Jess to a spot where they could study the clearing and see who was there.

There was no fire burning in the clearing this day but there were several large pieces of cardboard scattered around the edge. Lack of rain for the last few days left everything dry and clean looking. As near as the boys could tell there was only one man sleeping on one of the sheets but his feet were towards them and they could not make out his face.

Howie put his lips right up against Jess's ear and whispered, "Stay here and keep a lookout. I'm going to go around to the other side and see if that's the same old bum."

Jess grabbed Howie's forearm and shook his head violently but Howie just pulled away and started through the underbrush. Howie was gone so quickly and Jess could only stare in amazement after his friend. Howie moved quietly as he crept up on the sleeping man. There was no sound what so ever.

In less than a minute Howie had retraced his step and once again whispered to Jess, "It's him, it's the same old bum that we saw at the trestle."

"How'd you do that?" Jess asked. "I could never move so quietly."

Howie ignored the question, just remained hunched down as he stared away from Jess towards the old man.

"What are we gonna' do now?" Jess whispered.

Howie looked back at him and Jess saw a strange light shining deep in his blue eyes. Jess had never seen madness before but he was looking at it now.

"Whack, whack, whack," Howie whispered before he started back around the clearing, his stick held tight in both hands.

****

I'm scared, Jess tried to say but the words wouldn't come out. Icy water began running down his face and chest and he could hardly breathe. He knew what was going to happen but was unable to avert his eyes. He had seen it many times with animals and he knew the fate of the old man. In spite of what the old man had done, Jess wanted to stop things but there was no way without putting Howie in terrible danger.

****

Howie got to the old man without waking him and raised his stick. He never hesitated, even an instant, and brought the heavy stick down on the man's head. The weapon mashed wide and deep into the side of his head just over his ear. Almost before he had time to bleed, Howie brought the stick down again and again, mashing the head into a bloody mass. The body jerked and twitched a couple of times but Howie had done his work well.

Jess had not moved from his hiding place in the weeds but when Howie called for him to come and see, it was all he could do just to get to his feet and start back the way they had come. Jess had already seen much more than he wanted and after walking a few steps he fell to his hands and knees and vomited until he was so weak he could hardly get back to his feet.

Howie and Jess walked away from the hobo camp and headed back for their fishing spot on the river. There was no old man to fear anymore. When they got there Howie took off his clothes and rinsed them in the water and at the same time washed the blood and other goo from his face, hair, hands and arms. He was wearing blue jeans and a horizontally striped tee shirt along with black, high topped tennis shoes. After rinsing in the cold water, the blood was not very noticeable. Howie sat on the bank in his Fruit-of-the-Loom briefs and waited for things to dry out. He had his stick at his side and had washed it down as best he could.

"We fixed that old shit-ass," Howie said. Those were the strongest swear words he knew. "WHACK, WHACK," he said while he accompanied himself by beating the stick on the ground. "Now we can fish whenever we want and that old shit won't be around to bother us anymore."

"What if somebody finds out?" Jess said. "We could get into a lot of trouble for what we did."

"Who'll ever know?" Howie said looking straight at Jess. "Nobody would ever think we could whack some old man like that. Just you and me know and we sure ain't gonna' tell. I mean, you ain't gonna' tell anyone, are you?"

Jess felt a chill run throughout him and felt the intense scrutiny of his friend. "Sure, no, I ain't going to say nothing to nobody."

****

Nothing in the world could have made Jess tell anything about Howard Martin Lawson, age ten of Newton, Ohio.

CHAPTER FIVE

Cornelia felt that her life in Newton had only been adequate at best. She missed the city with its' high class stores and exciting night life. All the magazines she had delivered showed the latest fashions and what was new on Broadway. Her main pastime was seeing every decent movie that came to town but this was only good for a very few hours each week.

This particular day she sat in the front room, smoking and looking out the window when she heard the phone ring and Rosey answer it.

"Miz Corny," Rosey shouted, "come to the phone quick. It's Mister Martin calling from New York."

Cornelia got up, straightening her dress and brushing her hair with her hands before answering the phone.

"Oh Martin," she said into the phone, "I'm so glad you called. Is everything all right?"

"Everything is fine here," he answered. "I just got to thinking about you over the weekend and how much I missed you. I guessed you would be home on a Monday morning. How is everybody there?"

"Rosey and Howie are fine," she said, "and I'm okay except that I get a little bored once in a while. There's not a lot to do here and I miss Broadway and the shows with all of the big names. It has been good for Howie though. He'll be in the fourth grade this year and he's doing a lot better in school. I told you it was hard on him at first but he's made friends and doing fine now."

"I'm glad to hear that," Martin replied. "One of the reasons I called was to ask you what you wanted to do with the car you left here in the carriage house out back. I drive it once in a while just to keep it running but if you don't have any use for it I was going to sell it and use the space for storage. What do you think?"

"Well, I've been teaching Rosey to drive and if there was some way to get it here to Newton we could give it to her. Do you think you could arrange to get it shipped to Ohio? Of course I'd pay for the shipping."

Martin was quiet for a few seconds and when he answered he said, "How about me driving it out there for you? I could get away for a few days and after I delivered the car to you I could just take the train back home."

"Oh, Marty, could you do that, would you do that?" Cornelia said, so excited she could hardly talk. "Would you come and see me so we could talk and talk and talk and you could tell me about the city and..." she ran out of breath leaving herself speechless.

Martin was not immune to the excitement in her voice and he was very flattered that she wanted to see him so badly.

"Okay, we got a deal," he said, "but you need to tell me where you're at. I don't have any idea where Ohio is let alone how to find you when I get there."

"Hold on for just a minute," Cornelia said as she dropped the phone and ran to Howie's room for a big Atlas he used in school. She was back in a flash and flipped through the pages finding the information she needed. It took her more that half an hour to explain how to get to Newton and when she was done Martin had covered three pages with notes to help him make the trip.

When he finished writing, Martin said, "This is Monday and if everything goes right I'll leave on Thursday morning. I want to get the car checked out before I leave. That would mean I would probably get there sometime Friday afternoon. I'll just call you when I get to town and you can come and meet me and escort me to your place."

"Oh, that would be just wonderful," she said. "I can hardly wait until you get here."

When Cornelia finally got off the phone she rushed into the kitchen and hugged Rosey saying, "Martin is coming for a visit. "Oh Rosey, isn't that just wonderful?!"

"Lord yes, Miz Corny," Rosey answered. "It will sure be good to see Mister Martin again. When will he be here?"

"He's leaving New York on Thursday and he'll be here on Friday," Cornelia said. "Oh my goodness, I'm so excited I can hardly wait."

Cornelia was laughing and dancing around the kitchen in a way Rosey could never remember her doing and it was only then that it occurred to Rosey what a lonely life Cornelia had been living.

****

It wasn't until later that afternoon that Rosey wondered how Howie would react to Cornelia paying attention to someone else. Maybe the boy would behave, he had been more reserved since the hobo had scared him and Jess a couple of weeks ago.

****

Howie arrived home that evening just before dark. He and Jess parted company as Jess headed for home. Howie placed his good white stick against the porch rail and came in for supper. Later he, his mother and Rosie were sitting around the table eating when Cornelia spoke up.

"Howie, we're going to have company," she said. "Do you remember Martin Fields who lived in the same building as we did back in New York? Well, he's going to come and visit the end of the week," and she went on to explain how he was going to bring the car and then stay for a few days.

Howie listened intently as she spoke picking up immediately on her excitement and animation. When she finished speaking he said, "I kinda' remember him but not much. How long did you say he'd be here?"

"I don't know exactly," his mother said. "Four or five days I suppose."

Rosey was watching Howie intently as the conversation was taking place and she tried to read his attitude towards the news but she couldn't tell for sure how he responded. Howie just finished his meal and walked into the front room to watch television where Gorgeous George was parading around the wrestling ring. Howie was very quiet, obviously thinking over what he had been told.

The next morning at breakfast Howie ate in silence as his mother sat across from him working on a list of things to do in preparation for Martin's visit. Rosey was making out a shopping list so all of their meals could be taken at home instead on wasting time chasing around to the mediocre restaurants in Newton. Jess knocked on the back door and came in for cookies and milk while Howie finished eating.

"Me and Jess are gonna' go play," Howie said heading for the back door.

"Have fun and be careful," Cornelia replied absently without looking up from her notes.

Howie picked up his stick from the back porch and started walking towards the railroad tracks. His mother's inattention that morning had unsettled him and he was working towards a very sullen mood.

WHACK! He tossed a stone in the air and swung his stick like a baseball bat knocking it flying down the tracks. Whack! Whack! Two more went sailing. Jess recognized his temper and walked off to the side well clear of the swinging stick and large stones.

" I don't know why we have to have company come from out of town?" Howie said venomously. "We don't need some old guy comin' to visit."

"What are you talkin' about, Howie?" Jess asked. "What old guy?"

"My mom says some guy from New York she knows is comin' to our house in a couple of days and is gonna' stay for a while and I just don't like it, that's all."

Whack—Whack—he swung the stick downward, knocking the branches from a small tree along the tracks.

"Ain't nothing you can do about it, is there?" Jess asked.

"I guess not," Howie answered. "At least not now anyways."

"Then let's go to the show this afternoon," Jess said wanting to change the subject and get Howie away from this mood of violence. "Gene Autry and the Bowery Boys are on at the Annex and I got some money. What da'ya say, wanta' go?"

"Yeah, I guess," Howie answered. "I like them all pretty good."

The two boys had walked as far as the railroad trestle and as they crossed they looked down and saw some teen-age boys fishing in their usual spot.

Although they had no equipment and had not intended to fish, Howie being in a mood yelled down and said, "What are you guys doin' fishing in our place? Get out of there!"

The boys were several years older than Howie and Jess and one of them yelled back, "Go to hell, kid. You can't make us."

Howie was standing on the trestle and looking straight down at the boys and it only took him a second before he had opened the front of his pants and started urinating right down on them.

Within seconds the three boys under the trestle were on their way up the bank and Howie and Jess were running as fast as they could along the tracks and back towards town. Behind them they could hear the threats from the badly outdistanced pursuers but their head start would allow them to reach the safety of their hiding places downtown.

Howie led the way to the rear of a vacant building and he and Jess ducked quickly inside. Howie was laughing like crazy and soon his humor had affected Jess so that both were rolling on the floor in near convulsions.

"Piss on them, piss on them," Howie would chant and they would start laughing all over again.

When they had settled down Howie pulled several wadded up dollar bills from his pocket and turned to Jess saying, "Let's go get some candy."

Watching carefully for their potential assailants, they went to the nearest drug store and spent almost fifteen minutes at the candy counter picking out what they wanted.

A short time later as they sat on a park bench eating candy Jess asked, "What time does the show start?"

"One o'clock, I already told ya'," Howie replied impatiently.

Jess looked up at the clock in the steeple of the courthouse in the middle of downtown and saw it was nearly eleven o'clock. "Let's go play some pool 'til it's time to go to the show."

"Okay, let's go," Howie said getting up from the wrought iron park bench and leading the way to the alley where the poolroom was located.

The large sign in the front window listed the house rules and ended by stating that ABSOLUTELY NO ONE UNDER 18 ALLOWED. The boys had found that if the place wasn't crowded and they behaved themselves the owner would overlook this rule as long as they had the nickels to pay for the games they played. On this occasion they were the only customers in the place. With the loser paying it cost Howie five nickels for five games and after about an hour he was ready to move on.

They walked through a couple of grocery stores and Howie soon had an apple in one sock and an orange in the other. He also had two bottles of warm soda in the front of his pants. He and Jess found a large box in an alley at the rear of a furniture store and crawled inside to share the fruit and cola.

"Oh-oh, look who's coming," Jess said scooting deeper into the refrigerator box that was lying on its' side.

Howie saw the three boys from the trestle walking down the alley towards their hiding place. His stick was beside him and he grabbed it but the box was not big enough for him to do anything more than hold it in his hand. "Be quiet," he whispered unnecessarily.

Sure enough the older boys walked right past the boxes never suspecting their prey was there. As soon as it was safe, Howie and Jess crawled out of and headed for the movie.

It cost sixteen cents to get into the theater and there were not many there for a Tuesday afternoon. Howie and Jess took seats about ten rows back in the middle and scrunched down with their feet on the back of the seats in front of them. They would sit like this until an employee came along and made them put their feet down. This happened every time they went to the movie but they did it anyway. From behind only the tops of their heads were visible and Jess was hard to see once the light went down. Howie laid his stick on the floor under his seat.

The previews came on the screen quickly followed by Gene Autry and Smiley Burnette singing and shooting and, in the end, winning. The Bowery Boys had just started their escapades on the screen when Howie got a slap in the back of the head.

"Hey kid, that white hair of yours is like a sign. Com'ere you little shit!"

It was two of the three boys from the trestle and Howie had jumped up and leaned forward as soon as he had been hit but he had not neglected to grab his stick from under the seat. Both of the older boys were reaching over the seats, grabbing at Howie and Jess. Jess was down on the floor scrambling for cover when Howie swung his stick like a baseball bat as much in fear as in self-defense. He connected soundly with an outstretched arm, right at the elbow.

"Ow-Ow-Ow," the injured boy started yelling as he sat back in his seat holding the arm that had been struck.

Howie saw flashlights coming down the aisles on both sides of the darkened theater and discovered that there was no place to escape. He held his stick cocked back in case of further attack.

"Put that stick down!" the owner of the theater demanded as he approached the boys.

Howie, like most children, was intimidated by adult authority and lowered the stick. The injured boy was still yelling and all the other patrons of the theater were standing and trying to see what all of the hullabaloo was about.

The owner approached the boys from one side as the usher came in from the other side. The owner went directly to the injured boy.

"What's going on here?" the usher demanded shining his light on the hollering boy.

"Oh, Ow," the boy continued to yell, "I think my arm's broke. That kid with the stick hit me."

"Hey, Mr. Clark, looka' this," the usher said pointing his light at the damaged arm. There was a knot as big as a baseball at the boy's elbow and it was growing even as they watched.

"All right, you boys come with me," Mr. Clark said. "And you," he said pointing his flashlight at Howie, "Give me that stick," and he jerked it out of Howie's hand's. "Now all of you up to the office," and he led the parade with the four boys in the middle and the usher bringing up the rear.

Once in the office the owner called out to the ticket seller to call the police. The seller, Nancy Antritt, quickly made the call to the police station that was only a block away from the theater.

The owner didn't stand for this type of trouble in his theater and he lined the boys up along the wall of the office, allowing the injured boy to sit but making the others stand. At first the only sounds were the moans coming from the injured boy, the other three boys obviously frightened enough to keep quiet.

"You boys tell me your names and addresses and phone numbers," Clark said. "I'm going to call your folks and tell them what happened."

He got the information from three of the boys but since Jess didn' have a telephone he couldn't call his parents. Howie assured the owner that his mother would answer for Jess and take care of him. Howie also told Mr. Clark that once his mother arrived, she would take care of everything.

Cornelia arrived at the theater only minutes after the police and waited patiently as the police finished writing down the names of the boys and getting the story of what had happened and why. As the facts came out the boy with the injured arm sat in the chair and never said a word. The other boy told the story of how they had been fishing and what Howie had done to start the trouble. He had difficulty explaining what had happened with Cornelia standing there but he finally managed to tell the whole story.

Cornelia, the ultimate realist, was deciding what to do and in what order to take the necessary action. Her primary concern was to get her son away from the police and take him home with her.

"Officers," she said, "if my son happened to injure this boy while he was being attacked, I can somewhat understand his actions. I'm not saying that he was entirely right but when these bigger and older boys attacked him and Jess, it was only natural that they defend themselves. They obviously acted more out of fear than anything else. But since Howie has injured this other boy, I do feel an obligation to pay any medical bills to get the other boy's arm taken care of. I hope that payment and an apology all around will solve this problem."

****

While Cornelia had been speaking she had been fully aware of the appraisal of the officers and Mr. Clark. One thing Cornelia knew very well was the effect she could have on men when she chose to be charming.

Then she turned and spoke directly to the theater owner as she said, "Of course if there has been any damage to the theater, I will also agree to cover that expense."

Mr. Clark was at a loss for words. He was being confronted by a woman who made the movie stars that appeared on his screen appear quite plain.

"No, Mrs. Lawson," Clark said, "everything here is okay. I just don't want to see any kid get into trouble. I have children of my own and these young people are my best customers. But I do want them to behave while they are in my theater."

"Well then officers," Cornelia said, "if you'll just tell the parents of the boy with the hurt arm to send me the doctor bill, that should settle things up just fine. Now, if you don't mind, I'll take Howie and Jess with me and I will drop Jess off on my way home."

"All right, you can go," one of the policemen said, "but have a talk with your kid about hitting people with sticks. He could get in a lot more trouble if he keeps doing things like this."

✳✳✳✳✳✳✳✳✳✳✳✳✳✳✳✳

The other parents arrived shortly after Cornelia had left and they agreed to the solution the police had decided upon.

When the policemen left the theater they took Howie's stick and tossed it into the back seat of their cruiser. Later that afternoon at shift change, they were discussing the day's activities with the oncoming officers. Cornelia Lawson's name was mentioned and one of the afternoon shift said he had seen her when some old bum along the railroad tracks had scared her son and another little boy.

"You don't suppose it was the same old bum that someone rolled and killed over by the main line a couple of weeks ago, do you?" one of the officers said.

"Who knows?" another officer answered. "The detectives decided he fell off a train, rolled two hundred yards and landed on that piece of cardboard."

"Well it beats having an unsolved homicide, but I was there that night and it looked to me like somebody beat his head in with a ball bat," the first officer stated.

"Speaking of ball bats," the officer going off duty said, "I forgot to take that stick out of the back seat of the cruiser." He walked over to the car and retrieved the stick and attempted to break it over his knee.

"Ouch, damn this stick," he said. "It's as strong as a piece of pipe. No wonder the other kid had a broken arm. It's just lucky he didn't get hit in the head," and with that observation the policeman threw the stick in the general direction of the trash and went home for the day.

✳✳✳✳✳✳✳✳✳✳✳✳✳✳✳✳

CHAPTER SIX

It was Thursday afternoon and Cornelia was wound up tighter than a twelve-day clock. In the past three days she had not given any thought to Howie's transgression at the theater. When the parents of the injured boy had stopped at the house to present the doctor bill for the boy's arm Cornelia had quickly paid the two hundred dollars and given them an extra twenty for the boy's discomfort. Then she had returned to cleaning, cooking and scurrying around as she prepared for Martin's visit.

Howie had even helped by cleaning out one of the garages to keep the car Martin would be delivering. Howie had also agreed to sleep on the couch in the front room during Martin's visit and turning over his room to their guest.

Although he was not exactly happy about it, he was keeping a low profile due to the recent incident at the theater.

Howie had been lucky in one respect. The day after the trouble he had been walking downtown with Jess and had recovered his stick from the trash pile at the rear of the city building. It was not damaged so he took it home and put it under the back porch so it would be available for later use. Jess was also quiet because he feared his parents would find out about the trouble at the theater but so far they remained unaware.

****

Rosy was the most concerned about the theater incident and had considered talking with Jess's parents but she had decided to hang onto her good job and keep her mouth shut. She had been watching Howie much closer lately and had seen him bring the heavy white stick home and secrete it under the back porch.

****

When the phone rang a little after noon on Friday, Cornelia had it in her hand before it had a chance at a second ring. It was Marty and he was at a gas station on the south side of town a couple of miles from their home.

After hanging up the phone, Cornelia ran into the bathroom to check her appearance in the mirror. She had done this a dozen times in the last two hours and after one more stop for Rosey to look her over; she ran out the back door and got in the car. Howie was going with her and he was dressed in new Levis and polo shirt, fall school clothes that his mother had insisted he wear on this special occasion.

In less than ten minutes she was at the gas station and immediately spotted her old Volkswagen parked off to the side with Martin behind the wheel. She honked the horn vigorously and she came to a stop, jumped out and ran to meet her old friend. Howie just sat in the car watching, surprised at his mother's animation, a slight frown on his face.

Martin got out and grabbed Cornelia in his arms, hugging her tight as he kissed her on the cheek. He whispered something in her ear and she giggled and laughed like a schoolgirl. She kissed him on both cheeks and held his face in her hands as she continued to study him. Then she took his hand and led him over to her car.

"Howie, come here and say hello to Martin," Cornelia said.

Howie got out of the car and walked to them as gravely as if he were in a funeral procession. He scrutinized Martin with unabashed intensity as he said, "Hello".

"Hi, Howie, do you remember me?" Martin asked.

Martin was looking at the boy just as carefully as the boy was looking at him. Now was not the time for any revelations in Howie's life but when the time did come, Martin would be there to help with any explanations.

Martin saw that Howie had his mother's fair hair and blue eyes but he also possessed Martin's fine, elegant features and thin frame. Howie also had small hands and feet, a trait of which Martin was very proud.

"I guess I sorta' remember you," Howie said, "but not very good. I just know that you were our neighbor back in New York."

"Well I remember you and I brought you something," Martin said. "I've got it in the car and you can have it as soon as we get to your house."

Howie, who had never had any family and had never received gifts from anyone other than his mother or Santa Claus, was intrigued by this offer.

:"What is it?" Howie asked excitedly, "show me now". Martin had, at least temporarily, made a friend.

"It's packed in the car," Martin said. "I'll get it out as soon as we get to your house."

Howie was showing an uncharacteristic exuberance as he turned to his mother and said, "Can we go home now Mama?"

"Sure baby," Cornelia replied, "I think that's a wonderful idea. Martin, you follow us and we'll go right now."

As they parted Martin said, "And I've got something in the car for you too," as he walked swiftly to the Volkswagen.

As they turned into home, Cornelia motioned out the back window of her car for Martin to pull into the back yard as she drove into one of the garages. Rosey was on the back porch waiting their arrival and as Martin slid from his car she rushed to greet him. Her full moon face was a giant smile as she hugged him with her powerful arm and said, "Oh Lordy-Lordy Mister Martin, it's sure good to see you again. You comin' to see Miz Corny is the very best thing that's happened since we got here. She shore'nuff been excited about your visit."

Martin had his arms in the direction of going around her but his hands did not quite meet behind her broad back. He leaned slightly back from the embrace and said with sudden serious concern, "She's not been sick or anything, has she?"

"No-No, nothing like that," Rosey answered. "It's just that she don't have nobody but the boy and me to talk with and I can see how lonesome she is sometimes. When ya'all called and said you could come for a visit she perked up more than I seen her since we come to this here little old town. Here she comes now and you can see how happy she is."

Cornelia was running across the yard looking like a high school girl rushing to meet her date. She was as beautiful as he remembered and Martin was sure she was exactly the same as the day he had first seen her so many years before. Howie was following in her wake walking steadily but not running.

Martin broke loose from Rosey and put his arm around Cornelia's shoulders and walked her to the front of the Volkswagen where he opened the luggage compartment. Right on top was a long square box wrapped with white paper. He handed the gift to Howie saying, "This is for you."

Howie took the box and stood there holding it, his eyes darting swiftly from the box to his mother, to Martin, back to the box, over and over. He didn't say anything until his mother made the statement that mothers have been making for thousands of years, "What do you say, Howie?"

"Thank you," Howie replied as he walked to the back porch, sat on the top step and began to unwrap the long box. He didn't tear the paper off but instead carefully loosened the folds and peeled the covering back with deliberate care so he could inspect the treasures inside. He found two ball gloves, one ball bat and a baseball in the box. Joe DiMaggio, the Yankee Clipper, had personally signed all four items. It was obvious that Martin had gone to a great deal of trouble to get what he hoped was just the right gift for a ten-year-old boy. Howie put the gloves on the porch, pocket side up and placed the ball in one of them. Then he picked up the bat and began examining it very closely.

The items were not a gift that Martin had picked up on the spur of the moment. He had actually planned to mail the gift to Cornelia as a Christmas present for the boy. Martin had purchased the ball, bat and gloves at a sporting good store and then sent them to Yankee Stadium with a friend. This friend had connections and was able to get the famous player to sign each piece with the inscription-'To Howie Lawson with best wishes, Joe DiMaggio'.

"Howie," Martin said, "toss me one of those gloves then throw me the ball."

Howie did as he was asked and picked up the second glove and started throwing the ball back and forth with Martin. The bat he had carefully laid aside.

Martin continued to talk with Cornelia and Rosey as he and Howie played catch. Howie started throwing the ball to the side of Martin away from his mother, making him move farther and farther into the yard in order to make the catch. After about ten minutes of this Martin called for a pause and returned to the car.

"I've got a couple more boxes in the back seat and I'd like to see what the ladies think of these. Rosey, you can open yours here but I think Cornelia should take hers' inside for a more private showing."

Martin handed a medium sized carton to Rosey that was wrapped in gold paper with a big, white bow on top. Cornelia's package was longer and flatter with silver wrapping and blue bows. Rosey immediately sat on the top step of the porch and unwrapped her gift while Cornelia hugged hers' tight to her chest.

"Mama, can I go play?" Howie asked. "I want to show Jess what I got." Howie had left the ball gloves and ball on the steps and was holding his new bat in his hands.

Cornelia stood next to him and ruffled his hair with his hand as she said, "Go ahead but be back in time for supper and she bent over and kissed him on the forehead leaving a lipstick smear that she rubbed off with her thumb. Then she practically danced into the house, clutching her gift and pulling Rosey behind her. She was ripping paper and ribbons as she went through the door.

****

Howie stood for a few seconds watching as the adults entered the house before he started the walk to Jess's house, swinging his bat at imaginary targets. Whack-Whack-Whack, he was thinking.

Howie returned an hour later and Jess was with him. They went into the kitchen to find the three adults sitting around the table admiring the gifts that Martin had brought. Rosey had a sterling silver tea and coffee service on a tray with the attendant creamer and sugar bowl. Cornelia had a new dress and nightgown. The dress was a pale blue, sheer as tissue and low cut in the front for formal wear. The nightgown, or dressing gown as Cornelia referred to it, was all white and of the finest silk with a lush feather collar. In the old days she would have worn something similar to it with no qualms what so ever. Now she knew the only ones who would ever see her in it were Rosey and maybe Martin. Howie was getting a little old for her to be wearing this style of garment around the house. Before Howie had returned Cornelia had promised to model it for Martin when they were alone.

Jess was introduced to Martin and they gravely shook hands, Jess somewhat uncomfortable with the formality. Then Jess and Howie ducked out the back door and started throwing the baseball back and forth. The adults could hear the boys talking through the screen door.

"That autograph of Joe DiMaggio is really something," Jess was saying. "I bet these things are worth a hunnerd bucks. Boy, you sure are lucky to have someone give you stuff like this. I wish one of these gloves was mine."

Howie threw the ball back to Jess with a grunt and said, "Take which ever one you want. I don't need two gloves and besides you're the only one I'll be playin' ball with anyway. Just you better leave it here at the house 'til that guy leaves."

Martin and Cornelia snapped their heads towards each other checking the others reaction to this last comment.

Martin smiled at her and said, "Remember, he's just a little boy and it's good he wants to share with his friend."

"You're probably right," Cornelia said dubiously, "but I'd rather he had acted better and been more appreciative of the gift. Sometimes

I just don't understand how a boy thinks and I don't have a man to advise me." She was thinking back to the incident at the theater a couple of days earlier and wondered if her preoccupation with Martin's visit had caused her to mishandle the situation. For a minute she had doubts but as she continued to scrutinize Howie as he played ball with Jess, she knew in her heart that any boy that beautiful could only be good.

"Well," Martin said changing the subject, "tell me about your life here in Newton." He had spent the first hour of their visit telling her that nothing of importance had happened in the city since she had left, which wasn't exactly accurate. What he had meant was that nothing unusual had happened in his life.

Now it was her turn and she told him essentially the same story about her life here in Newton. As they talked Rosey was bustling around the kitchen fixing supper. They were having fried chicken, smashed potatoes, (as Howie called them) corn on the cob and pineapple upside-down cake for dessert. With Rosey cooking it would be a feast fit for a king.

Jess stayed for supper as he had done on so many occasions and after the meal was over, he and Howie went out the back door leaving the grown-ups sitting at the table with their coffee. Each boy had a bottle of cream soda in one hand and Howie had his best white stick in the other as they wandered towards the downtown and found a seat on a park bench on Main Street. Jess was animated and talked excitedly about the gifts Howie had received and their great evening meal. Howie, who had always taken these things for granted, said very little.

Howie was not happy with their visitor from New York but, being only a child, he did not understand the real reason for his resentment. He only knew that his mother was paying more attention to Martin than she was to him and he didn't like it. The more he thought about it the more agitated he became.

"Cum'mon, let's walk around a while and fine' something to do," he said to Jess.

They began walking through an alley heading south towards the railroad and the gardens that people kept in the unused land along the right-of-way attendant to the tracks. Almost every type of vegetables was grown on these plots but late summer was the time for tomatoes and watermelons. As they crossed the tracks Howie lobbed his pop bottle at a parked car but missed and the bottle shattered in the street sending glass fragments in all directions. Now he started walking through the gardens. It was getting to be dusk and there were no people around so Howie just walked slowly and swung his stick at the plants and vegetables. The objects of his furibund activity turned immediately into useless pulp. The watermelons got the most attention as he mashed them again and again all the time muttering, "Whack-Whack-Whack".

****

Jess followed along a few paces behind him keeping well clear of the slashing stick and couldn't help but compare the force Howie used as so similar to the way he had beaten the old man some time ago. Also Jess disapproved of Howie's vandalism mostly due to the fact that it was destroying good food but he noticed that it was getting dark and Jess knew Howie would soon head for home.

Within minutes Howie turned to Jess and made his usual excuse, "I'm getting a little tired so I guess maybe I'll head for home."

The dark didn't bother Jess but he had gotten used to Howie's habit of being home before the streetlights came on and he accepted his friend's idiosyncrasy.

"What'chu going to do?" Howie asked as they walked towards his house. "Do you wanna' come in and watch TV for a while?" He knew Jess's family did not own a TV set.

Jess was watching Howie closely and could see that he was much calmed down after his spree in the gardens. "Okay with me if your Mom don't mind," he answered.

"Naw, she won't care," Howie said. "Besides she's busy with old what's-his name from New York an' she won't even know we're there." Whack-Whack, Howie brought his stick down hard in the dust of the alley where they were walking.

Jess studied his friend out of the corner of his eye and hoped that the visitor would not cause any further frantic outbursts from Howie.

The boys entered the house through the back door and found Cornelia and Martin sitting in the front room drinking coffee from Rosey's new silver service. Even the creamer and sugar bowl were full and setting on the tray with the cups. Rosey was in the kitchen finishing up the cleaning after the evening meal and humming a gospel song as she worked. The boys went straight to Cornelia.

"Mama, can me and Jess watch some TV?" Howie asked.

"Sure baby, you go ahead," Cornelia answered as she turned to Martin and said, "You don't mind sitting in the kitchen, do you?"

"Of course not," he replied getting out of his chair and, picking up the tray with their café au lait, heading for the kitchen.

****

Howie and Jess settled in on the couch to watch their favorite show, 'Six Gun Playhouse'. Jess was completely engrossed in the action but Howie was paying much more attention to the conversation in the kitchen.

Martin was talking about the entire latest goings on in the city and Cornelia was listening with enchantment to his every word. "I believe that Truman was the dominant force in bringing the United Nations to New York. The Berlin airlift gave this country so much good publicity that the other nations could hardly consider anyplace else for their headquarters."

"They've broken ground for the complex and it is supposed to be finished in a year. When they get it open you'll have to come back and see it for yourself," Martin continued.

In the other room Howie squinted his eyes on hearing this offer and filed it away in memory to be meditated about at a later time. He was reasonably certain that he did not want to go to the city just so his mother could spend all of her time with this guy. She was ignoring him much too much as it was.

Martin went on talking and said, "Oh, I almost forgot that I brought something else for you. Let me run out to the car for a minute and I'll get it." Martin hurried across the kitchen and out the back door.

Within a couple of minutes he was back with a smallish square box under his arm. He sat it on the table and ripped off the paper to reveal a record player for the new .45-rpm records that had recently come on the market. In the bottom of the box were a dozen of the latest releases in popular music.

"I know how much you like music so I brought you these," Martin said with a smile.

Cornelia immediately unwrapped the cord and said, "Plug this in and let's listen to what's here. Marty, this is so nice of you I just don't know what to say," and she leaned across the table and kissed him on the cheek.

Howie, seeing this, did more than just squint. He stared at Martin with a hatred that was nearly verbal.

Martin's head snapped around and his eyes locked up with Howie. Martin felt as though he had been wrenched by a force from within and found himself staring into a hostile face such as he had never known. He shivered from the hatred before he could calm himself and pull his eyes away.

Cornelia, seeing his sudden reaction, said, "What's wrong, Martin? You look like you saw a ghost."

"Nothing. Nothing's wrong. I just felt a chill for a minute. I must be tired from the drive." He could not bring himself to look back into the front room to see if the boy was still watching them.

Soon after, Jess came quietly into the kitchen and announced he was going home and slipped out the back door. Howie was still sitting in the front room faintly illuminated by the glow of the television set and Cornelia went to him. "I'm going to bring in your pillow and blankets and make up your bed on the couch. You can watch TV for a while yet but go ahead and sleep here tonight and take your bath in the morning.

She was only minutes making up the bed and with a quick kiss on the forehead, wished him good night and went back to her chair at the kitchen table.

Howie turned off the television and lay still trying to hear the conversation coming from the kitchen but mostly it was covered up by the music from the record player. He could hear occasional laughter and each time his eyes would squint and his expression became very grave. He lay back and gave no thought to going to sleep.

****

In the kitchen Martin's eyes kept darting back to the now darkened front room. Martin knew he must have been imagining things. No child could be that hateful and display all of that malevolence with just a look. Maybe it had just been the way the light had been shining or maybe—or or—he wasn't sure. He had to be mistaken; he just had to be.

Martin forced his mind back to what Cornelia was saying, trying to concentrate on the conversation and put the boy out of his mind.

"—made a movie of the book "All The King's Men" and it is supposed to be excellent. It's playing here and if you haven't seen it maybe we could go tomorrow night."

"Sure we can," Martin answered, "if that's what you would like to do. I came here to spend time with you so anything you want to do is fine with me. You know I'm something of a fan of Mercedes McCambridge."

Martin leaned back in his chair and glanced again into the adjoining room. The distraction of the boy was upsetting him and he was having trouble concentrating on the conversation.

As it approached midnight, Martin realized how tired he really was. With Cornelia showing no sign of slowing down, he was finally forced to mention the fact that he was nearly exhausted and beg off the talk for the night.

"Just show me where I'll be sleeping. I can hardly keep my eyes open. We can start again in the morning," Martin said, "but right now I'm just all in."

Rosey had discreetly vanished a couple of hours earlier. She was a master at understanding the feelings of others around her and she knew that Martin and Cornelia needed to be alone to reminisce and enjoy the other's company.

Cornelia begrudgingly agreed to call it a night and she took Martin to Howie's room. Martin glanced quickly in passing into the now dark front room of the house but he was unable to see if the boy was still awake.

****

Howie was awake. He was lying on his back looking at the ceiling and having bad thoughts. He wanted Martin gone but he was not sure how to orchestrate his departure. He knew his mother was happy with Martin's visit so she wouldn't be of any help to him. In fact she would probably object most strenuously if Howie caused a fuss. She might even take Martin's side against him. Howie continued to stare into the dark until his eyes started to ache. The house was now quiet and everyone was in bed. Slowly Howie slipped from the couch and walked to his own room where Martin was sleeping.

****

The object of Howie's consternation was having a hard time going to sleep. When Martin had first laid down he felt as though he would be asleep in a matter of minutes but this was not the case. The proximity to the passing trains was unsettling as well as the surprising hostility of the boy.

Martin was sure that he had not imagined that the boy resented him. He felt that he understood the reason and this was that the boy was jealous of the attention Cornelia was lavishing on him. He knew, of course, that the boy did not suspect whom his real father was and it was not a subject for discussion in the foreseeable future.

Could the boy be as bitter as he appeared or was Martin just imagining it? It was so very obvious that Howie was intensely jealous of Cornelia. Martin stared into the dark of the front room and tried to come to an intelligent conclusion.

An hour later as Martin lay on his bed hovering on the edge of sleep he saw and heard the door to the room where he was sleeping swing slowly open. Howie was standing in the doorway outlined by the moonlight. The boy walked up to the side of the bed and stopped as he looked down at the man he believed to be asleep. There were no trains within earshot and it was deadly quiet. Martin did his best to breath regularly, simulating sleep. Through eyes barely open he watched the boy at his bedside.

Howie stood and stared, lost in thought for several minutes before he seemed to shake himself into movement. Howie turned and left the room as quietly as he had entered, pulling the door shut ever so softly as he left Martin in the darkness.

A strange word popped into Martin's head as the boy left, something he was not sure he had really heard. But then again, maybe he had heard it---whack---just barely whispered.

CHAPTER SEVEN

Martin slept later than usual, partly because of being tired from the trip and also because he had not rested well. He had been awake thinking about the boy for a good while after the late visit. He had nearly convinced himself that Howie was only jealous of his mother's attention and would eventually see that there would be no contest between the two of them for Cornelia's affection. Should his friendship with Cornelia trigger such hostility; he didn't know. Anyway he would be leaving early Sunday morning to return home and after he was gone, any problem should go away.

Martin went into the kitchen and joined Cornelia and Rosey at the table for coffee and juice. Rosey insisted on fixing Martin a country breakfast and he consented before retreating to the shower while the food was being prepared.

After his ablution, Martin re-entered the kitchen just in time to see a uniformed policeman going out the back door. "Is everything all right?" he asked.

"Oh, just a minor thing," Cornelia said. "The officer said that Howie and Jess ran through a few gardens and ruined some plants. I had him give me the addresses of the people and told him I would take care of the damages. Nothing serious. Boys will be boys," and she shook her head and gave Martin a wry smile.

Cornelia passed it off so easily that Martin never imagined it was the second time in one week that Howie had been bought out of trouble with the police.

****

While this had been going on, Howie and Jess were fishing in a new spot about half a mile downstream and on the other side of the river. The location was only a few hundred feet from where the waters of two small rivers joined into a bigger river.

"This has got to be a better place than up there under the trestle," Howie was telling Jess.

Howie had caught two catfish and Jess had landed four cats and two big carp. On this day Howie didn't mind being out-fished. His mind was on other things. He had accepted the fact that there was nothing he could do about the strange man being in their house. The good thing was that he had heard that the man would be leaving tomorrow morning on the train to go back to the city. But Howie had heard the invitation for his mother to visit the man at his home in New York and he didn't like that idea at all. His mom was an old woman anyway and she didn't need some man hanging around her. She had told him about his dad being killed in the war so what would she want another man for anyway?

****

That same morning, while the boys were fishing, Rosey had been dispatched to settle with the owners of the damaged gardens. Cornelia had given her sufficient cash to deal with the claims and the police had supplied them with the names and addresses of the injured parties. Rosey was not happy with the chore. If questioned she never would have admitted to anything but devotion to Cornelia and the boy, but in her heart, she really didn't care much for Howie. From her observations over the years she knew how mean and malicious the boy was and she was sure that Howie was long overdue for a good, old fashioned ass kicking and she would have loved to be the person to administer the punishment. She was equally aware that any efforts on her part to interject her feelings in the matter could meet with an extreme reaction on Cornelia's part. Now as she walked briskly along the street she mumbled to herself and vowed to keep her promise of long ago, do as she was told and keep her opinions to herself.

Rosey visited the five homes on the list and paid in full whatever was asked to cover the damage to the gardens plus an extra ten dollars for the inconvenience to the owners. Now, as she was headed home, another thought occurred to her. Howie was clearly unhappy with Mr. Martin and Rosey could not imagine that his mother was unable to see this. It would only be a matter of time before there would be some sort of blow-up between Martin and Howie. She hoped that it would not happen before Mr. Martin left in the morning to go back to the city. Rosey wanted to protect Cornelia against such an incident but she was not sure she would be able to do this. She could only pray with one day to go that nothing would happen.

Rosey continued to stomp along the street, a woman on a mission with much on her mind.

****

Howie hid his stick behind a drainpipe at the rear of a hotel adjacent to the movie theater. After the trouble at the theater he was sure the owner would be watching for him to come to the show and he wanted to see the movie so he prepared for the worst. When he and Jess got to the theater the expected happened. The woman in the booth selling tickets called the owner to check on whether or not to admit the boys.

"Well, are we gonna' have any trouble with you kids?" Mr. Clark asked.

"No sir." "No sir." Both boys answered in unison.

"We'll be good and not cause any trouble," Howie said looking up at the owner with such innocence that he could hardly be denied.

The owner turned to the lady selling tickets and said, "Okay, Nancy, let them in but I'm going to tell the usher to keep an eye on them and at the first sign of acting up, out they go!"

Howie was learning that if he acted a certain way, people would respond to his assumed innocence and the more he practiced the more proficient he became.

On this day the boys behaved themselves and there were no more incidents at the theater. The owner even smiled at the boys on their way out.

****

Rosey's day had gone from bad to worse. She arrived back home with a load of groceries to find the police once again at the house. Lordy, she thought, what's that boy done now? But this time it wasn't

Howie; it was one of the railroader/tenants who lived in one of the rooms upstairs who was the problem. He had gotten drunk that morning and started a fight with two of the other tenants resulting in the police being summoned. With Cornelia gone, Rosey was expected to handle the problem. As it turned out there was nothing for her to do since the drunken brakeman took a punch at one of the cops and was then promptly removed from the scene, bleeding profusely from a cut inflicted by a blow from a hickory stick. Now all Rosey had to do was inform Cornelia of what had happened and let her decide if anything needed to be done.

****

The drunken railroader had only been living there for a couple of weeks and when he had rented the room he had been sober and nice enough. But when he was drinking he was one of the meanest, dirtiest and most foul-mouthed men that ever lived. The police knew him well and he had been locked up more than five hundred times in the past few years, mostly for drunkenness and fighting. When the man was drunk he was capable of anything.

****

Now, with Cornelia and the cleaning lady gone, Rosey headed upstairs to see if any damage had been done. What she found was the cause of the fight. Dewey House, the drunk, had vomited in the hall and then fallen down and spread the mess all over. When the other tenants had objected, Dewey had urinated on the doors of their rooms and was going to do more before they dragged him down the steps and into the front yard.

The men had worked together at different times over the years and everyone knew Dewey to be aggressive and obnoxious when he was drinking. Out in the yard the other tenants had turned the garden hose on Dewey to both sober him up and wash him off. Dewey had attacked them and that was when the police arrived.

Rosey stomped back down the stairs to get the equipment to begin cleaning up the mess. If she hadn't been a good Christian woman, she would certainly have told someone off, for sure and certain!

****

Howie and Jess left the theater and ducked into the back of the poolroom. The money games always happened on Saturday and they liked to watch the good players demonstrate their skills. There was a game of nine-ball going on with the winner getting five dollars from each of the other players every time he won. The boys watched for about an hour and then headed for Howie's house. They arrived just shortly after Martin and his mother and were just in time to hear Rosey tell about the incident with the old drunk getting in a fight with the police and being taken to jail.

Howie listened with interest. He had little contact with the other tenants in the house, particularly the railroaders who came and went early in the morning and late at night. Howie had seen the man they were talking about and had not liked his looks. He felt the man looked and acted towards him in much the same manner as the old bum at the trestle. He had the feeling that the man could be dangerous.

When the story was over, Howie and Jess picked up the ball gloves from the back porch and went into the yard and started throwing the ball back and forth while they waited for supper. Jess had, as usual, been invited to stay and eat and he had accepted. Martin sat at the kitchen table talking with the women as the food was being prepared.

The sudden impact of a metal garbage can on the ground between Jess and Howie caused both boys to jump for the back porch. The noise brought the adults to the kitchen door and they all saw the cause.

Dewey House had gotten out of jail and he was back, drunker than ever. He had staggered into the back yard and thrown the can towards the house. His clothes were covered with vomit, blood and dirt and somewhere he had lost one of his shoes. His skimpy gray hair was frizzed out in all directions and he was cussing everybody and everything in sight. Dewey was heading directly towards the back porch so both boys beat a hasty retreat into the kitchen.

Dewey House fell up the back steps, got back to his feet, opened the screen door to the kitchen and walked right in.

"It's supper time so fix me somethin' to eat," he said as he pulled out a kitchen chair. He tried to sit but missed the chair and fell to the floor. Then he began cussing with a fervor that none of them had ever heard before.

Cornelia calmly turned to the boys and asked them to go into the other room where they continued to watch from the doorway. Now she turned to Dewey and said, "Mr. House, please leave. This is my home and you're not welcome here." She had her arms folded across her chest and she did not even raise her voice.

Dewey struggled up from the floor and looked Cornelia up and down with an obscene leer on his face. "You know, you're kinda a good lookin' piece. How's about me an' you goin' somewheres an' gettin' a drink?" He looked at Martin and said, "It don't look to me like your fancy-pants boyfriend could handle anything as fine as you."

Rosey, who had seen more than enough was in just the proper mood to get involved. "Move over, Miss Corny," Rosey said, "and let me throw this white trash bum out'ta here."

"Dewey quickly rounded on Rosey as he said, "Shut up, nigger. You ain't kickin' nobody, nowhere. You just get your ass busy fixin' food."

Cornelia turned to Rosey and put her hand on her arm as she said, "It's okay Rosey. He's just drunk."

But drunk or not, Dewey House had said too much. Martin had slowly walked around the table to confront the drunken man. House immediately balled up his fists, preparing to fight, but what happened next was a surprise to everyone but Martin.

"Cornelia, would you open the back door please, and hold it open for a few seconds?" Martin asked.

As soon as the door opened, Martin grabbed the drunk's wrist and pulled him so that the man turned in a half circle. Then he grabbed the drunk's belt in the small of his back with one hand while he gripped a handful of greasy hair in the other hand. Dewey House was then propelled through the kitchen door and thrown from the back steps, to land at least twenty feet out in the yard, coming down with his face in the dirt and grass. The wind was completely knocked out of Dewey and he just lay there, gasping for air. Martin did no more than walk back into the kitchen where he went to the sink and started scrubbing his hands.

"It's a dirty job but somebody has to do it," Martin said with a grin.

During supper Cornelia had tried to apologize to Martin for the incident but he had just laughed and said, "That wasn't so bad. I just hate to see a bully try to intimidate women and children. In the neighborhood where I grew up there was always someone coming around to pick on the Jews so I learned to defend myself. That old drunk was no problem but I have to admit, I'm not as young as I used to be. There was a day when I could have thrown him a lot farther."

He said this last for the benefit of the boys who he thought had been duly impressed by his actions and had been looking at Martin in silence as he spoke. Howie's contemplation of Martin was caused by something entirely different. In Howie's own mind he was sure that he could have done just as good a job of defending his mother. He knew he could have taken his stick and—Whack-Whack. That old drunk would have never bothered them again. But for tonight something unusual had happened and that would temporarily make him happy.

After eating they all went to the front room to relax. Cornelia and Martin were planning on going to the movie to see "All the King's Men" and they asked Howie and Jess if they would like to go along. Both boys declined; they didn't want to see a show without any cowboys or monsters.

The boys listened as Martin and Cornelia discussed whether it was safe to leave the house with the threat of Dewey House still lurking around somewhere but Rosey put a stop to those worries by saying, "You just go on to your picture show, Mister Martin. I can take care of things just fine around here. If that troublemaker comes back I can give him what-for just as good as anyone. You'all don't need to worry your heads about us."

Martin thought for only a minute before agreeing with her. Rosey certainly would be able to handle things.

As it grew dark, the boys sat in the front room watching television. Rosey was there but she was only paying scant attention to the wrestling matches. When she had free time in the evenings she would read her Bible and just take it easy as she was doing now. Several times men had come and gone through the front door but always quietly. There were no more disturbances because, unknown to them, Dewey House had ended up back in jail after starting another fight in one of the downtown bars.

Earlier, when Rosey was in the bathroom, Howie had brought his best stick into the front room and hid it behind the couch. He had cautioned Jess with a finger across his lips and Jess had been cooperative with his silence as he had been afraid of the old drunk and he knew that Howie would not hesitate to use his stick if it became necessary.

****

Martin and Cornelia had gone to the eight o'clock showing of the movie and they arrived back at the house shortly after ten. They had come straight home just in case they were needed for anything but everything was fine. Martin had loaded Jess in the car and drove him home. The big Buick attracted envious stares from Jess's neighbors, many of who were sitting on their front steps enjoying the late summer evening. Martin got out of the car and walked to the front door with Jess and explained to his mother that he was a friend of Howie's mother and was just giving the boy a ride home.

Martin was smart enough to know that Jess's parents would want an explanation of why a stranger was bringing him home in a big car, late at night.

When Martin returned to the house, he found Cornelia sitting at the kitchen table. Rosey had gone to bed and the front room was lit up by the glow from the television set. Howie could be vaguely seen on the couch where his bed had been made up.

Cornelia had changed from her 'going-out' clothes and was now wearing flannel pajamas and blue fuzzy slippers. Her hair was still down and she had not taken off her make-up.

Martin stared at her for a few seconds and said, "Lady, time has certainly been good to you. You're just as beautiful as the first time I saw you all those years ago."

Cornelia looked back into Martin's eyes and saw all of the love and devotion she had accepted in the past. She saw no thoughts of seduction, only a true and loving friend who worshipped her without reservations. And she felt the same towards him, love without any complications.

"Martin," she said, "it's been so good to have you here. You can't imagine how I've missed having you to talk with. When I left the city I knew it was time for me to stop working and start a new life for Howie's sake. But to tell you the truth, I've been so very lonely. There is nothing for me around here and I miss the night life and the shows and everything back in the city."

She stopped speaking and looked at Martin with tears in her eyes. He saw that she was not the happy person he had known so well back in the city. As he watched her she lit a cigarette and started talking once again.

"It's not that I miss work, I don't. And I know I'm doing what's right for Howie. He would never have a chance to grow up back in the city. There would always have been someone to slap him down because of me. Here, he's got a chance to be in school without pressure from the other kids and to make friends of his own. But, oh Martin, I miss you and the city and all the excitement. This place is quite a change from New York."

Martin didn't know what to say. They had been so happy since he had arrived on the visit; he hated to see her spirits change because of his upcoming departure. He also knew that he had to go back and that he could never, ever stay in this town. If it hadn't been for Cornelia he would have gone nuts in just the few days he had been away from the city. There was absolutely nothing that could keep him in this little town.

"Is there anything I can do to make it better for you here?" he asked softly, already knowing the answer.

"No, there's nothing anyone can do," she said as she looked down at the tabletop and shook her head. "I'll just need to tough it out, at least until Howie grows up and I'm back on my own again."

Martin had glanced into the front room a couple of times but he could not tell if Howie was awake and listening or asleep on the couch. They had been talking in fairly low tones so even if the boy had listening he shouldn't have been able to hear their conversation.

Suddenly Cornelia looked up and smiled, showing off the radiance that had made her one of the most beautiful women in the entire city of New York. "I don't want to spoil our time together," she said. "Let's just relax and be happy this evening. Just because you have to go back in the morning is no reason we won't be seeing each other. You know that you can come and visit any time you want."

"Sure, I know that," Martin answered, "and you could come to the city and visit me anytime you wanted. You have always loved to shop so you could just come back for a few days before Christmas and we could see some shows while you're there. From what I've seen here, Rosey could handle things around the house and give you some time off for yourself."

"Oh, Martin, I don't know. I'd hate to stick Rosey with all the work around here."

"You don't need to decide right now," Martin said, "just think about it. You can fly from here to the city in no time at all and can return home just as quickly. I'm not trying to pressure you but I wish you would at least think about it."

"I can do that much," Cornelia answered with a smile as she got up from the table. "Now you wait here. There's something I want you to see."

Cornelia left the kitchen and walked into her room. Within seconds she was back wearing the white silk robe that Martin had brought her. She had it on over her flannel pajamas and the costume was outrageous.

Martin gasped and they both started laughing at the same time. He reached out and took both of her hands in his and looked her up and down before they collapsed on chairs with the table between them.

I wanted to model your gift for you but I wasn't sure how to do it. This seemed the safest way with other people in the house," Cornelia said.

"You look as lovely as always," he said seriously as the laughter died, "and I'm so very grateful to be your friend. This has been a wonderful vacation."

Her smile remained but her eyes were serious as she answered, "I know what this means. Tomorrow is going to be a long day and you must get your rest. I understand and I will think about what you said. Maybe a trip before Christmas could be worked out. If there is any way I can do it, I will surely try."

"Promise?" he said.

"Yes, I promise," and she leaned forward and took his arm as she kissed him lightly on the cheek. They stood and parted towards their separate rooms.

During the night Martin slipped quietly out of bed to visit the bathroom. As he walked past the door to the front room he could see Howie sitting up at the front window, looking out. He paused and the boy turned his head to look at him. Martin could only see the silhouette of his head and shoulders and could not see his face but Martin felt sure the boy was not smiling. Howie turned slowly back to the window, saying nothing and ignoring the man's passage.

School had started and Howie was in the fourth grade. He was getting along better with the other kids and his teacher but it was plain he would never be a good student. All of his teachers found him to be lazy and inattentive but extremely bright. It was frustrating for them to have a potentially gifted child that refused to apply himself. Along with his intelligence he had such striking good looks. Slender and fair with pale blond hair and blue eyes, he had the most engaging smile of any child the teachers had ever seen. But all this beauty was a sham once you were around him for any period of time. In fact he was conniving, devious and utterly untrustworthy. He wanted his own way at everything and would become sullen and petulant whenever he felt he was thwarted. These traits did not show up at home because he was always allowed to do pretty much as he pleased. Cornelia always doted on him.

****

Now Howie was forming a plan. He had an enemy he could focus on, Dewey House, and he was plotting action against the man. In the evenings Howie would sit on the porch and watch the railroaders come and go through the front door of their home. The target of his hostilities was working as a brakeman on one of the yard engines that moved freight cars in and out of local factories. Their duties also included placing cars in proper order to be moved over the tracks from point to point in full sized trains. Dewey's job was to couple and uncouple the cars as the huge steam engines pushed them around. Howie often saw him go by hanging from the side of the cars on the attached steel ladders. That job, plus the fact that Dewey drank all the time, had given Howie an idea. Howie started his plan by going out of his way to make Dewey dislike him.

Dewey, not being very bright, fell easily into the scheme. When Dewey had seen Howie sitting on the porch, he had spoken to the boy in a passing manner. In return, Howie gave him the finger. After this happened the second time Dewey got into the habit of cursing at the boy whenever he saw him and nobody was around. This suited Howie just fine as long as he had room to retreat if it had become necessary.

Actually Dewey had not caused any more trouble around the rooming house. He had used up all the money from his last paycheck and was restricted for funds until his next payday. Also some of the other men who had rooms at Cornelia's house had talked to him telling him to settle down of they would take strong action against him. This was the nicest rooming house where any of them had ever stayed and they didn't want Dewey spoiling it for them. The tenants liked Cornelia and Rosey and they would not allow Dewey to abuse the women. They had also heard Dewey speak disparagingly about the boy and they were concerned the Dewey might try to harm Howie. They well knew that Dewey would pick on anyone or anything that was weaker than he was. The boy looked so angelic and helpless.

Howie had learned that the railroads operated on the same schedule as the factories, twenty-four hours a day and seven days a week. Most of the men who worked on the yard engine crews worked a forty-hour week so it was easy to figure out when a man would be on duty. Dewey worked almost exclusively on the day shift starting at seven o'clock in the morning until three o'clock in the afternoon. The days off would vary but the work hours remained pretty much constant. Alternating days off among the crew were common. This allowed for some of the crew to have always worked the previous day so they were able to make known to the men what the crews of the day earlier had completed or promised to complete.

Dewey had Sunday and Monday off each week unless something unusual occurred or another of the crew reported off for some reason. When this did happen a replacement worked had to be summoned but it was seldom that Dewey got this call because of his propensity for drunkenness. This suited the other men as well as the company because he was a general pain in the ass to everyone who had contact with him.

Howie had noticed that on Saturday morning the yard engine was used to weigh rail cars full of coal. The procedure was fairly simple. The engine would push about twenty cars towards the scale. The scales were on top of a hump with the tracks going downhill as the cars crossed the weighing platform. The cars were pushed across the scales, weighed and uncoupled and allowed to down roll into the yard where they came to rest, once again part of a long string awaiting transport to their destination. It was the duty of the brakeman to walk beside the cars as they were pushed onto the scales and uncouple them after the weighing was complete. Howie had watched the routine for hours on end and decided how he would proceed.

On this Saturday morning, the day after payday, Dewey House was working with a pint of whiskey in his pocket. It was no secret that he was drinking and the men he worked with were accustomed to his actions. Because of the powerful railroad unions the company had never been able to dismiss Dewey and make it stick.

Each railroad car was nearly fifty feet long and, when loaded with coal, weighed about one hundred tons. On this push the engine had twenty-two cars in front of it, more cars than were generally handled at one time. The
crew was so familiar with the operation that everything had become routine. The Engineer could not see the front end of the cut of cars he was working but he knew just how far to move and how often to go forward in order to push the cars over the hump. Dewey was walking beside the cars, ready to pull the drawbar between the cars and release it after being weighed to find its' way through gravity to the correct location.

Howie was riding on top of the second coal car and out of sight. His plan was simple, even childish, but absolutely deadly.

Dewey released the first car just as some small lumps of coal came showering down on his head and shoulders. He looked up to see the boy peeking over the edge of the coal car. Howie had another lump in his hand that he promptly threw down at Dewey.

"You little son-of-a-bitch, get down offa' that car!" Dewey yelled up at the boy.

"You go to hell you dirty old shit!" Howie yelled back as he chucked another lump of coal at the man.

"If you don't get down outta' that there car I'm gonna' come up there and beat your skinny ass black and blue!" Dewey shouted furiously.

"Just try and catch me you ass-hole!" Howie shouted back. "You couldn't even if you tried, you shitin' drunk."

That was all the encouragement Dewey needed to begin climbing up the steel ladder to the top of the car. Dewey was aware that the car was moving but he was drunk and mad and in no mood to fool with this kid. Besides he didn't like the kid and it would be a good excuse to beat his ass.

Dewey reached the top of the ladder and looked over the edge of the coal car. He expected to see the boy trying to get away over the coal. He was wrong as he had been so many times in his life but this would be the last mistake he would ever make.

Howie was waiting just back from the edge with his good white stick firmly in his grasp. The first blow he struck came crashing down onto Dewey's left hand where it held to the top of the coal car, breaking and nearly severing three of his fingers. Dewey screamed long and loud but nobody could hear him because of the noise of the railroad. Dewey tried to hold on with his good, not daring to let go. The car was still attached to the train and was moving back and forth as the engineer jockeyed the train in the weighing procedure. Dewey looked down at the turning wheels beneath him and one foot slipped off the ladder. He was flapping his wounded hand and holding tight with the other as he attempted to attract the attention of the engineer and get him to stop the train. That was when Howie struck his next blow. It came smashing into Dewey's face, across his eye and mashing down onto his nose. Dewey was stunned as he lost his grip and fell towards the huge steel wheels.

****

It was about half an hour later when the police arrived in the railroad yards. After looking things over they called for the coroner to be sent to the scene. The only people present were the railroad crew and a little blond boy standing back by a fence that bordered the tracks.

The police were required to call the coroner to view any unattended death even though there was no doubt in their minds what had happened. The smashed whiskey bottle in Dewey's pocket helped confirm their beliefs.

The injuries to Dewey were horrendous. The train had gone forward and back several times before the engineer had become curious about the weight on the front of the cut of cars and sent the fireman ahead to check. Dewey was lying across the rails and the train had passed over his body from top to bottom starting below his right hip to the top of his left shoulder. There was not much blood due to the fact that Dewey had been pinched in two but in the jostling from the cars, part of his head had also been run over.

One of the officers grabbed his partner and pointed down at Dewey as he said, "Hey, you old drunken bastard, pull yourself together." They both laughed and then glanced around self-consciously but detected no disapproval from the railroaders who were present

When the coroner arrived the first thing he did was tell the policemen to send all the onlookers on their way. As they did Howie lost sight of his foe for the last time as the policeman said, "This ain't nothin' for a little kid to be lookin' at. Ga'wan, get out of here."

****

Howie walked away along the automobile access road that led into the railroad yards and headed for Jess's house. He was carrying his stick as proudly as Moses had once carried his wooden staff. In his own mind he felt totally justified in the action he had taken against

Dewey House. The old man had disrupted his home and threatened his mother so he had done what had been necessary to correct the situation. Anyone would agree he had done the right thing. Not that he planned on checking with any third party on the off chance they wouldn't agree.

When he arrived at Jess's he first asked to use the bathroom and cleaned the coal dust from his hands and brushed his clothes so there would be no telltale stains. The few smudges on his pants and shoes were negligible so he ignored them.

As Howie exited the bathroom he took Jess by the arm and said to his friend, "Let's go get somethin' to eat. I wanna' get a big cheeseburger an' a milkshake. I got enough money so's we can both get one down at Jake's restaurant.

"Sure," Jess answered. His family didn't eat out all that often so it was an even bigger treat for him than it was for Howie.

After their snack in the diner, Howie and Jess sat on one of the park benches placed conveniently around the center of town and Howie pulled a new jackknife out of his pocket. He rested his stick on the ground and held it on both sides with his knees as he scraped it with the knife, a new three-blades he had shoplifted from a hardware store.

Jess watched with interest. There were black smears all up and down the stick and he was curious. "Where did all that dirt on your stick come from?" he asked.

Howie only paused for a second before he answered. "Oh, I was walking down the tracks on the way to your house and I dropped it." Then he looked curiously at Jess and said, "Why you askin' me that?"

"No reason," Jess replied. "I was just thinkin' about the last time that stick got all messes up," and he looked knowingly at Howie.

Howie didn't reply. He squinted his eyes and started mulling over Jess's curiosity. He was forming a reply when one of the policemen who walked the downtown beat came by, spinning his nightstick on its' leather strap making it practically dance along the sidewalk. Both boys were fascinated by the display.

"Hi, Mr. Johnson," Jess said.

"Lo, Mr. Johnson," Howie echoed.

"You boys goin' to the show today?" Officer Johnson asked.

"Yeah, we are," Howie answered for both of them. "We gotta' get our cards punched for the serial that's on," and they both pulled the four by six cards from their pockets as way of proof and held them up for inspection.

Johnson looked at the card as if they really meant something and nodded his head as he said, "Okay, but like you've been told, no more trouble like you had a while back. I keep my eye on everything that goes on around here and I'm gonna' be watching you two."

Howie looked up with his most engaging smile and said, "Yessir, you bet, Mr. Johnson," as he continued to scrape his stick with the stolen pocketknife.

After the movie when Howie had recovered his stick from its' hiding place behind the drainpipe, they had gone to the poolroom where they sat quietly in chairs along the wall and watched the pros play nine-ball. One of the players was telling the others in the game about an accident that had happened in railroad yards. It seemed a drunken worker had fallen under the cars and got himself run over. The dead man's name was Dewey House and he was a well-known troublemaker around town.

"Hey," Jess said looking at Howie, "that's the guy who was drunk and caused a fuss at your house a while back."

"Is that right? I didn't remember his name," Howie lied so casually without taking his eyes from the pool game.

"Yeah, we won't need to worry about that old bum anymore and I'm glad," Jess said.

CHAPTER EIGHT

Things had changed for Howie in school. He no longer had any trouble with the other kids. He had learned to go his own way. The boys ignored him since he didn't join in any of their games or activities. The girls all tried to attract him because of his looks but he never paid the slightest attention to them. He never felt flattered because he kept so much to himself he didn't even know girls existed. Howie felt he satisfied all the school requirements by going to his classroom every day and passing from grade to grade. His teachers, while upset by his lack of initiative, were grateful he was no longer disruptive in their classrooms.

At home things were going very smoothly. Now that Dewey House had been removed as a threat, Cornelia had decided to visit New York between Christmas and Thanksgiving. Everything was going so fine with Howie she felt comfortable leaving him under Rosey's care for a few days. Cornelia would be flying to New York on a Monday and returning on the following Friday.

It was the middle of November while they were eating dinner that she told Howie of her decision. She brought the subject up by asking, "What would you think about me visiting Martin in New York for a few days?"

Howie just looked at her for a few seconds before he responded by saying, "You never went away before. Why are you going now?"

"I'm not really going away," she answered. "I'm just going to the city for a few days to do some Christmas shopping. You want me to get you something special, don't you?"

Howie thought for a few more seconds before he answered slowly, "Are you going to be seeing that Martin guy while you're there?"

"Yes, I'll be seeing Martin while I'm there. Does that bother you?"

Howie was looking down at his plate as he said, "You're not gonna' stay there with him and leave me here, are you?" When he looked up his eyes were starting to tear.

Cornelia immediately got up from her chair and stepped around the table and knelt down to put her arms around the boy and held him close. Kissing the top of his head she said, "There's no reason for you to ever worry about that. I love you more than anything and nothing can take me away from you."

"But how long are you gonna' be gone?" he asked.

"Just for a few days, baby. I'm going to fly there and back so I won't be gone long at all. I'll leave on Monday morning after Thanksgiving and come back by Friday. Only five days."

Howie pursed his lips and tipped his head to the side, obviously thinking and then said, "Could Jess come over and stay all week while you're gone?"

Cornelia got to her feet and put her hands on Howie's shoulders and looked down into his eyes as she said, "Honey, you know Jess can stay anytime he wants. You'll just need to check with his mother to see if it's okay for him to stay for a whole week."

"All right then," Howie said enthusiastically. "I'll ask him tomorrow."

Cornelia let out a sigh of relief at Howie's acceptance of her trip proposal. Now she could call Martin and start making her plans and already she was excited. She leaned over and kissed Howie on the head as she said something he really didn't understand, "I'm really not as much of an old woman as you might think. Sometimes I need to play and have a good time too."

Thanksgiving came and went with only a modicum of fuss. There was no large family to gather about so Cornelia, Howie and Rosey ate their turkey and just relaxed. Cornelia didn't mind at all since she was busy making plans for her trip and Rosey was helping her prepare.

After dinner, Howie had wandered off to Jess's house to see what was going on. The boys had been making plans for what they would do the week Cornelia would be gone. Since they would both be in school during the day, that left only the evenings free and Howie had an idea of how he wanted to spend that time. He wanted to learn about the dark.

Howie knew that Jess had no trepidation about the night and Howie had decided he wanted to overcome his fear. The main reason for this was that Howie was tired of being needled by Jess and, even more importantly, he hated loosing all of that time when he could have been prowling the streets. Howie thought of himself as a creature of the streets and now he wanted to also be a creature of the night. For more than a year he had been having trouble sleeping and had taken to getting up and looking out the window of his room for hours on end. He was getting used to the dark and since he already knew every bush, tree, building and bump for miles around he had decided to venture forth and see them after dark. He knew Jess would be with him and he was looking excitedly towards the adventure. He had said nothing to Jess about his intentions intending to surprise him with his daring.

Now it was ten o'clock on a Sunday morning, the day before Cornelia's departure and Howie and Jess were in the back of the poolroom playing a game of eight ball. The owner was dozing in an easy chair behind the counter obviously recovering from the night before. He had told the boys they could play for free as long as they held down the noise. Howie and Jess were passing a cigarette back and forth from a pack Howie had taken from home. They were the only customers in the place.

"Let's go to the show the 'safternoon," Howie said. "There's a Tarzan movie on at the Mainline."

"Okay with me," Jess said as he shot in the eight ball and won his third game in a row.

Howie put the wooden triangle on the table and racked up the balls for the next game saying, "We'll go in the back door five minutes after the show starts."

Jess nodded in agreement. Both boys knew the fifty years old edifice with the loose fitting exit doors was as easy to enter as their own homes. The trick was to open the door and duck inside and sit down in the crowd before an usher would hear the door open and close and spot the boys. They had only been caught one time and all that was done was to march them out the front door and onto the street. Thirty minutes later at their second attempt they had been successful.

They played pool until just after noon and then Howie reached in his pocket and pulled out a handful of crumpled up dollar bills. He waved them towards Jess and said, "Lets go over to Jake's Sandwich Shop and get a couple of cheeseburgers an' a milk shake." Howie always had money and he readily shared with his friend who seldom had more than change in his pockets. Howie could have easily paid their way into the movie but that was just not done. Howie believed that if you could sneak into a place or steal what you wanted it added enough excitement to make life interesting.

Three hours later when they came out of the theater it was drizzling a cold November rain. The boys had been disappointed in the movie. Watching Tarzan swim with a bunch of women was not their idea of entertainment. They hurried along to Jess's house where they picked up his belongings for the week long stay at Howie's and listened politely to Jess's mother's orders about how they should behave while Cornelia was gone on her trip.

The rain had stopped as they headed back to Howie's house but it seemed to be getting colder. As the boys talked, a cloud of vapor formed in front of their faces and this caused Howie to think of his cigarettes. He gave one to Jess and took one for himself as they stopped on the corner of an alley and, after looking both ways, lit up.

Howie was tapping his stick on the sidewalk, becoming restless about his mother's upcoming trip and Jess recognized the signs. Trying small talk to cheer Howie up, Jess said, "What'chu think your mom will bring you back from her trip?"

"I don't know and I don't care. There ain't nothin' I need. Just so long as she don't bring that asshole Martin back with her, I'll be happy." Howie's vocabulary was improving as he hung around the poolroom more and more.

"I thought that Martin guy was kinda' neat," Jess said. "He gave you those ball gloves an' stuff. Besides the way he fixed that old Dewey guy was really great."

"Oh yeah," Howie said belligerently, "because he didn't fix him near as good as I did!"

"What'chu mean," Jess asked.

"Nothin', I don't mean nothin'," Howie said.

"Cum'mon Howie, what happened?" Jess pleaded.

Howie realized he had already said more than he should but now he couldn't resist telling Jess the whole story of how he had knocked Dewey from the coal car to his death.

Jess eyes got big as he listened with rapt attention as the story unfolded, realizing that this was exactly what he had suspected all along but didn't want to admit even to himself.

The boys were now smoking another cigarette and were so engrossed in the story that they failed to notice the policeman walking their way. When he spoke both boys jumped and looked guilty.

"What're you boys doing here? You're to young to be smokin'."

"We ain't doin' nothin' Mr. Johnson," Howie said quickly. We're just on the way to my house."

"Where'd you boys get those cigarettes?"

"We just found them back there along the street. We was just foolin' around like, you know, smokin' to show off," Howie answered.

Both boys immediately dropped their cigarettes in a puddle and tried to look contrite. It never occurred to Johnson that finding dry cigarettes along the street on a rainy day was quite a trick, even for these two.

"What were you boys talking about when I walked up?" Officer Johnson asked. "You sure had your heads together about something."

"We was just talkin' about the Tarzan show we went to see at the Mainline," Howie said. "We didn't like it to good."

"Okay," Johnson said as he started to walk away, "but I thought it was a pretty good movie. Anyway, you boys quit that smokin' or your gonna' be getting into trouble with the law. Remember, I got my eye on you two so you better behave."

The boys cut through an alley to get out of Johnson's sight and hurried on to Howie's where they went leaping up the back steps and into the kitchen to see what Rosey was fixing for supper. There was a large pot of beef stew simmering on the stove and Rosey was just removing a pan of fresh biscuits from the oven. It looked like a perfect meal to Howie and Jess.

Cornelia was in the front room talking to a tall, thin woman about renting a room. Like all of Cornelia's tenants the woman worked for the railroad but she was a telegraph operator. She had just taken over the midnight shift at the depot just across the tracks from the rooming house. The fact that all the other tenants were men did not bother her at all. She had been working at this job since the war and was accustomed to being 'one of the boys'. She was in her mid-thirties and was not exactly a pretty woman but was neat and clean in appearance. Cornelia did not hesitate in renting her a room.

The boys had plopped down at the table only to have Rosey immediately bounce them back up and chase them into the bathroom to wash up. They were back in a flash and sat side by side, watching Rosey ladle the stew into their bowls and a platter of biscuits was placed between them. A large plate of semi-soft butter was on the table along with a dish of strawberry jam. The food was everything two boys their age could possibly want.

Cornelia and Rosey were busy talking about the details of the upcoming trip. Rosey was writing herself notes about what she should do while she was home alone including all of Cornelia's instructions. There were enough notes to cover the rest of the year instead of the five days Cornelia would be gone. Then there was the packing. Cornelia was taking one large suitcase for her clothing and a smaller one for her cosmetics. She intended to buy a whole new wardrobe of clothing and have her purchases shipped back to Newton.

The chatter and bustle of the women had no effect on Howie. He had resigned himself to his mother's trip and no longer paid any attention to the planning. He and Jess finished their meal and went into the front room to watch television. As he left the kitchen he heard his mother say, "The plane leaves Columbus at six-thirty in the morning so I want the cab to pick me up at five o'clock. That will give me an hour to get there and a half-hour to find my plane. Rosey, do you think that's long enough or should I leave at four-thirty?"

"Lordy, Miz Cornelia," Howie heard Rosey answer, "you know a lot more about those things than I do. I'm just so glad that you're taking a few days to see to your own self after being here in this skimpy little town for so long. It'll do you really good to take this trip."

Howie went through the door with Rosey's words in his head and he paused, not at all sure he liked the sound of Rosey's approval for the trip. It made him uneasy but he could not really put his finger on reason for his concern.

The worry slipped from his mind as Kukla, Fran and Oliver J. Dragon started entertaining the boys on the television. The boys laughed at the basic, unsophisticated humor of the program and Howie studiously ignored the continuing preparations from the women in the back of the house.

Earlier, in the privacy of his room, he had been making plans for what he intended to do while his mother was gone and he intended to discuss them with Jess after they went to bed. Howie was well aware of Rosey's creed of 'early to bed and early to rise' and those habits suited Howie just fine as long as he was excluded from the program. Ever since Cornelia had told him that she was making the trip, Howie had been planning and by tomorrow night, those plans would be in effect. Tonight the women would stay up late, sleep little and arise early. He could wait one more day.

The boys retreated to Howie's room when the more adult shows came on the television. They sat on the floor, reading comic books about Batman, Superman, Captain Marvel and World War Two. The adventure stories were the only ones they read and these were scanned over and over. The boys had removed their shoes and sat with their stocking feet on the register that fed warm air into the bedroom.

After it had been quiet in the house for a while, Howie got to his feet and said, "Com'ere, I wanta' show you something," and led Jess to his bedroom window. He pulled back the curtains and raised the window to reveal a second storm window on the outside. It was fastened with a hook at the bottom and hinged at the top. When the hook was released, the window swung open to allow a rush of cold air into the room. Howie pointed over the bottom sill at the ground only three feet below the lever of the window and then closed everything up and stepped back. "What'taya think of that?" he asked.

"I don't know," Jess answered somewhat puzzled. "What you got in mind?"

Howie answered with a knowing smile. "I was just showing you that we could get out the window anytime we want after Rosey goes to bed. She'll never know we're gone."

"You mean you want to go out at night?" Jess said. "You never wanted to do that before."

"Well I do now. I ain't afraid to go out and if you don't want to go then
I'll just go by myself. I can find my way around real good in the dark," Howie said.

"Course I'll go with you," Jess said. "You know I ain't afraid. When you want'a go?"

"Not tonight," Howie said. "They're gonna' be stirring around most of the night and my mom always comes in to check on me but Rosey never does cause she goes to bed real early. Tomorrow night will be soon enough when mom's gone."

The boys settled back on the floor. Howie was more excited than he wanted Jess to know. Nothing much had happened since Dewey and he was looking forward to what adventures he might be able to have in the dark.

****

The cab arrived shortly after four o'clock in the morning and Rosey carried the suitcases out front. She sat the large one at the rear of the cab for the driver to place in the trunk and the small one on the back seat under Cornelia's care. The driver opened the trunk and grasped the suitcase preparing to lift it into the trunk. The case didn't move and the driver let out a gasp as he said, "Damn, lady. What'chu got in this thing, bricks?"

"Move boy," Rosey commanded and easily flipped the suitcase into the trunk with apparent ease. The driver, standing well back out of the way, knew in a flash that Rosey was not a woman to be trifled with and nodded in respect before getting behind the wheel of the auto. He watched as the two women hugged good-by and then Cornelia got in the back seat and they were off.

Howie, watching surreptitiously from the window, saw her leave and then scurried back to bed before anyone saw him. He had been awake when his mother had slipped into his room earlier to kiss him on the forehead as he feigned sleep. Now he crawled quickly under the covers, lying still in case Rosey should look in but she walked past his room with a pause. He heard her heavy, carpet slippered steps pass into the kitchen where the light immediately went out and she retired back to her room. The house was completely quiet with the only noise coming from the nearby railroad but no one heard that rumbling.

CHAPTER NINE

It was five minutes to ten and Rosey had been in bed for almost half an hour. Howie came back into his room after listening in the hallway, closed the door softly and went immediately to the window. He raised the sill and unhooked the storm window, shoving it outward. He and Jess tumbled out onto the ground and Howie reached into his pocket for another treasure.

"Look here," he said as he pulled an old fashioned clothes pin from his pocket. He grasped a prong in each hand and split the pin into two pieces. He then pushed the storm window closed and wedged half of the clothes pin under the frame, holding the window shut and preventing it from banging in the night breeze.

"That's real neat," Jess said. "All we have to do is pull it out and we can get back in when ever we're ready."

Both boys had made up dummies in their beds of blankets and pillows so it would look like they were sleeping. Now they headed out dressed in dark, warm clothing into the early winter night. Howie was wearing a dark blue stocking cap to cover his blond hair.

"Cum'mon this way," Howie said. "I know where we're going and you're gonna' like it real good."

They boys crossed the south end of Newton, keeping to the alleys and shortcuts they knew so well. They crossed streets in a dash after looking both ways to check for car headlights. Howie soon led Jess to the rear of a sleezy bar in an alley several blocks from the middle of town. They stopped at the back door, which was slightly ajar.

"You wait here," Howie cautioned Jess. "This guy don't know you so I better go in alone this time." With those words Howie disappeared into the open door.

The kitchen he entered was filthy beyond belief. Open containers of garbage and trash were all around the room, every one filled to overflowing and each with it's own fragrance. Spiraling strips of fly paper hung from the ceiling in profusion, some of them left over from the previous Christmas eleven months earlier. The grease covered grill was a trap for the crawling creatures that were the bar's most numerous residents. Of course they only came out in the dark. One 25-watt light bulb burned from a wire hanging from the roof somewhere near the door that led to the front room of the establishment. This light only seemed to accent the darkness instead of dispelling it.

As Howie crept across the room he heard the uneasy scurrying of small creatures just beyond the edge of his vision. He stepped over a man's leg projecting barely into the light and silently hoped it was attached to a body. No way could he be sure of that. Howie pushed open a swinging door that led into the front and was immediately standing next to a large card table where several men were sitting and playing poker. There were literally hundreds of beer bottles around the table and Howie was careful not to step on any.

"Hey, kid, what'chu want?" the owner called from his seat at the table. He was a short, stocky man of late middle age with a very dark complexion and lots of curly black hair. Whether his dark skin was ethnic or environmental was difficult to say.

Howie had been here before and knew what to say. "I need two quarts of beer for my grandpa," and he held up two one-dollar bills in his hand. "I got the money right here."

"Yeah kid, sure. For your grandpa," the owner said with a guffaw as he got out of his chair and walked behind the bar with a lurching gait. He immediately returned with two big quart bottles of Burger beer and handed them to Howie after sticking the two dollar bills in his shirt pocket.

"Here you go, kid," he said with another laugh, "for your grandpa." and a couple of other men at the table joined in the chuckles.

Howie quickly retreated through the kitchen, stepping carefully over the leg and maintaining his balance on the greasy floor. Jess was waiting right outside the door and Howie held up his prizes.

As they walked away, Howie had his stick in one hand, a bottle of beer in the other and was trying to smoke a cigarette. He was one hand short. Finally he sat down on a stack of concrete blocks at the rear of a garage in the darkest part of the alley. In the ten minutes since they had left the bar Howie and Jess had swallowed about half of their beer and were getting a bit dizzy. Howie tried to hold the cigarette in his lips but the smoke kept making his eyes water. He didn't think this was manly so he set his beer on the ground and took the cigarette from his mouth. He kept his stick in his hand.

Neither boy cared much for the taste of the beer and would have preferred Pepsi Cola. On the other hand drinking Pepsi was not much of an adventure.

"How did'ja ever find that place to get the beer?" Jess asked.

"I just figured it out," Howie replied. "A quart of beer costs fifty cents so I offered the old guy a dollar a bottle and he sold it to me. I told him it was for my grandpa but he didn't believe me, he just acted like he did. My guess is the old man would sell anything if the price was right."

"What'chu want to do now?" Jess asked as he tipped up his bottle and drained the last of his beer, spilling some on the front of his shirt and giggling. There was a decided slur to his voice that was understandable for a third grade boy who had just downed a quart of beer.

"Watch this," Howie said. He was in the same shape as Jess and staggered slightly as he picked up his beer bottle and threw it over a garage. It sailed towards a house but fell short and exploded with a crash in the back yard. Both boys were already running down the alley, laughing uncontrollably as the lights came on at the rear of the house.

They headed back for the Five and Ten Cents store on Main Street and went up the fire escape at the rear of the building and crossed the roof, keeping low, to the front of the building where they could see without being seen. It was getting close to midnight and there was not much going on. The movies had all let out earlier and the only real activity they could see were the coming and going around the poolroom and some of the local bars. Both boys had the giggles from the beer and they took turns spitting on the different cars parked along the street.

"Ya suppose we better be gettin' back before something happens?" Jess asked.

"Yeah, I guess," Howie answered. "Besides I'm getting kind of sleepy. Let's head home."

Both boys walked back across the roof and down to the ground. Jess fell the last three steps causing both boys to laugh hysterically as they ran down the alley for home and bed.

****

The days had rushed by and Howie's mother was due back tomorrow and Jess would be going back home. It had been an exciting week and Howie was thrilled with the adventure of prowling the streets at night. It was something he wished he had started sooner. He was well accustomed to the dark and his intimate knowledge of the town had made it easy to get around.

It was now two o'clock in the morning and Howie sat looking out his window at the activities around the train station across the street. The last passenger train had left shortly after midnight and the next one wouldn't go until after six o'clock in the morning. The freight trains arrived and departed at the rate of a couple every hour. The engines moving freight in the railroad yards came past every few minutes. Howie had grown used to the phone in the upstairs hallway ringing at all hours of the night. It would soon be followed by a heavy tread on the stairs as the workers reported for duty on the train crews.

Howie slept very little for a child, generally less than four hours a night and as a result was generally lethargic in school. Most of his teachers put this down to indifference. Actually he was one of those 'night people' who only seemed to function after the sun went down. No matter how tired he was, once it got dark he came to life. When he was not prowling, he could look out the window for hours, engrossed in whatever he saw. Tonight was such a night.

He and Jess had roamed the streets until well after midnight. Now Jess was sleeping soundly and Howie was still watching. The woman who had recently moved in upstairs came out of the depot across the tracks and handed a handful of papers to a group of trainmen standing near a hissing steam engine. Her duty satisfied and in deference to the cold weather, she hurried back inside and sat down at a desk placed in a bay window where she could watch the passing trains. Three of the trainmen climbed up the ladder and into the engine while the other two started the long walk to the caboose at the end of the train.

Howie had a blanket that he had pulled from the bed draped around his shoulders. He sometimes dozed in this position as he watched the night hours go by but he almost always managed to wait for sunrise before going back to bed. He wanted to carry the colors of sunrise back to his dreams. Howie always dreamed in color and he found the iridescence of morning to be very satisfying because it seemed to help his dreams.

Flying was what he enjoyed the most. In his dreams he struggled so very hard to get into the air and, quite often, he would only just begin to soar before he would be dragged back down to earth, crashing clumsily to the ground. On rare occasions he would sail high above the town, looking down on all of the lesser creatures that were earthbound. That vision was pure ecstasy.

Now the sun started to rise, breaking through the morning clouds with the red and golden colors that, Howie knew, promised a dreary winter day. He concentrated on the colors, imprinting them on his mind before crawling back into bed, holding the brilliance behind his eyelids. He was immediately asleep, searching for his dreams and holding the colors like a security blanket wrapped around his mind.

The next day at school while Howie was at recess, he sat in a swing on the playground. The wooden seat hard was under his rear end, his hands holding onto the steel chains. Of the dozen swings in the schoolyard, his was the only one occupied.

Howie felt the push between his shoulders at the same time he heard the voice say, "Hey kid, get out'ta my swing!"

Howie looked around to see Moosie Miller and two of his cronies standing behind him. Moosie was the biggest kid in the whole school and he was a sixth grader. He had noticed that Howie was a loner and since Moosie was a predator, he had wrongly assumed that the smaller, younger boy was legitimate prey for him and his friends.

"Hey, I said for you to get out of my favorite swing," Moosie repeated, grinning at his cohorts.

Howie just sat, looking down at his toes resting in the shallow, foot worn trench beneath the swing. He wasn't really afraid of Moosie and thought if he just sat quietly, the boys might go away and leave him alone. No such luck. Moosie reached out and grabbed the chain that supported the swing and began jerking it back and forth.

"You quit that and leave me alone!" Howie said as he scowled at the three older boys. "There're lots of other swings, use one of them!"

In answer, Moosie gave Howie a push in the middle of the back that sent Howie sprawling on his hands and knees in the gravel of the schoolyard.

"I said I wanted THIS swing," and Moosie sat down and laughed as Howie got up off the wet ground.

Howie didn't run away, he just stood his ground looking intently at Moosie.

"What'chu lookin' at, you little creep?" Moosie asked from his seat in the swing.

"Nothin' much," Howie answered.

"Yeah, well look at this," said Moosie's bully buddy, Lester Lee, as he stepped forward and pushed Howie solidly in the chest, again knocking him to the ground. Lester, who was not much bigger than

Howie, would never have had the nerve to do anything without Moosie to back him up.

Howie got up again and stood looking intently at his foes. He was deciding what to do next and Lester, not sure of what might be coming, took a couple of steps back. The third boy, a kid Howie didn't know, just stood and watched.

"Okay," Howie said with his most captivating smile, "you guys win," and he turned and walked away as unconcerned as if he was the only child on the playground. What the other three boys didn't see was that, as soon as his back was turned, Howie allowed all of his rage to show in his face. In his head he could hear only one thing. WHACK-WHACK-WHACK!!

When school let out that afternoon, Howie hurried to the corner where Jess was waiting. The first three grades got out ten minutes before the second three and it was Jess's custom to wait for his friend.

"Do you know some big kid in the sixth grade they call Moosie?" Howie asked Jess.

"Yeah, I know who he is, that's all. He's pretty tough an' I stay away from him. Why, what'd he do?"

"Oh, nothin' much," Howie said. "Just him an' a couple other kids pushed me around a little bit at recess. What do you know about him?"

Jess thought for a minute before he answered. "His dad's a cop an' he's always got two or three guys with him an' he's pretty tough. He likes to push people around and he calls me names whenever he sees me. I stay away from him 'cause those guys could really hurt you if they got the chance."

Howie calmly recounted the story of how he had been pushed around on the playground and he finished by saying, "an' I ain't gonna' put up with them pushing me around."

Jess studied Howie intently as the story concluded and he saw all of the anger shining in Howie's blue eyes. He was no longer afraid of what Moosie might do, now his fear was what action Howie would take.

"I gotta' be getting on home," Howie said suddenly changing the subject. "My mom should be home by now an' I wanna' go see her. Are you coming over in a little bit to get your clothes and stuff?"

" Yeah," Jess answered. "I'll be over after I stop at home. What'chu want to do?"

"Oh, I don't know. Maybe just walk around for a little while. I'll think about it and let you know when you come over."

"Okay, I'll be over as soon as I can," Jess said as he headed for the railroad tracks and his shortcut for home.

Howie started walking slowly but steadily, the cold air making a cloud in front of his face. He pretended he was smoking and tried to blow smoke rings in front of his face. It didn't work. He was thinking mostly about Moosie and his trouble in the schoolyard.

Howie was now deep in the world of his imagination and that was a very private place. He could imagine all sorts of improbable scenarios that would feature him as the hero, always having the last word and saying just the right thing. He also involved himself in confrontations where he was the quickest and strongest and most cunning. These thoughts helped him with his planning of revenge and also made him more patient. Now Howie was already planning for an attack on Moosie Miller and he was looking forward to watching his enemy. Howie felt that Moosie's attack on him was totally unjustified and he was now going to retaliate in the most forceful manner he could devise. There was absolutely no rationale for the actions Moosie had taken against him. Nobody would have been able to convince Howie that Moosie was a semi-literate, lonely, abused child who should be ignored.

****

"Oh, Rosey, it was wonderful," Cornelia was saying as Howie came in the back door. "Martin has a car and he met me at the airport and we…" she broke off talking and grabbed Howie and hugged him tightly, burying her face in his blond hair and kissing the top of his head.

"Hi, Mama," he said wrapping his arms around her waist. "I'm sure glad you're home."

"And I'm glad to be back home," she replied. "You didn't have any trouble while I was gone, did you?"

"No Mama, I just missed you," Howie said.

"I missed you too, Baby. Now sit down and I'll tell you all about my trip." Rosey made a suggestion that was greeted with enthusisiam when she said, "How about some cookies and milk while we talk. I baked peanut butter cookies, your favorite, this afternoon and they're still hot from the oven."

"Oh boy," Howie said, "but can I have coffee with mine like you guys do? They're better with coffee than they are with milk."

Of course Cornelia indulged his request, flavoring his coffee heavily with sugar and milk as she drank hers' along with him.

With their snack in front of them she began her story. Howie was only moderately attentive as he listened to her talk about the new United Nations Building and the Broadway show, 'South Pacific'. He grew more restless as she talked about seeing a thirty-three year old Frank Sinatra perform his nightclub show singing the new tune 'New York, New York' and when she started talking about the old neighborhood and Martin's car, a Lincoln Continental, he lost interest completely.

Jess had slipped quietly into the kitchen while the story telling was going on and was eating cookies, preferring milk with his snack.

"Mama," Howie interrupted, "would it be okay for me an' Jess to walk downtown?"

"Sure, Baby," Cornelia said, "just be back in time for supper."

"We will, Mama," Howie said as he jumped up and headed out the back door, pulling on his coat as he thundered down the back steps with Jess right on his heels.

They ran for about a block before Howie stopped and turned to Jess, saying, "Let's go up to Pear Street. There's something up there I want to take a look at."

"What's that?" Jess asked.

"Moosie Miller lives somewhere on Pear Street and I wanna' see if I can figure out which house it is. I just wan'ta look around a little bit."

"You ain't gonna' do nothing, are you?" Jess asked apprehensively.

"No, I ain't gonna' do nothin'" Howie said in a whining voice as he mocked Jess's concern. "I just want to have a look around in the daylight."

Pear Street was only three blocks long, dead-ending at a cross alley. It was four streets on the other side of downtown in what used to be one of the better sections of Newton. That had been fifty years ago and now the houses were slightly run down and showed more wear than they did maintenance. The street was lined with large maple trees with an occasional hickory or buckeye thrown in.

The boys walked slowly as Howie studied the area and stopped when Howie grabbed Jess's arm with one hand and pointed with the other.

At a house across the street there was a twelve-foot stepladder leaning against the spouting on the front porch and a fat man was half way up with a roll of Christmas lights hanging from his arm. One end of the string was attached to the edge of the porch roof and it was obvious that the man intended to string the lights as decorations. Standing on the ground, looking up at the man on the ladder was Moosie. Howie and Jess moved to a spot directly across the street and stationed themselves where they would be hidden by the trunks of some large maple trees.

"Can't you do nothin' right," the man was saying. "I said hand me those pliers and another handful of them goddam staples."

Moosie extended his arm over his head with the pliers in his hand. The man on the ladder, who was in fact his father, looked down and said, "Get your lazy ass up this ladder and hand those to me and bring the staples with you. Jesus, do I have to tell you everything to do?"

Even from across the street Howie and Jess could tell that the man was about half drunk and they settled down to watch the show. All of old man Miller's Christmas cheer was in his stomach.

In the process of grabbing the pliers from Moosie's hand and holding on to the ladder, Miller dropped his hammer barely missing Moosie's head and causing him to jump from the ladder and glance up at his father for the first time. Moosie just stood, looking at the hammer at his feet until his father said, "Hey dummy, wake up down there and hand me up the hammer. You're supposed to be helping get these decorations hung up for your Ma."

Moosie picked up the hammer and handed it back up to his father. He wasn't smart but he had learned to keep his mouth shut when his old man was drinking and in a bad mood. Not that old man Miller was ever in a good mood, it was just that when he was drinking his fist could come from anywhere, at anytime, with astonishing force.

"Hell's bells," the old man said, "I might as well get one of your sisters out here to help. At least I don't have to tell them every goddam thing I want them to do."

Howie and Jess, watching from their hiding place behind the tree were enjoying themselves immensely. They kept grabbing each other and giggling as they cautioned each other of the possibility of discovery.

"Ga'wan in the house and get me another bottle of beer," they heard old man Miller order. Of course after Moosie brought it out, his father had to send him back in the house to open it.

The show was obviously going to last longer than the boys could stay and when about half the lights had been put up, they slipped away and headed for supper at Howie's house. It had been a wonderful excursion into Moosie's world. Although he looked big to the boys, Galen Miller, Moosie's father, was not all that tall. At about five foot eight, his two hundred and thirty pounds made him physically formidable.

****

Galen Miller's uncle was the Chief of Police and, because of this, he had joined the police department and been appointed Sergeant over many more qualified men. But if you had asked him what the word 'nepotism' meant you would only have received a blank stare. But then anyone was more qualified than Galen Miller. He had an eighth grade education and a forth grade mentality. Even when he had been drafted into the army, he was the only soldier anyone ever heard of who had to go through boot camp twice.

After the war his uncle had helped him get on the police, a move that was soon regretted. Galen could not cope with even the most minor problem of patrol duty so it had been necessary to appoint him Sergeant and give him a desk job out of the public eye. Galen had managed to learn the rudimentary operation of the radio and the telephone.

Galen Miller had been married when the war had broken out, having been responsible for a fifteen-year-old neighbor girl becoming pregnant (he was twenty-one at the time) and Moosie was a result of that union. His wife had a second child while he was in the service stationed in Europe. He had been gone from home for fifteen months when the child was born but it never occurred to his that his wife had not been expecting when he left home as she had claimed. The third child was born about seven months after he returned home, slightly premature his wife claimed.

These last two children, both girls, were exactly like their mother, sluggish, sullen and none too clean. They had learned to beware of their father who was apt to bring them around to his way of thinking in a sudden and forceful manner if they became too insolent. Their mother had learned the same thing years earlier, but now she had become as clever as a fox…or maybe mink would be a better description.

Dinner that night in the Miller household was pretty much

standard fare. Round steak fried in an iron skillet and boiled potatoes cut into chunks with butter over them. The kids had milk to drink and Moosie's mother, Angela, drank coffee. Galen Miller drank beer before, during and after his meal. It was a normal evening with the Miller clan.

After eating, the old man went back to finish the job of putting up the Christmas lights. After he had them strung around the porch he was pretty well drunk having finished off more than a dozen beers.

"Angela, com'ere and hand me something," Galen yelled at his wife.

She came into the front room to see him standing next to a front room window with an extension cord in his hand. He opened the window and stepped out onto the front porch. "When I get up on the ladder, you hand the end of this cord up to me," he told her.

She followed him through the window and waited as he climbed the ladder before dutifully passing up the cord so they could plug in the lights. To her surprise, the lights all came on with a glow that caused the front of the house to look somewhat attractive. The only problem was that now the front window would not completely close due to the fat extension cord. Galen Miller looked at it only a few seconds before wedging the window down as far as it would go and heading for the kitchen and another beer. He was thinking that when he set the Christmas tree in front of that same window the cold air would help to keep it fresh and green.

Now, armed with a fresh beer he plopped down into his favorite chair to watch the television for a while. Midget wrestling was just coming on and he did not want to miss that latest display of American culture.

****

Back at Howie's house the boys were also watching the midgets chase each other around the ring and through the referee's legs. They had been giggling and happy since they had returned to the house and Jess had phoned his mother for the first time in his life. Jess's father had gone to work at a local glass company and there were a few luxuries starting to come their way.

****

Cornelia was happy with Howie's good humor but Rosey was watching him much more closely. Rosey knew well that happiness on Howie's part usually meant bad news for the rest of the world. That Jess was also in a good mood allayed her fears somewhat but she still intended to keep a watchful eye on Howie for the next few days.

****

As soon as supper was done, Cornelia had gone into the front room and started unpacking a huge portmanteau that had been delivered from the railroad that afternoon. She had shipped it from New York by rail and it contained most of the purchases she had made on her trip. Some of the packages were already gift wrapped and had card on them. Howie's name was most prominent on the cards but 'Rosey' and 'Jess' appeared often enough to keep everyone wondering. There were even some marked 'Cornelia' and the others thought that was strange until Cornelia explained by telling them that Martin had sent some packages for all of them to open at Christmas.

She went on by saying "I saw Santa Claus when I went to Macy's Department store and he also sent some packages along for all of us."

The packages were sorted by name and put in groups awaiting placement under the Christmas tree that was soon to come.

Howie spoke up and asked if he and Jess could go out for a while to attend a basketball game at the gymnasium near the high school.

Cornelia expressed concern and surprise that the boys were going out after dark but, after extracting numerous promises to be careful, she gave each boy five dollars and sent them on their way.

As they headed for downtown, Jess said, "Your mom's really neat. She lets you do about anything you want and she is always given' you money and stuff. I really like her, you know?"

"Yeah, I guess she's okay but she is old," Howie said. "She don't really know much about stuff 'cause she ain't never really be around."

CORNELIA

In the early years of the twentieth century, pregnant single women did not have the options available to them that they now have in this so-called modern day and age. Legal abortions were almost non-existent and the main method of dealing with this situation was to farm the girl out to distant relatives, let the baby be born and then put the child in a home of some kind. Most of these facilities were holdovers from the middle ages and the children left in them had a chance of survival but little hope of a productive future. There were exceptions.

The baby girl Smith was left in such a facility in central Ohio in the year 1907 and she survived. She was a pretty baby with the blond hair that was almost white. Such hair usually darkened as the child got older but hers' stayed that platinum color and with her blue/violet eyes she was truly a beautiful child. Because of her looks she could have been adopted many times from the orphanage except for the fact that the couple who ran the facility wanted her for their own. They managed to keep her until she was seventeen years of age and then one night she just disappeared.

When the baby had first been taken in, she had been named Cornelia by the combination cook/housekeeper who had developed a special affection for the girl. This woman was trapped by her race in a menial job far below her intellectual ability. She could see that the baby girl Cornelia was in the same trap.

By the time the girl was five years old, the male half of the couple who ran the home had developed a feeling for the child that would last for as long as the girl was available to him. It started with him holding the girl on his lap for long periods of time and continued on from there. By the time Cornelia was eleven years old she had been exposed to every type of sexual practice the warped mind of the man and his wife could imagine. Alone or together, they used her in ways that bordered on insane.

Only the black housekeeper was aware of what was going on with the three of them. The housekeeper spent as much time as she dared trying to shield and comfort the girl and soften the blows that life was dealing forth. She countered the abuse with all the love she had to give.

****

As Cornelia approached adulthood, she started to understand what she was told by the housekeeper, her self appointed guardian. Cornelia started to make plans of her own. She had learned the quiet subterfuge of women and the lust of men and she would use these lessons to make a new life for herself.

Cornelia left Ohio by train on June 12, 1924 and headed East towards New York City. She had all the money she had been able to steal from those in the home. That escape was the start of a streak of good luck that was to continue for many years. On the train she rode out of town were many of the delegates from the Republican National Convention in Cleveland. They were returning to Washington, D.C. and they immediately asked her to join their party on the train. It was just what Cornelia needed. She passed herself off as being twenty-two years old and accompanied the men back to their home base of Washington. She knew she would eventually get to New York and was in no hurry to be anywhere.

She ended up in a suite of rooms at a hotel on the outskirts of Washington with several of her suitors splitting the bill and keeping her in spending money. They were also generous with gifts of merchandise that she converted to cash and hid away for whatever the future might bring.

Cornelia stayed there through the summer and fall but, when the Republicans actually won the elections in November and fearing a possible scandal, her paramours gave her traveling money and had her move on. This suited Cornelia just fine and after adopting the last name of Lawson, she moved on to New York City.

She took a small apartment on the edge of the garment district and began to establish her trade. She had become more beautiful than nature should have ever allowed and this made her plans work perfectly. She let herself be seen and noticed by the important men of the area and in subtle ways let them know that she was available. But she was not available to just anyone, only to the men who could pay the price for top quality companionship.

Cornelia soon had a list of admirers who supported her in lavish style. And she always remembered the most important lesson of her youth, never be poor because then others can use you however they please. She saved every spare penny she could get her hands on because even at this time, still in her teens, she knew she could not go on forever. She could only last as long as her looks held up.

CHAPTER 10

It was February of 1925 and Cornelia was cold. She lay in bed in her room trying to read a book about 'The Great Gatsby' but the cold was seeping into her body and she had trouble trying to concentrate. She got up, put her coat on and headed for the basement to try and get more heat up to her third floor apartment.

At the bottom of the basement stairs she called out, "Mose Cole, are you down here?" He was the building custodian and lived in one room far in the back of the basement.

"Yas'am, I'm back here," came a voice from somewhere in the gloom. Mose was as black as the darkness and she could not tell exactly where he was except by following the sound of his voice.

Mose came into view and he was bundled up with what looked to be all the clothes he owned. "I know what you want, Miz Corny," he said, "but we only got a little bit of coal left and I don't know when we're gonna' get any more because of the strikes."

New York was suffering one of the coldest winters ever and people were freezing to death in their own homes caused by a lack of coal because of a strike by the United Mineworkers of America. Unions could do good and bad at the same time.

"I'm trying to keep enough heat in the building to keep the pipes from freezing," Mose went on, "and that's about all I can do."

Cornelia was on good terms with Mose. He understood what she did for a living but was not one to pass judgment. They were both alone in the city and were getting by, although she was doing a little better than he was doing.

"Well it looks like back to bed for me," she said with a grin, "even if it's only to try and keep warm." She took her leave of the basement and went back to her room knowing well that nobody, no matter how motivated, would go out on a night as cold as this.

Back in her room she piled all the blankets she owned on the bed and, her coat still around her, crawled back under the covers. She hoped the phone would not ring but, if it did, she would probably make the house call as long as the price was right.

Cornelia had started working from the telephone about a month ago. Shortly before that she had been in a delicatessen eating lunch when she had seen the waitress, busy on the phone, taking call in orders for food and realized the potential for her own business. Within a month she had a phone installed and had made her growing list of customers aware of the convenience. Now all she could do was wait out the weather and hope the phone didn't ring.

****

It was June and winter was long gone. Cornelia left the building and walked two blocks to where she was meeting one of her better customers for a two-day trip to Philadelphia. His name was Arthur Flegenheimer but he went by a couple of nicknames, one of them being Dutch Schultz. He always treated her rather casually and she believed that the only real reason he took her out was so that he could be seen with a beautiful blond on his arm. They were going to spend the day walking around the current World's Fair, then stay the night in Philly and return the following day. She knew he would take a couple of his men with him and was thinking that if she did any work at all, it would probably be for them. It made no difference to her because she knew that Arthur would give her good money for the trip and that was what really mattered.

She arrived at the corner and only waited a few minutes before the car pulled up and Arthur, who was in the front seat but not driving, motioned her into the back of the big convertible. She sat quietly and listened to the men discuss the problems they were having with bad liquor at the speakeasies they were running around town. This situation did not concern her so she just sat, her suitcase between her feet, and enjoyed the passing scenery. She knew that the reason the men spoke freely in her presence was a tribute to her intelligence and her known ability to keep whatever she heard strictly to herself.

The trip went pretty much as she had imagined it would go and

Cornelia spent that evening strolling past the various displays at the fair. She held the left arm of her escort and, though she appeared to only have eyes for him, she was well aware of the stares of appraisal of her face and form from the passing crowds. Her job was to make Arthur look good and she was the very best at her job. That evening they went to the best hotel in Philadelphia where a suite of rooms had been reserved. The men sat in the largest room talking and smoking their cigars while she sat alone back in a corner, waiting. Late in the evening several more men arrived and Arthur spoke to her for the second time that day, telling her to go into the bedroom and that he would be in later. Every man in the room ogled her openly as she walked across the room and through a door but she kept her eyes demurely downcast, knowing well her part in Arthur's life.

In the bedroom, she undressed and crawled into a huge bed, completely naked, and pulled the sheet up to her shoulders. After a while she went to sleep and as far as she could tell, nobody else came into the room all night.

The next morning, after an elaborate breakfast in the hotel dining room, they drove back to New York where she was handed two five hundred dollar bills and dropped off on the same corner where she had been picked up. As she got out of the car, Arthur spoke to her for the third time telling her he would call again soon. As the car drove off down the street, Cornelia started her two-block walk back to her house. It had been a pretty much normal excursion, she thought.

At home, she was surprised to find a large moving van parked in front of the apartment house. The small, used furniture store at ground level was moving out of the building. She walked inside to find old Mr. Eisenberg almost in tears. He grabbed her hand as she entered his apartment/business and squeezed it with both of his hands.

"Oy, Oy, I have to leave all of my security," he explained. "My brother has died and I must go clear to Long Island and help his wife." He went on to explain, sometimes with tears in his eyes that he and his brother had come to this country from Russia just before the turn of the century. Not wanting to compete in business they had lived this distance apart. Both had small shops run out of where they lived but his brother's place had been in a building all by itself. Now he would be going further from his home than he had ever been since he came to this country and because of his advanced age, he was frightened.

Cornelia put her arms around the old man and comforted him as best she could before retreating to her room, well aware she would never see Mr. Eisenberg again. It just helped prove to her that the bad people would always be around but the good people disappeared from your life for no rhyme or reason. She hid her money at her cache in her apartment just as the phone rang. She put the old man out of her mind and got back to business.

The next morning as she returned home, a tall young man was standing in the doorway of the shop so recently vacated. He spoke to her as she entered the building and told her his name was Martin Fields. He was opening a rare coin and stamp shop in the now refurbished first floor rooms. Cornelia knew that Martin was destined to become a part of her life.

CHAPTER ELEVEN

More than a year had passed since Martin Fields had moved into the building and during that time he and Cornelia had become fast friends. He watched her come and go at all hours of the day and night, suspecting what she did for a living. After much thought he asked her if she would like to see a movie with him. He was not interested in romance, at least not with a woman, and she understood this and accepted him just as he was, never passing judgment.

She readily accepted and arrived at his door dressed fit to kill. Nice clothing was a part of her business and since she was not working this evening, she had decided to dress up and enjoy herself.

"You ready, Marty?" she asked as she stood in his doorway.

"I sure am," he answered. "Boy, you certainly look nice. If I didn't know better I would guess you were still a teenager." Although Martin was several years older than Cornelia was, he believed them to be nearly the same age.

He was dressed in his best and though it was not in her league, he didn't really care. Her straight blond hair fell exactly to her shoulders held in place by a red hair band around her brow. A fashionable, gold spangled flapper dress and medium heeled red slippers with sheer white cotton stockings completed her outfit. She was carrying a white cashmere sweater casually over her shoulder in deference to the early October weather.

They started walking towards the theater and Martin said with great admiration, "Good God, Corny, any man in New York would give almost anything to have you walking by his side," then lowered his voice to add, "and some of them probably have." They both laughed out loud causing others on the sidewalk to turn and smile at the handsome man and beautiful woman as they walked hand in hand, totally at ease.

Cornelia dropped his hand and took his arm, resting her cheek against his shoulder as she whispered back, "And maybe some of those same men wouldn't mind being out with you either."

They continued to laugh as each enjoyed the company of the only friend either had in the city.

They were going to see a new movie that had just been released called "The Jazz Singer" and it was the first talking picture to ever appear in New York. They were both big movie fans and attended as often as they could, seeking escapism in the thrill of motion pictures. Martin ran his business twelve hours a day, every day and closed only on holidays or when the weather made it impossible for people to visit his shop. Tonight the two of them had agreed to relax and indulge themselves. As she had been leaving the apartment, the phone had rung but she had never looked back.

They sat through the movie and then followed the crowd where he stopped her and suggested they see it again. She happily agreed and so he bought two more tickets and they went back inside, still laughing like a couple of kids.

****

They spent Christmas of 1928 sitting in the front room of his apartment that also served as his shop. The chairs were comfortable and the windows were low enough to allow a good view of the passing populace. There were sweet rolls and coffee on the table between them and they were quietly enjoying the day. She had surprised him with the gift of a pearl gray fedora and had been surprised in return. He had for her a velvet box containing a new twenty-dollar gold piece in an ornate bezel on a gold chain.

Earlier they had walked together to the basement where she had given Mose Cole two new pairs of Levi's and two woolen work shirts and Martin had given him a twenty-dollar gold piece less the holder and chain.

Now, as they sat comfortably in their chair, the main topic of conversation was a wax carton that sat in the middle of the table. The day before when Martin had gone to the front step to get his milk delivery, instead of the usual bottles, he found the wax quart cartons waiting near the front door.

"What won't they think of next," he said as they poured milk into their coffee.

Cornelia smiled but her mind seemed to be on something else. She was staring at large new steel safe Martin had recently moved into his apartment. "Martin, can I ask a favor of you?" she said.

"Of course you can. What is it?"

She hedged a bit at first as she said, "Do you like living here and are you planning on staying and keeping your business here?"

"Yeah, I like it here and business had been pretty good. I wouldn't want to move and start over again somewhere else. Besides it takes a lot of work to get a shop set up with that big safe and all," Martin answered.

Aware of his curious look, Cornelia went on. "It's about the safe that I want to talk to you. Would you have room to keep a small box in it for me?"

Martin nodded as he said, "Sure, Cornelia, you know I would. We'll put it separate and make sure that no one ever touches it but you. Hell, you don't even have to tell me what's in it if you don't want to."

Cornelia smiled as she continued; "I don't mind telling you. It's some money I've saved up and I worry more about a fire than anything else. I'm not crazy about doing business with a bank and having anyone else know my business but I would like my money to be in a safe place."

"Just bring it here and we can lock it up right now," Martin said.

Within minutes Cornelia had gone to her apartment and returned with a cigar box with string tied around it. Martin opened the safe and she put it inside, on the bottom, way in the back. She had said there was money in the box and Martin suspected it was her life savings, nothing formidable but important to her. At a time when the average woman working in New York was making thirty-three dollars for a fifty-hour week, Cornelia had just put over seventy-five thousand dollars in the safe. Martin knew she was good, he just didn't know how good she was and who her customers were. They closed the door with a solid thump and shook hands on their deal.

****

It was the summer of 1929 and Cornelia had taken Martin shopping with her at some of the most fashionable shops in the city. She had bought many of the latest fashions recently put on the market by CoCo Chanel, the newest and, quite possibly, the finest designer of clothes in the world. She spent so much money that Martin started to get scared she wouldn't be able to pay for her purchases, but this was definitely not the case. She needed the clothes because she had several customers who worked at Tammany Hall and she had to look extra nice when they took her too political functions and dinners. Besides they were the ones who were really buying the clothes.

After shopping they went to the Cotton Club in Harlem. There were very few black people in attendance except as employees. That day they heard Bessie Smith sing and saw Bojangles Robinson dance up and down his special stairs. When the show was over, because of all the packages and the late hour they hailed a taxi for their ride home.

During the ride Martin was telling Cornelia, "I've taken all of my money out of the bank and cashed in all of my stocks and bonds. Everything seems to be in turmoil and I believe something bad could happen. Things have just been going great for too long of a time. If anything did happen, a person with cash on hand could be in a very strong position. I've never stuck my nose into your affairs but if you have money in any bank or own many stocks and bonds, I would advise you to sell."

"Thanks for your concern, Martin," Cornelia said, "but I've avoided making any investments. I do agree with you though, all the talk I've been hearing indicate the stock market could be in trouble. You know some of my customers are in that business and some of them have been pretty nervous lately." She didn't add that the only security she believed in was the cash you could hold in your hand.

"Now that you have brought up the subject, I would like to put another package in your safe if I could," she went on. She had spent several days in Washington D. C. and made a lot of money in tips as well as the money from her regular business and she wanted to put it away.

When they returned home she dashed up to her apartment and returned with a cardboard milk carton she had rinsed out and was now sealed on the end with adhesive tape. She put it in the safe on top of her cigar box. Neither knew it but, as good as times had been up to now, the best times of their lives were only three months away.

****

The stock market crash at the end of October in 1929 ruined a lot of people but Martin and Cornelia worked it to their benefit. They had cash and his business improved in leaps and bounds. He was able to buy coins and stamps for pennies on the dollar from the formally rich and famous. Her business stayed pretty much the same but the only BIG tips came from the politicians and gangsters.

In November Jimmy Walker was elected Mayor of New York City and Cornelia was well acquainted with him and the Tammany Hall boys and she knew they had most of the money in the City.

The following summer Cornelia purchased the building where they lived and moved her apartment to the second floor. She had all the apartments rented to married couples and did not allow children in the building. Any who had kids had to find someplace else to live. All the tenants believed Martin was the landlord and paid their rents to him. Not even Mose Cole knew that Cornelia was the real owner. She had bought the building through Martin at a foreclosure sale from the bank and only had to pay a fraction of what it was worth since nobody else had money to bid against her.

The years passed quickly and early in December 1933, prohibition had been repealed. Martin and Cornelia were again sitting in his front room but now they were drinking rum and Pepsi-Cola to celebrate the new law. They had called Mose Cole to join them and he was also fitted up with a drink in his hand. They had talked well into the night. Tomorrow was Sunday and Martin never opened his shop until noon. Jimmy Walker had been defeated in his run for second term as mayor and now Fiorello LaGuardia was in office and Cornelia was telling the two men about how he was running the politics.

"Everyone who works for the city has to give their boss at least a dollar a week for an election support fund and the higher paying jobs require a bigger donation. On top of that they only hire relatives or people who actually buy their jobs. Getting on the police or fire department can cost as much as five hundred dollars but then they have a position for life. I really don't expect much to change with the new administration because it's been going on for too long." She was slightly drunk, an unusual condition for her, and she was talking about things she normally would keep to herself. Her slightly slurred speech was amusing to Martin and embarrassing to Mose.

A year ago Franklin Roosevelt had been elected president and soon after had started his 'fireside chats' on the radio. Listening to him was how the three had started their evening. He had spoken at great length about promises for economic recovery but they, like so many others, were skeptical of any politician.

"I met him a couple of times both here in New York and in Washington," Cornelia told the men. "I do believe he is sincere in trying to help the country get out of this depression but there are so many crooks in office that every time he takes two steps forward, they jerk him back at least one. It's going to take a lot more than promises to get this country back on its' feet."

Martin agreed, knowing very little about politics beyond what Cornelia had taught him while they sat around listening to the speeches on the radio. Mose said nothing at all. He was just happy to have friends who cared enough to have him visit and imbibe the rum and cola. If you would have got him to admit it, he would have preferred the cola without the rum but he was being sociable and besides no one had bothered to ask.

As the clock passed midnight, Mose trundled off to his room down below after promising to check the heat on the way. They had talked later this night than usual and it was getting a little cool with the fires burning low in the two huge furnaces in the basement. A second furnace had been added last summer and all the tenants had thanked Martin for his thoughtfulness not knowing that it had been Cornelia's doing. She hated being cold and now there was one furnace to heat the four apartments on the first floor and a bigger unit to heat the eight apartments on the second and third floors.

Only minutes after Mose left for the night, Cornelia crossed the hall to her apartment and the three friends turned in for the night.

****

In the summer of 1934, Cornelia did some business with several men who were in town from Hollywood and they persuaded her to accompany them on their return trip to the West Coast. They all flew out and she stayed two weeks before returning home alone. She was disappointed in the trip to the movie capitol. All the men wanted was the same thing they wanted in New York but in Hollywood they wanted to pay her with promises to put her in the movies, Not Money!

She did manage to return with lots of new clothes from the stylish West Coast boutiques. And she also found the plane travel to be very exciting and the eighteen-hour trip much superior to four days by train.

She did notice there was a lot of money in Hollywood while the rest of the country was pretty well broke. Still she decided that the only way she would return to California was if she was working.

****

By the spring of 1936 the country was slowly coming out of the depression. Germany was much in the news but the only time any of them thought about that foreign country was when Cornelia took Martin for a Sunday drive in her new automobile. It had been a gift from one of her clients, Mr. Luciano, who had become her best customer. Arthur was no longer around having been shot to death the previous fall while doing business over in New Jersey.

She had converted an old carriage house at the rear of the apartment building into a garage for the snub-nosed Volkswagen Beetle. And she turned a lot of heads when she putted around town. The car had been promoted worldwide by that Hitler fellow and because of this not many people would buy it. This did not bother Mr. Luciano due to the fact that a friend of his, Benito Mussolini, was also a friend of Hitler. Besides Luciano had little compunction about flouting public opinion. 'Lucky' received the first of the cars to come to this country. They had been delivered to his home and he, in turn, gave them away to his friends. Cornelia had received hers' after spending the weekend at his home and, when it came time to leave, he had no one available to chauffeur her. He gave her one of the cars and told her to drive it home and keep it.

She had never driven a car before but she knew a good thing when she saw it so she just hopped and jumped the vehicle back to the front of her apartment house and arranged for Martin to teach her how to drive.

Soon after he had given her the car, Luciano had been sent to jail for promoting prostitution but Cornelia knew that would only be a temporary condition. Several times he had tried to get her to come to work for him but she had always been able to charm her way out of that situation.

****

The following summer she got up one Sunday morning with no appointments ahead of her and, after scanning the papers, walked across the hall to knock loudly on Martin's door.

"Marty, are you up?" she called through the door.

He opened the door and she entered. He had been sitting near the front window reading the morning paper and drinking coffee. "Come in and have a cup," he said. As she poured her coffee, he went on, "What got you up and stirring on this fine morning?"

Cornelia sat down on the arm of a large chair with the china cup held in both hands and said, "I don't have to work today so if you want, I'll take you downtown to see a jazz concert. Benny Goodman is playing at the Paramount Theater and I'm buying if you'll go with me."

"Sure," he said. "You know I can't pass up a deal like that. Are we driving or taking the street car?"

"Driving, but you'll have to drive. These new long dresses make it hard for me to work the pedals in the car." She was not happy with the tight, long dresses with the high collars that were now in fashion because, as she put it, they didn't allow her to show off her merchandise.

They arrived at the theater a little early and she paid the seventy cents it cost to get in. Their early arrival let them get good seats up close and they thoroughly enjoyed the show. When it was over, as they had done so many times before, she bought two more tickets and they went right back inside.

CHAPTER TWELVE

It was now the first of August in 1938 and Cornelia and Martin were taking a vacation. They were going on a cruise to England and the 'Continent', as Europe was called by Cornelia's clients. The plans had been made by accident as they sat around one night talking about the war clouds that were building over Germany.

"There will be a war," Martin had said. "That man Hitler won't stop until he's the emperor of the world and kills every Jew in Europe." He spoke with such vehemence that Cornelia and Mose were taken slightly aback by his outburst. He was usually quite contained during their discussions, making analytical deductions of the things they talked about.

"What's bothering you tonight?" Cornelia asked, slightly disturbed by his outburst that was so out of character. Mose also looked at Martin with concern as he sat drinking his Pepsi minus any booze as had become his custom. Mose could afford to buy Pepsi for their little get-to-gethers but booze was a little beyond his means and he felt he should contribute to the refreshments.

"Not that it's ever mattered but I'm a Jew. It never came up before and I don't practice my religion the way I should but I still feel that this new trouble for the Jews in Europe is just beginning. I would really like to know what is going on over there."

The weather combined with their slow summer business prompted Cornelia to make an unusual suggestion. "How about you taking me shopping next week and we'll just check the situation out? We can go to Paris and I can shop as I've never shopped before."

Martin looked at her in astonishment and then leaned back in his chair to mull the suggestion over. He had never considered something like that in his whole life. It was not a matter of money for he had done very well these last several years and now that times were improving, he was doing even better. He had read books about Europe all of his life and now this would be a chance to go there and see things for himself.

"You know," he said with a wry smile, "I wouldn't mind going as long as we don't have to go to Germany. It might still be safe for tourists but I still despise what Hitler is doing. If you're willing to avoid that country, I think I would love to take you shopping."

"Fine," Cornelia replied, "I'll call around tomorrow and find out what it would take for us to go over there."

The talk really livened up now that the decision had been made. Mose would be more than capable of handling things. They decided to travel by ship and Martin knew that Cornelia would make top-flight reservation because that was the only way she would go.

The reservations were made in the name of Mr. and Mrs. Martin Fields. They both felt it would cause fewer problems in their travel and would effectively cut down on the costs, a concession to both of their basically frugal natures.

They left on the fifth of August for Paris.

****

Cornelia was pleasantly surprised when they arrived in France and she discovered that Martin could speak enough French for them to get by in the stores and restaurants. They went on a grand tour of the country and finally arrived in Paris. They spent three days sight seeing and then Cornelia could no longer contain herself. She went shopping.

She looked long and hard at all the latest fashions, purchasing with a discriminating eye. She had all of her purchases carefully packed and shipped back to New York. She kept just a few items for the rest of their excursion.

After the adventure in Paris, they boarded a plane for London and more shopping where, among other things, she bought two new suits made for Martin by the finest tailors on Bond Street.

The only cloud on the trip was the constant threat of war that prevailed everywhere they went. Italy had allied with Germany and many governments of the other European countries were bowing down to Hitler and allowing him to do what ever he pleased. Each concession, they assured the rest of the world, would surely lead to peace. Only fools believed this and Martin and Cornelia were not fools. They could see better than ever that war was sure to come and they felt sure that the United States would become involved in the conflict.

Their last night in London was one they would both remember for the rest of their lives. They had dinner and went to the equivalent of a Broadway show and then on to a nightclub for drinks and the floorshow. They had some difficulty understanding the British comedians and the number of drinks they were having did not improve their comprehension. It was nearly two o'clock in the morning by the time they returned by cab to their hotel. They had been traveling as man and wife since their departure from New York and sharing accommodations all during the trip. Tonight they were full of life and happy to be heading home the next day. They were also slightly drunk.

They were staying in a suite with a large living room separating two bedrooms, each with its' own bath. The man at the front desk had called it the 'Cecil Rhodes Suite' whoever he was.

"Come over here and undo me," Cornelia called from the door of her bedroom.

Martin walked across the ornate living room and, as he approached Cornelia, she turned her back to him so he had access to the row of fasteners that ran down the back of her dress. His fingers trembled as he tried to undo the tiny buttons. When he finally finished, she leaned back against him and said, "Marty, I've never been so happy in my whole life. This has been the most wonderful trip and I feel like I'm living in a fairy tale. I only have you to thank for it."

His arms went forward encircling her body and he felt a shock through his whole being like he had seldom experienced in his entire life. He continued to hold her, enjoying the deep excitement of the physical contact. She could feel him against her body becoming aroused by the contact and she wanted to give him a gift he would never forget. A gift only she would be able to give.

They walked slowly towards the bed and she felt reluctance on his part to make this total commitment. She turned and kissed him and then he responded to her with more tenderness than she would have imagined. They were both totally in love and it would last all through the night.

****

The next morning they acted subdued around each other until she spoke, saying, "Martin, I will never have a permanent man in my life. It just wouldn't work, you know it and I know it. I am sure of one thing though; you are the only man I have ever loved. I didn't know that until last night but I know it now and will always remember all you have done for me."

She walked to where he stood and took his face in her hands, looking directly into his eyes and said, "Nothing like this can ever happen again. If you continue to be my true friend, be sure that I will love you forever."

Martin looked back at her with tears in his eyes and answered, "I love you too. Right now I'm so confused about last night I don't know what to say except that I know you're right. It would never work to try and carry this any further. It would tear me apart. Just being friends is fine with me. But I want you to know I will never forget what happened and how special you have made me feel." He hugged her tight against his chest for a second and as they parted, he turned and became extremely busy with his packing. Each kept their head turned so the other could not see the tears that flowed down both faces.

When they had left New York, Cornelia had brought some books with her. She had put two of them, 'Of Mice and Men' and 'The African Queen' in Martin's luggage for him to find and enjoy. She had kept two others, 'The Yearling' and 'The Grapes of Wrath' and now they exchanged books for the trip home. The first day on the boat they mostly just laid around in deck chairs enjoying the ocean breeze and relaxing from the hectic schedule of traveling. They were aboard the 'Queen Mary' out of London and headed for New York. They departed on Thursday morning and would arrive back in New York on Sunday evening.

By the second day they were beginning to enjoy their first class accommodations. They dined at the Captain's table and he fawned over Cornelia as much as he dared. Without a doubt, Cornelia was the most beautiful woman on the boat with her slim figure and pale blond hair. She created an illusion that she was little more than a girl although she had turned thirty-one on her last birthday. She had enjoyed much good fortune and it would continue for several more years.

Upon their return they both went immediately back to work and it was not until early October that Cornelia showed up one morning for their coffee and sweet rolls with some startling news. She was pregnant.

In all the years she had been working this had never happened and because of the trip, she had been careless.

"I've decided to have the baby," she told Martin. "I have the means to raise a child and give it all the love I never had growing up. I'm going to convert the whole side of the first floor into one big apartment and make room for a maid. I'll make a nursery out of one of the middle bedrooms." It was evident that she had thought everything out and made up her mind.

Martin, of course, knew better than to disagree with her, and besides it really was none of his business. He congratulated her saying, "You know I'll do anything I can to help. I'll even baby-sit and change diapers if you will let me."

"Wait and see," she replied. "Just wait and see."

It wasn't until she had left his apartment that Martin started to wonder. Could it possibly be? He would just have to wait for the birth date to be sure.

CHAPTER THIRTEEN

The baby, a little boy, was born on May 13, 1939 in the apartment Cornelia had so recently remodeled into her home. A very competent doctor and nurse attended the birth and they both had experience in delivering babies in places other than hospitals. In the last few months before the birth Cornelia had spent a great deal of time sitting in Martin's front room with Martin and the new housekeeper.

Mose Cole had recommended a middle-aged black woman by the name of Rosey as the prospective nurse for the baby. Cornelia had moved her into the back bedroom and had been checking her out to be sure she would be capable of doing the exacting job that the new mother would require. Because of her own childhood, Cornelia was being extremely protective of how her child would be raised. The others sometimes became impatient with her preparations but they had no idea of what Cornelia had gone through and she wasn't about to explain.

It was a Saturday night and the four of them were sitting and listening to the radio, laughing happily over the talk of George Burns and Gracie Allen, when suddenly Cornelia started to gasp. Everyone knew what to do and within twenty minutes the doctor and nurse arrived and were on the job. Everything had been prepared and the birth was normal in every respect.

On Sunday morning they had a crying baby in the house, the only baby that had been in this house for many years. He was named Howard Martin Lawson and only then, in a very private manner, did Cornelia reveal to Martin what he had suspected all along, Martin was the baby's father. She told him that was the most important reasons she had decided to keep the child.

By August, Cornelia was back to a full work schedule and Rosey was in charge of the baby. Mose and Martin were part time supervisors and they offered more advice than actual help. Life returned to normal.

****

By Christmas of 1941, the baby was over a year old and in spite of the war that had broken out they had a celebration that was exciting for all of them. Cornelia had not bought gifts for Mose and Rosey and instead had given them money, an envelope containing a five hundred dollar bill. They knew Cornelia was well-to-do but it was more than they ever expected, in fact it was the most money that either one of them had ever had at one time in their whole lives.

A month before Christmas, Cornelia and Martin had taken Howie, as the baby was called, to the movies for the first time. They had seen 'Dumbo' and all of their subsequent decoration would be on the theme of that movie including a huge, stuffed replica of the title character in the movie. The baby spent most of Christmas day alternating trying to ride the toy and rolling with it on the floor. They were all very happy and, knowing the world situation, knew the good times might not last much longer.

****

Martin and Cornelia sat in her front room listening to the radio and watching the baby play on the floor. Mose and Rosey were in the kitchen.

"I went to see the army recruiter on Friday and the army is going to take me," Martin announced somewhat nervously.

Cornelia took a long minute to reflect on what Martin had just said before she replied. "Why, Martin? You're too old for the draft and you don't believe in violence. You don't really have to go." There was more pleading in her voice than Martin had ever heard before.

"You know how I feel about Hitler," he said. "I want to do something to help so I went to the army and asked what I could do. They tested me and I'll be going to Fort Monmouth in New Jersey to teach the French language to officers going overseas. At least I'll be doing something for the war effort."

Cornelia slid from the chair where she had been sitting and fell to her knees at Martin's feet, taking his hands in hers'. "Martin, I don't want you to go," she said looking up at his face. "Stay here and help me with things, the house and the baby and all. Don't go away."

"You don't need me to help," Martin answered. "You've got Rosey and Mose to keep everything in order and to take care of Howie. I'm going to close the shop and, if it's okay, have you watch everything until I get back."

"You know I'll do that if you want me to but I'd rather you wouldn't go."

She rested her cheek against his knee and for one of the few times in her life, she cried. She strongly felt that the good times had come to an end and things were going to get a lot tougher.

****

Rosey didn't know what to do about little Howard Martin Lawson. At four years old he was positively the meanest kid that Rosey had ever seen and his mother was not doing anything to improve his disposition. Cornelia indulged him with whatever he wanted and when he was denied, he threw a temper fit until she gave in and allowed him to have or do whatever he wished.

Rosey dearly loved Miss Cornelia but she had come to despise the little boy. Whenever she tried to express her misgivings about the child, Cornelia would listen patiently and then go on about her business, completely ignoring whatever Rosey told her. If only Mr. Martin had been here, Rosey thought. He might be the one able to talk some sense into Cornelia's head. But this was not the case.

****

Cornelia sat looking out the window, smoking a cigarette. It was fall and the weather had been rainy and cold for this time of the year. She had opened Martin's safe earlier in the evening and placed another package on the bottom shelf. He had given her the combination before he left, just in case, and this had been the fourth time she had used it. She was still making good money but not getting as big of tips as she once had. Food rationing had started and even if you had money, a lot of things were scarce. Sugar, coffee and gasoline had been first but now all of the essentials were under government control. A client had given her some extra ration books but so far she had gotten by without using them. Cigarettes were the only things she really abused, having picked up the habit on the trip to Europe and she enjoyed them too much to consider doing without.

She worried about Martin. He had only been back once in the two years and she missed having a friend to talk with. Rosey was there all day, every day, but all they ever talked about was the baby and Cornelia was tired of listening to her complain about not being able to control little Howie.

Cornelia was seldom home more than one full day each week and she did not see any real problem. The baby wanted attention from his mother and Cornelia gave it to him, what could possibly be wrong with that? After all, he was only a baby and how much trouble could a child cause for full-grown adults. She lit a cigarette from the butt of another and continued looking at the raindrops running down the windowpane. Face the fact, she thought, she was lonely and depressed.

****

Rosey had brought a kitten home for the boy to play with and he loved the cat…for a while. That evening the cat had scratched Howie and before Rosey had a chance to intercede, he threw the cat down on the kitchen floor and stomped, killing it and then walking away without a thought about anything except the tiny spot of blood on his hand. When Rosey attempted to scold the boy about the incident, he sat and looked at her as though he couldn't understand a word she was saying.

This was not the first trouble she had experienced with him. Earlier in the summer Rosey had found him in the carriage house where Cornelia kept her car. She taken a pair of scissors away from him and started back in the house when she heard a sound coming from underneath the car. She looked and discovered one of the neighborhood dogs. When she got a broom and attempted to shoo it from under the Volkswagen, she found the dog to be covered with blood and both of its' eyes had been punched. She had grabbed the scissors out of her pocket and, sure enough, they had blood all over the tips. Rosey was appalled and went to Mose Cole for advice.

"I reckon the best thing to do is to tell Miss Cornelia and do whatever she says. You know how she is about this child and if you make a big fuss, why then you're gonna' be out the door and somebody else will have this fine place to live and all of this good food." Mose was a realist and could see things exactly as they were, getting to the bottom of any problem instinctively.

Rosey mulled over what he said and, looking at Mose intently, said, "Are you telling me not to do nothin' because if you are, you're wrong. We both know this baby don't have no daddy and his mama just wants him for a toy when she come home."

"No," Mose said, "what I'm telling you is to do what you're supposed to do. What do you think would happen to you if Mizz Cornelia was to kick you out? Where do you think you could go? You got it mighty good here except for that child and you should think about that first of all."

Rosey thought about what he said for a few seconds and relented. She was no small woman and when he had mentioned the food, he had hit a soft spot. There was no doubt she would ever find work anyplace that had all of the benefits she had here. Her own room and bath, all the food she wanted to fix and only the apartment to keep clean and one child to watch. She also received more wages than any other workingwoman she knew, a fact she kept strictly to herself.

"I know you're right," Rosey said, "but I hate to see a nice lady like Mizz Cornelia with such a bad child. And that's what he is, just plain bad. No body will ever be able to change that. I'm afraid he's gonna' be the death of her before it's all over and he's full grown."

CHAPTER FOURTEEN

Martin returned home in July of 1945. In May he had been sent to France to aid in some negotiations with the French government and had returned to the States on the steamship Queen Elizabeth. The war was over in Europe and he was mustered out with the rank of Major.

Martin was little changed by the war. He had adapted well to military life and he had made the best of a bad situation. His natural intelligence had caused the army to take him into the cryptography section of military intelligence and he had moved up rapidly in rank. His part in the war effort, though considerable, was something he would not discuss, even with Cornelia.

Now back in his original apartment, Martin discovered the behavior of little Howie since he had contact with the boy every day. He was appalled at the actions of the child. Not that the boy wasn't handsome, quite the opposite. Howie was extremely attractive with pale blond hair, blue eyes, thin fine features and delicate hands and feet. He looked amazingly like his mother. It was his disposition and personality that were so unsettling.

Howie was selfish and demanding about whatever he wanted and Cornelia and Rosey waited on the boy constantly. Howie had become so accustomed to the treatment that when Martin expressed misgivings about the way the women treated the boy, only Rosey stood by him in his views. Before long the child avoided Martin because of his outlook and Martin could see that if he maintained his position, Cornelia would also be against him. As a result he kept as much as possible to himself and worked at re-establishing his coin and stamp business.

One of the first things he had noticed on his return was the number of packages on the bottom shelf of his safe. There were more than twenty packages, obviously full of cash, and he could not begin to guess the total amount except to realize that it was considerable.

He had estimated his own personal fortune since returning by adjusting the value of his coins and stamps to post-war worth. If he sold out he would be worth nearly two million dollars. He had no way of knowing that Cornelia was worth even more than that staggering figure.

****

On September 2, 1946, Howie went to school for the first time. He had very little experience with other children since there were none living in the building where he had been brought up. Other kids who lived in the neighborhood who were younger than he avoided him because of his meanness. Kids who were older than he was always picked on him and Howie in turn avoided them. None of them had ever liked him and now he was going into their world.

Cornelia had not had to work that first day of school and, like so many young mothers had walked him the four blocks to the school where she left him tearfully at the door to his room.

Later that day she was waiting in front when he came out the door of the schoolhouse. He started talking a mile a minute. Nothing had suited him. He said his teacher was old and ugly, the seats were hard, the other kids were mean to him and he ended with the question, "Mama, what's a whore? The other kids in school said you was a whore and I don't know what that is."

Cornelia stopped in her tracks like she had run head on into an invisible steel wall. She was so stunned that all she could do was stare down at the boy who was holding her hand and let the tears run down her face. She had never considered the viciousness of children or that her son might be exposed to it so suddenly. It was a monstrous oversight on her part.

"Don't you even think about that, baby," Cornelia said as the walked the last two blocks to their house. "You won't ever have to listen to them again because you will never be going back to that school." It had taken her just that long to make up her mind about what to do.

As soon as she arrived home she started her preparations. Cornelia called Mose, Rosey and Martin together in her apartment and made her announcement. "Martin," she said, "I'm giving this house to you. I want you to have it so let's not argue. The deed is in your safe so I'll just sign it and you can do whatever you want. I would like for you to agree to keep Mose as caretaker."

The others were to stunned to speak as she turned to Rosey and said, "I have decided to move to Ohio and, if you will, I'd would like for you to come along with me. I won't ever be coming back but you would have time off to come here and visit if you so wish. Your job will be the same and I intend to find us comfortable living quarters when we get where we're going."

Rosey only hesitated for a second before she answered, "Of course I'll go with you, Miz Cornelia." She trusted her boss explicitly and knew she would be safe in her employ.

Martin was still dumbfounded by her decision and he asked her again and again what had prompted this sudden move. All that she would answer was that she was moving and that was that. It would be several days before Martin associated the move with the first day of school and figure out what had probably happened.

Rosey and Cornelia immediately began packing the items they would be taking with them and Mose returned to his duties after being assured he would have a job as long as he cared to stay. Howie sat at a table in Martin's front room having cookies and milk. He watched Martin open his huge safe and take a number of small packages from the bottom shelf and put them in a cardboard box. Cornelia carried the box across to her apartment. She left Howie with Martin to finish his snack.

Cornelia knew there was a lot of money in the packages but not even she knew exactly how much. She got busy counting and sorting, keeping her account on a sheet of paper close at hand. When she was done she was sure that there was enough to last her the rest of her life.

The next morning with many tearful good-byes on the part of the adults, the two women and the child left in a taxi for Grand Central Station. A second taxi loaded with luggage followed close behind. Cornelia did carry one suitcase herself and would not even let the porter help her with it when they boarded the train. She had bought tickets for them on the train going to Columbus, Ohio. She would decide when they got there if she wanted to keep going. The huge B&O steam engine pulled the train out and headed west, back the way she had come twenty-two years earlier.

She sat in her seat and watched as Howie ran up and down the aisle, staggering with the motion of the train. She thought back when she had taken the train east so many years before and felt no regrets about her life. She felt more as if she were going home than once again running away.

CHAPTER FIFTEEN

Howie and Jess had to pay their way into the basketball game. The event was attended mostly by students and, try as they might, the boys couldn't find a way to sneak into the gymnasium. Neither one of them knew much about basketball so they spent most of their time roaming around eating popcorn and drinking Pepsi. They left the game when it was over and wandered downtown to the Mainline Theater and went in one of the fire exits. They got there just in time to catch a 'Tom and Jerry' cartoon. They both liked to watch these best of all for the unusual reason that the old black woman reminded them of Rosey. When she shuffled through the house in her floppy slippers and beat Tom's ass with a broom, they howled with laughter. Jess even suggested that Howie should get a cat and take it home so they could have a show every day.

Next they walked through a newsstand and, while Jess distracted the clerk, Howie swiped two packs of Cavalier cigarettes. They moved on to the big poolroom and sat in the rear as they smoked and watched the money games being played. It was after ten o'clock when Jess said he had to head for home so Howie gave in and called it a night right along with him. Howie didn't want to stay out late and get his mother worried to the place where she would start keeping an eye on him. He knew that if he wanted he could always come back out later after everyone else went to bed.

****

Howie woke up sitting by the window. He had a blanket wrapped around his shoulders and his head was resting against the wall. He had been dreaming and had a feeling of apprehension as he came to his senses. In his dream, he had been trying to fly but he kept coming to obstacles such as tree branches, chimneys and phone and power wires. They kept popping up in front of him and forcing him ever closer to the ground. Then he tried running, faster and faster trying to get back into the air but was unable to get off the ground.

He was out of breath and totally exhausted when he awoke.

It took him a few seconds to get oriented to his surroundings. Within minutes the dream started to fade from his mind and after looking out the window for a short time the dream had become impossible to recall. Howie started to think about the problem of Moosie and what he intended to do. In every scenario he was always victorious and Moosie in terminal trouble. The final solution continued to elude but he was sure he would come up with something in the next few days.

****

Howie knew he had to go back to Pear Street and look for ideas on what to do but he decided not to go tonight. He turned on a small lamp beside his bed and sat reading comic books for the next hour. Then back to the window with the light out so he could see more clearly through the glass into the darkness. He alternately dozed and watched until the sun started to come up before crawling back into bed and falling into a dreamless sleep.

The next morning, Saturday, Howie was up and ready to go when Jess arrived at nine o'clock to start their day. The only thing they were sure of was that they would go to the weekly matinee and get their cards punched for the 'Zorro' serial they were currently attending.

After the movie Howie headed for Pear Street to do a little scouting around. Jess went along, albeit reluctantly, not happy with being in the proximity of Moosie Miller and his cohorts. Jess did have faith that Howie would be able to get them out of any trouble they might run into. In this case Jess's confidence was misplaced.

They had just turned the corner onto Pear Street when they saw Moosie about fifty feet away and walking directly towards them. As usual he had two of his cronies with him and Howie and Jess knew that immediate and rapid flight was their only course of action. Without a word they turned and ran back towards downtown seeking sanctuary in the alleys and buildings they knew so well. Howie was slightly encumbered by his stick but this was definitely not the time to abandon their only weapon.

"Run for the back of the Mainline Theater," Howie yelled as they plunged through an alley with Moosie and his buddies pounding along behind them. "If we can make it inside they won't be able to find us in the dark."

As they made it to the fire exit, they both grabbed the loose fitting door and pulled as hard as they could. Making noise and getting caught by a teen-age usher was the least of their worries at this point. They jumped inside and pulled the door closed with a second crash that caused all the people in the theater to jump with fright.

Jess started to go into the audience but Howie grabbed him, pulling him instead the other direction towards the backstage of the old edifice. The boys ducked around a corner and into the dark where they found themselves standing amid a tangle of dusty, dirty ropes. The fire door banged open and shut for a second time, admitting their pursuers. Howie and Jess stood frozen as the other boys went into the front of the theater searching for their quarry.

"Com'ere," Howie said, "I wanna' show you something. We can watch them without them seeing us."

He pulled Jess to the rear of the huge movie screen and the two boys walked out behind it. Jess was surprised to find the screen was porous and they could see through it and had a clear view of the people in the audience watching the movie.

"Can the people out there see us?" Jess asked.

"Heck no," Howie replied. "All they see is the movie on the screen. I've done this lots of times and if they could see me someone would have run me out before this. When the show's bright, it lights up the people real good and you can see everything out front."

Howie and Jess watched as Moosie and his friends walked slowly up the center aisle looking for them and Jess's faith was restored in his friend. Howie had once again pulled them through. Now they had the additional fun of watching as the usher met Moosie and the others and escorted them briskly out of sight in the direction of the front doors.

"What'daya wanna' do now?" Jess asked. "It probably wouldn't be a good idea to leave. They'll be out there somewhere waiting for us to come and if they catch us now, oh boy, you know what they're going to do."

Howie's head was swiveling all around when he answered, "Let's look around back here for a while." He was looking mostly up when he said this and Jess raised his eyes to see a whole world hanging above their heads.

At least twenty racks of old, moldy scenery were suspended by ropes from the very high ceiling, props left over from vaudeville days. The ropes ran through pulleys near the roof and were tied off at one side of the stage near where the boys had first entered. When they started to investigate, they found a narrow winding staircase that was little more than a ladder leading up into the darkness. Howie immediately started to climb. As he went up with Jess close behind, he discovered some of the steps were cracked or broken and others missing entirely. It was a scary and dangerous climb and Jess hesitated to go on.

"Hey, Howie," Jess whispered, "you sure you wanna' climb these old steps?"

"Yeah, I wanna' go up and see what's up there. You don't have to come if you don't want to."

"Okay," Jess answered. "I'll just wait here on the steps." He sat down to wait and watched as Howie disappeared onto the darkness.

Howie was in a very touchy situation because he was unaware of the frailty of the abandoned equipment. His small size and light weight were the only things that saved him from crashing through the wooden walkway and dropping to the stage seventy-five feet below. At the top he could barely make out the metal pulleys that were used to raise and lower the scenery. The walkway was right up against the ropes and he could easily reach out and touch them. Looking down at Jess, Howie could see the ropes running parallel to the stairs all the way back to the stage floor. Without any hesitation, Howie grabbed one of the ropes, swung out into space and slid slowly down the rope until he reached the level where Jess waited. In as deep a voice as he could muster, Howie said, "Hey, boy, what'chu doing up here?"

Jess nearly wet his pants when the voice came out of the air so close beside him and, luckily, he froze in fright right where he was. Howie started laughing at Jess's fright and Jess saw what Howie had done.

"Holy Jesus, you really scared me," Jess said. "I'm getting down out of here."

"Okay, let's go," Howie answered as he wrapped his legs around the rope and loosened the grip he had with his hands. "I'll race you to the bottom."

Back on the floor of the stage the boys continued to look around. Off to one side of the stage they found a row of abandoned dressing rooms. They were in extreme disrepair and obviously had not been used in a very long time. The first one contained nothing but a broken mirror scattered on the floor. In the next one they had more luck. There was a light bulb in the fixture on the ceiling and when Howie closed the door and flipped the switch, it lit up. There was a sink on the wall and when they turned the faucet on, they got a stream of water, first rusty and dirty looking but eventually clearing up. There was also a small table and one chair in front of a wall hanging mirror. A window in one wall had long ago been painted shut.

With the light on Howie was surprised to see how dirty he was. When he had slid down the ropes he had wiped decades of dust and dirt onto his hands and clothing. He went to the sink and tried to wash himself in the cold water and he did manage to get most of the dirt off his hands and face. Using a rag he found on the floor he brushed his clothes and looked semi-normal. After inspecting himself in the mirror he said, "Let's look around some more. This is a really neat place."

Making sure the light was off before opening the door, they went to see what else they could find. There were four more dressing rooms, all similar to the ones they had already been in so they kept going until they came to a stairway leading down at the rear of the stage. It was pitch black and there were no light switches that the boys could see. Jess pulled a pack of matches out of his pocket and lit one. It didn't help much as the stairs were to wide and deep for the light to penetrate.

"I know what we can do," Howie said. "We can go get a flashlight and come back and see what's down there. I know just where to get one."

"Okay, let's go," Jess replied, not really liking the idea of going down the steps with only one pack of matches to chase back the darkness.

Making their way back to the fire exit, they opened the door as quietly as possible and, after looking around for Moosie, headed for the hardware store. Howie was so anxious to get back to the theater and go exploring that he broke down and bought a flashlight and extra batteries instead of taking the time to try and steal one.

They ran back to the theater and were soon at the staircase, descending into the darkness. "What'daya thinks down here?" Jess asked softly.

"I doan'no," Howie answered as he shined the light around. "There's no people, that's for sure. It's too dark and quiet for anybody to be around."

The only sound was coming from the speakers at the rear of the theater screen and it was fading fast away. They continued down and Howie counted thirty-one steps. At the bottom they were mystified to find a large pool of water. It was about twenty feet wide and thirty feet long with a boardwalk extending across the middle of it. High dirt and stone walls were all around and the only way to proceed was to cross the pool.

The walkway was solid and in good repair and the boys crossed swiftly to the other end. Here they found a giant circular fan about twelve feet across and it was pointed directly at the pool of water. On a panel beside the fan were a number of switches and gauges. Howie inspected them and found a large temperature gauge right in the center of the display.

After a minute of study, Howie said, "I know what this is. This is the way they cool the theater in the summer. Someone turns on this fan and it blows across the water and sends cool air onto the people out front."

He returned to the pool and stuck his stick down into the water and discovered it was nearly two feet deep.

Jess, not having a light of his own was forced to walk close behind Howie so he could see where he was going. Now he spoke up and said, "I don't like it down here. It's awful dark and if that fan happened to come on it could blow us away. Let's get out of here."

Howie reluctantly agreed even though he was having an adventure. He knew he would come back alone at the first opportunity and look around at his leisure.

CHAPTER SIXTEEN

It was twenty minutes past four in the morning and Howie was prowling. Twice he had circled the Miller's house while looking things over and making his plans. One of the first things he had found was the unlocked window where the extension cord fed electricity to the outdoor Christmas decorations. He had slipped his finger under the sash and gently raised the window about a foot before pushing it back down. Inside the window had been an open space devoid of furniture. He got the impression that furniture usually sat there but had been moved for some reason. He would continue to check and see what developed.

While he was going around the house it had occurred to him that if there had been snow on the ground it would curtail his surveillance. Fresh tracks around the house when the family first got out of bed would have been a warning of his intentions. Such an advantage should not be sacrificed through carelessness.

Howie crossed the street and looked back studying the shadows surrounding the house before starting for home. He wanted to get back to his room where he could sit in quiet and think about what he had found. He had not yet decided what he was going to actually DO about Moosie.

The next morning was Sunday and Cornelia announced at breakfast she would be going to a movie that afternoon and she wanted Rosey and Howie to go with her. The movie 'Gone With The Wind' had been re-released after ten years, partly because Hollywood moguls were sentimental. A hit-and-run driver in Atlanta had killed the author of the original story and, being sentimental for the money, the studio was capitalizing on all of the free publicity.

Cornelia, being a movie fan, had seen the movie when it had first come out. Now she wanted to give Howie and Rosey the chance to see it.

"Mama, can Jess go with us if he wants to?" Howie asked.

"Sure baby, you know he's welcome to go. Why don't you call him and ask. I want to go to the first showing at one o'clock so tell him to be here by twelve-thirty. We'll just walk to the theater from here."

It was at this point in the conversation that Jess knocked on the back door and they all laughed at his timely arrival, embarrassing him with their attention. Jess sat down shyly at the table and Rosey immediately fed him his second breakfast as she put a plate of pancakes and sausage in front of him. He started to eat, mumbling answers to questions around his mouthfuls of food. He happily agreed to go to the movie knowing he was as near to their family as he was to his own.

Breakfast over, the boys went outside for a walk after promising to be back home by noon. It was overcast and cold with a brisk north wind foretelling snow soon to come. So far the weather had been fairly decent for this time of year but it couldn't last forever. The boys were looking forward to snow and this was their topic of conversation.

"I wouldn't mind snow for Christmas," Howie said, "but I got some things to do before then an' snow will only get in the way."

"What things you gotta' do?" Jess asked.

"Oh, just some things I been thinking about," Howie replied. You know---Moosie. I got'ta figure out some way to make him leave us alone."

Jess studied his friend out of the corner of his eye and saw that Howie was using the stick he carried to hit tree limbs, bushes, rocks and anything else he happened to pass. As Howie had talked about Moosie, he became more agitated, swinging the stick harder and harder.

Howie turned his head and looked at Jess and said, "WHACK! WHACK! for that damn Moosie. I don't like him chasing us around and I'm gonna' make him quit it."

Jess, being well aware of what Howie could be capable of tried to calm his friend and said, "Let's just stay away from where he lives. If we see him and he does chase us we can get away easy. He's to fat and slow to ever catch us. Just forget about Moosie and maybe he'll go away."

"What'chu mean, forget about him! Do you think we should have to run every time he comes around?" Howie was starting to get upset even with Jess. "You do what you want and I'll do what I want. You ain't gonna' try and tell me what to do, are you?"

Jess looked at Howie and his huge brown eyes were pleading for understanding as he said, "I just don't want you to get in no trouble. You're my friend and I don't want nothing bad to happen."

Howie was partially mollified by Jess's pleading and he answered, saying, "Ain't nothing bad gonna' happen to me but don't be to sure that Moosie ain't gonna' have some trouble before long."

Jess hung his head and looked down at the ground as they walked, deathly afraid for his friend and what he might do. Jess knew that he had already said as much as he dared and now all he could do was wait and see what was going to happen.

When the boys returned to the house they were subdued. As they walked with Cornelia and Rosey to the movie, neither said a word. When Cornelia asked if they were feeling okay, both said they were. She dismissed their attitudes to the vagaries of childhood.

Cornelia bought the tickets for the movies, fifty cents for the adults and twenty cents for the boys and into the movie they went. Four boxes of popcorn were obligatory to their attendance and four more at the intermission half way through the feature.

Nearly four hours later they came out of the theater and Howie was a changed person. He laughed and jumped all the way home. It was the best frame of mind anyone had seen him display in a long time.

****

Howie was standing behind a tree across from Moosie's house. He had been there for about fifteen minutes. He had almost made a mess of everything earlier on his way to Pear Street. When he had turned the corner that brought the house into view, he heard a noise some distance behind him and had jumped into some bushes in order to conceal himself. From his hiding place he watched as old man Miller came walking up the street, obviously drunk. It was quarter to three in the morning and Howie guessed that the man had been the last patron to leave a drinking establishment.

Miller was half-dragging and half carrying a large Christmas tree and the vision of the empty space in front of the unsecured window flashed into Howie's mind. That was where this Christmas tree would go.

As Miller walked up the sidewalk to the front porch, he dropped the tree and left it in the middle of the front yard. After he had gone inside, Howie saw a light come on in the back of the house in the kitchen area. Howie stealthily crossed the street and ducked into the shadows near the houses' foundation. The front porch was dark, the Christmas lights having been unplugged long ago. Howie circled to the rear of the house and looked in the kitchen window. Galen Miller was sitting at the kitchen table drinking more beer. He drained the bottle and opened another, carrying it with him as he headed towards the front room. He sat down on the couch and began to undress, first removing his shoes and his shirt. He tipped up the bottle he was holding and drained half of it before slumping over sideways so he was full length on the couch. Setting the bottle on the floor, he was asleep within seconds.

Howie could see him from the kitchen window but decided to move around to the front where he would have a better view. He watched from his new position for a couple of minutes and was about ready to leave when he heard a noise inside the house. A woman, Miller's wife, was walking towards her sleeping husband. Howie watched as she picked his shirt off the floor and felt through the pockets as though looking for something. Unsuccessful, she dropped the shirt back to the floor. Next she bent over the sleeping man and started feeling his pants pockets. Slowly she put her hand in his pants, carefully so as not to awaken him, and withdrew a handful of paper money. Clutching it in her fist, she scurried out of the room and away from the sleeping man. The thought crossed Howie's mind to go into the house and check the sleeping man for something she might have missed but he decided against it. He had more important plans for the Millers. The movie he had seen that day with his mother had helped him get his mind straight on the proper course of action.

****

It was Friday night, the twenty-third of December in the year 1949 and Howie was ready to do his thing. He had made a trip to Pear Street every night this week. The Millers had put up their Christmas tree exactly where Howie expected. It was three-thirty in the morning and old man Miller had come home an hour ago and went straight to bed. Howie raised the window and reached inside to touch the green, brittle branches feeling their sticky sap. Moosie's two sisters had decorated the tree and the job was less than artistic. Howie paid little attention to the decorations, being more interested in the size and fullness of the tree.

He looked around the front room and could see that all was quiet. There were packages under the tree, wrapped and labeled, awaiting Christmas morning. Howie had no way of knowing that one of them was a 'gag gift' from Moosie's father to his wife. Twice within the last year she had run out of gas in her car and had called her husband to send a cruiser with gasoline to get her going. Galen had bought a two-gallon can, filled it with gas and placed it under the tree neatly wrapped and tagged with her name on it.

From under his coat Howie removed a single sheet of newspaper that had been crumpled into a loose ball. He shoved it into the branches of the Christmas tree and reached into his pocket for the Zippo lighter he had stolen for just this occasion. He spun the wheel with his thumb and applied the flame to the newspaper. After pulling the window sash back down he walked across the street to watch the fun.

The tree burned slowly at first, but then flared, igniting the curtains. The burning curtains fell among the packages with a high degree of heat warming the cardboard box containing the can of gas to the burning point. The gas heated to an explosion point and when it flared it was the equivalent of two sticks of dynamite going off. Every window in the downstairs was blown out creating a draft that turned the whole house into an inferno in a matter of two minutes.

The Miller family, sleeping upstairs, never had a chance at escape. By the time the fire department arrived and began pouring water on the fire it was apparent that anyone in the house would only come out one way, in a body bag.

Howie had been half way home by the time the fire trucks got to the house on Pear Street. He was thinking about the movie 'Gone With The Wind' and how the burning of Atlanta looked a little like Moosie's house. Then it occurred to him—Jess will know—and he wrestled with this thought in his mind. Howie decided to wait and see about this development, but he was concerned. Jess knew an awful lot of his secrets.

CHAPTER SEVENTEEN

It was summer and Howie sat under a tree reading the book 'Beau Ideal', the third of the 'Beau Geste' series. Jess lay on the ground next to him, sound asleep. Both boys were relaxed along the riverbank near where they had so often gone fishing. Howie's eyes flicked from the book to the trees overhead. Something had moved and caught his attention. He remained still, watching, until the next movement revealed a large red squirrel moving through the branches that were interwoven over their heads

Howie liked to read and, at least in his own mind, it was the only thing he had learned in school that was any benefit to him. He had progressed from 'Alice and Jerry and Jip' to the adventure novels of Wren, Haggard, Burroughs and most of all, Arthur Conan Doyle.

It was of 1953 and this school year he would be starting the seventh grade for the second time. At least he and Jess would be in the same class. Howie was not getting along well in school. He read books but only the ones he liked. He would ignore any assignment given to him by his teachers. In the classroom he would sit and read in spite of the program that was being conducted by the teacher. If he was reprimanded, he ignored the teacher and just went on reading. If the instructor said what they usually said, "Pay attention or get out!" he would calmly get up and walk out of the room, going automatically to the principal's office where he would sit and read until chastised by a higher authority.

Howie was the bane of teachers, a child with an IQ in the upper two percent of the school who was failing every subject except Gym. He was only passing this because he attended regularly. Although the school had been reluctant to do so, Howie had been held back for a year. They knew he was intelligent but if they allowed him to make a sham of the educational system it would be a bad example for the rest of the students. The flaw in their plan was that Howie was not cooperating. When he had been told he would have to go through the seventh grade a second time, he just shrugged and walked away not really caring one way or the other.

When the squirrel had passed from view, Howie folded his book and elbowed Jess in the ribs. "Hey, wake up," he said. "You gonna' sleep all day?"

Jess shaded his eyes from the sunlight and looked around, orienting himself. "Yeah, I'm awake. What'chu want to do? You want to go swimmin'?"

Of course he meant to swim in the river. Although there were no signs posted and it was cleverly handled, no black people were expected to patronize the Newton City Municipal Pool. This condition didn't bother the boys in the least, they just accepted it. If Howie did go to the city pool as he sometimes did with his mother, Jess didn't go along. On the whole, though, the boys preferred swimming in the river having done so for the last several years.

"Yeah, let's go down and swim for a while," Howie said.

The boys headed for the river, walking through the wood and undergrowth as easily as a person would walk through their own living room. In a manner of speaking, this area was as familiar to the boys as their own homes.

Arriving at the water, they found two boys fishing near the swimming hole. Howie and Jess knew both boys on sight. One was Mike McConnell, a high school student and the other was Bob Bailey who was currently attending Ohio State University. Bailey's mother had been Howie's first grade teacher.

Howie and Jess walked directly to the other boys and stood quietly until they were noticed. They didn't hesitate to approach the fishermen because these two had the reputation of being 'good boys'. When they did look up and notice Howie and Jess, Bailey spoke first and said, "Hey, guys, how's it going?"

"Goin' okay," Howie answered. "You catching anything?"

McConnell answered, saying, "We've caught four nice channel cats in the last hour. What are you guys up to?"

"Oh, nothin'" Howie said. "We're just walkin' and lookin'. See you around," and the younger boys started down the riverbank. With people fishing on the edge of the swimming hole, swimming would have to be put off until later.

****

When they were out of earshot, Bailey said to McConnell, "That's the kid my mom was telling me about. Supposed to be real strange and nobody can figure him out. The only kid he's ever with is that colored boy. I heard he failed a year of school so that they could be in the same grade. I wonder if he's a queer?"

McConnell watched them walk away and said, "He sure is a pretty boy with that blond hair and blue eyes. I sure don't know. I never heard anyone say he was but those two are a lot younger than most of the guys I know so maybe I just never heard. He don't act queer but most of the time you can't tell for sure."

****

Howie and Jess continued along the riverbank until they came to the trestle and the railroad tracks and started following this path back to the center of town. Until this summer Howie had been bigger that Jess but now that was changing. Both boys were still about the same height but Jess was starting to gain weight and was at least twenty pounds heavier than his friend. Howie was as thin as ever.

"What'chu want to do now?" Jess asked.

It was the middle of the week and there were not a lot of options. Howie avoided the playgrounds and all other kids his own age except Jess. They had seen every movie playing at the theaters so those were not an option.

"Let's just go downtown and sit on a bench on Main Street and see if anything's happening," Howie said. "If we can't find anything else to do we can go play pinball for a while."

Jess didn't reply. He was thinking that Howie was in a pretty good mood for not having anything to do and wondered what was the cause of his good humor. Like he had learned from his friend, Jess adopted a 'wait and see' attitude and hoped for the best.

Howie walked along and thought back to last night, a very good night in his estimation. Not even Sherlock Holmes would have been able to track him.

****

In the 1930's, the city fathers of Newton had an idea. They would develop an indoor shopping area with a variety of stores that would be sheltered from the elements. Over a period of two years they built the complex not realizing they were thirty years ahead of the times.

In the downtown area there was one square block that had two large cross alleys that intersected in the middle. The decided they would cover these alleys with a glass canopy and close off the ends with walls. Doorways would be placed at all four of the entrances and the ground would be covered with tile flooring. All of the stores in this block, and there were quite a variety, would access the enclosed area from their places of business. It was an experiment that would prove eminently successful.

While construction was underway, someone had the idea of digging a large, common basement under the alleyways. Since there would be no vehicle traffic allowed overhead, this was a fairly simple undertaking. It would also double the storage space for the businesses as well as providing easy access to go from one business to another for cleaning and maintenance.

There were a large variety of businesses including a furniture store, theater, Kresge's 5 & 10, book store, two beauty shops, meat market, barber shop, drug store, music store, candy store, two restaurants, and three clothing stores. There were also several other one-room establishments for businesses that would come and go over a period of time. Upstairs over most of the stores were apartments. Some of these were used for storage and others were rented out as living quarters. Actually it was a small city within a city.

****

Howie had discovered this area by accident but now it had become his favorite area to prowl. Almost every night for the last year he had gone there. A month earlier the big furniture store connected to the complex had hired a night watchman. Maybe he had been there longer than that but it had just been a month since Howie's first encounter with the man. Although the watchman was totally unaware of Howie's presence, Howie strongly resented having the man roaming around in his domain.

It had first come as a shock. It had been three o'clock in the morning and Howie was walking calmly through the huge basement when he heard a noise. He immediately ducked behind a pillar and stood quiet as the old man approached. There were ceiling lights but they were a hundred feet apart and only sixty-watt bulbs. The lights cast more shadows than they dispelled the darkness and were only good for navigational references. Without turning on a flashlight it was impossible for the man to walk through the cluttered underground area.

Howie always carried a small flashlight but, having young eyes, he seldom needed it as he was absolutely at home in the dark. The old watchman always used a light when he went into the basement but kept it pointed at his feet for safety's sake. On that first night Howie watched as the old man walked to the far end of the basement, paused at the wall and then retraced his step and went up the stairwell to the furniture store. Howie followed along, curious to see where the old man was going.

The old man was easy to follow and Howie just watched the bobbing light as it went through the furniture store. Soon it stopped and went out. Howie approached cautiously and soon made out the form of the watchman stretched out on a couch. Howie did what he was good at and waited. Soon he was rewarded as the man started snoring. Moving closer, Howie heard the loud ticking of an old fashioned alarm clock that sat on a stand near the man's head. It wasn't hard to figure out what was going on.

Howie made his way back through the store, down into the

basement and up the abandoned elevator shaft onto the street. After a quick look around, he headed for home. He had some serious thinking to do.

****

Howie stood in the basement of the primitive mall and waited for the watchman to come down the steps. He was halfway between the steps from the furniture store and the far end of the basement well away from any lights. He knew if he didn't move the man would never know he was there. At the far end of the basement, where the time clock was fastened to the wall, a light bulb hung from a cord in the ceiling and it was on. The old man had to walk the entire length of the basement to reach the clock and insert his key to keep the alarm from going off. This had to be done within five minutes, one way or the other, of three o'clock AM. Howie had watched him do it numerous times. The old man was always precisely on time and tonight was no different because Howie could see him coming down the steps. Soon Howie would start having fun.

The old man walked hesitantly down the dark center of the underground and passed within ten feet of where Howie stood concealed by a pillar. Howie waited until he reached the far end and conducted his business with the time clock before he made a sound. Then the boy let out a piercing, high-pitched scream and ran from one side of the basement to the other where he ducked through a door that led to a restaurant and fastened the door behind him.

The old man spun around and stared in the direction of the noise. Howie had wanted him to see a woman who would suddenly appear and then disappear from view. The watchman walked cautiously to the place where he thought he had seen the figure of a woman dressed all in white run across the basement but there was nothing there. He checked the doors in the vicinity and found they were all fastened. The batteries in his flashlight were starting to fail so he abandoned his search and headed for the furniture store. He was concerned and shaken by what had happened but he was too mature to panic.

The watchman climbed the steps to his home base in the furniture store and made his way to a large reclining chair. He would rest here tonight. He never overused one piece of furniture for his nightly naps, not wanting anything to show wear and give away his secret. Leaning back, he pondered what had happened. Nothing he could imagine would offer any solution to the puzzle. Soon he dozed off in the comfortable chair.

Howie was less than twenty feet away from the old man, perturbed by the fact that he had not reacted as Howie had hoped. The ticking of the alarm clock was soon accompanied by the snores of the watchman. Howie silently crept away to return the clothing he was wearing to the women's store where he had found it.

When Howie had started to dress up for his prank, he had arranged the clothing he was going to wear on the counter of the deserted women's clothing store. Next he entered one of the beauty shops and found a blonde wig. When everything was ready he took off all of his clothes and began dressing. Partly as a lark he put on women's underwear. He found bra pads of all sizes and used them for augmentation. For outerwear he put on a full slip and a cream colored summer dress of what he thought was silk but was actually nylon. He had stockings that were held up by a garter belt and when he added the wig the result was striking. He looked in the mirror, using his flashlight, and decided he was successful. From a distance he looked like a woman. He had been unable to find any women's shoes that suited him so he had worn his own Keds. As an afterthought, he added a fur stole. This should really scare the old man.

Now, as he carefully put the clothes back where he had got them, he was thinking how much more comfortable the ladies panties were than his own 'Fruit of the Loom' briefs. The smooth, cool feel around his hips was very pleasant. He almost kept the panties on but finally decided against taking them home with him. He knew they would be there for him whenever he wanted to put them back on.

He also knew he was going to make the old man see the woman again and if it didn't get rid of him, Howie intended to take a more direct approach.

****

Cornelia sat at the table reading the newspaper. One story was about a man named Kennedy, the son of one of her former clients. He was about to marry a woman named Jacqueline Bouvier and it would be the social event of the summer in the New England area. She thought back nostalgically for a few moments and then turned the page. She, Howie and Jess were going to the movie that evening to see 'From Here to Eternity' and she checked the paper for the feature starting time. She got up and started to get ready. It took her longer to prepare for an evening out than it had some years ago. Cornelia was now forty-six years old and putting her face on had become more complicated. Though she was still a very handsome woman there were a lot more wrinkles to contend with than before.

Howie and Jess were in the front room watching television. For them to get ready was just a matter of standing up and walking to the door. When Cornelia announced she was ready, Howie went out to the garage and started the car. He wasn't old enough to drive but she did allow him to start the car and pull it up close to the back of the house. This year she was driving a Lincoln and had only owned this car for about a month. It had nearly one hundred miles on the odometer, most of those from trips to the grocery store.

Howie looked closely at his mother as he came back into the house paying particular attention to her make-up and how it made her look younger and more attractive. He had never noticed much before but now he had become an ardent student of how make-up was used. He wondered if he could look more like his mother if he learned to use all of the various cosmetics that she employed and applied them skillfully to his own face.

Cornelia was aware of his scrutiny and asked, "What's wrong, Baby? Did I do something wrong to my face?" and she touched her cheek and turned to a mirror.

"Oh no, Mama. I was just thinking that you're about the prettiest woman I ever saw, specially since you're kinda' old."

"What'chu mean old!" Rosey said. She had heard Howie's statement and had spoken before she even thought. "Why child, your mama is still just a young girl!"

"Now Rosey, he didn't mean anything," Cornelia responded quickly to Howie's defense. "All grownups look old to boys their age," and she nodded her head towards Howie and Jess.

Í think you look pretty too," Jess said and then looked down, embarrassed by his own forwardness.

"Why, thank you, Jess. That's very nice of you," she answered as she reached out and put her hand on his cheek. "Now let's go to the movie."

All three of them liked the movie but Cornelia saw it in a different way than the boys. They liked the fighting and the war scenes while she liked the story of the romantic entanglements. It was dark outside when they left the theater so Cornelia took Jess home before driving to the garage and allowing Howie to put the car away.

As they walked into the house, Cornelia asked Howie a question that had been on her mind for quite a while. "Baby, what's wrong in school?"

Howie removed a bottle of Pepsi from the fridge and opened it before answering. "Nothing's wrong, Mama. I just get bored with some of the stuff they want us to learn. I get more from the books I read than they teach in those dumb classes."

Cornelia thought back to when she had been in school and had to memorize all of the counties in Ohio and understood some of what Howie was saying.

"Does it bother you that they kept you back a year?" she asked.

"Maybe a little bit but now me an' Jess are in the same class so that helps a lot."

"Well, what are you going to do this year?" she asked.

Howie had sat down at the table and he took a big drink of cola before answering. He could see the way the conversation was headed so he spoke saying all the things he knew she wanted to hear, true or not. "I'm gonna' try and do better, I really am." He looked directly into her eyes when he said this being as persuasive as possible.

As was usual, Cornelia believed him and didn't press the issue, preferring to trust in her son. Abruptly she changed the subject and said, "Martin is going to be coming for a visit in a couple of weeks. I talked to him on the phone today and he is going to let me know the exact dates. It doesn't bother you to have him come for a visit, does it?"

Howie had, more or less, become accustomed to having Martin show up once or twice a year. He just went along, avoiding Martin as much as possible and waited for him to leave. "No mama, it's fine with me if that's what you want," he said.

"On this trip Martin wants to talk to you about something he feels is very important," Cornelia said.

"What's that, mama?"

"I'll let him tell you when he gets here. I just hope you will listen to what he has to say," she said.

Howie was mildly curious but deep down he didn't think that anything Martin had to say would be of much interest to him personally but he answered, "Sure mama, I'll be as nice as I can and listen to whatever he has to say."

Cornelia, satisfied with the course of the conversation, said she was going to bed and walked out of the kitchen. Howie followed along and stood in the doorway of her bedroom as she sat down at her dressing table and began removing her make-up. They made idle small talk but what really interested Howie were the different creams and lotions she was using to bring her face back to its' natural look.

When finished, she undressed as far as her underwear, put on her robe and walked back into the kitchen for a glass of milk before she went to bed. Howie sat with her at the table finishing his Pepsi.

They parted for the night with Howie going to his room to read and look out the window.

As he looked at the moon he was thinking that he and his mother were nearly the same size and he wondered what it would be like to wear some of her clothing. He decided that the next time he was alone in the house he would find out. Tonight he wouldn't go out. He had made his plans about what to do about the night watchman and within the next two weeks the problem would be solved, one way or the other.

****

The night watchman had not told anyone about the woman who was haunting the basement. Five times in the last two weeks he had seen the apparition and it was starting to put him on edge. This night he had walked to the clock and inserted his key, then spun around quickly expecting to see where it was coming from but nothing had happened. He walked back to the staircase and, just as he put his foot on the bottom step, he glanced back the way he had come. It was hard to see in the dark because it was dressed in black, but it was definitely there. It stood in the middle of the long basement not making a sound. He flashed his light at it but was to far away to be able to illuminate the object. The fact that he had just walked through this area was what upset him the most. He had watched, both going and coming back and he was sure nothing had been there. His eyes were not what they had once been and it was hard to stare into the darkness for very long. He blinked his eyes a few times, shook his head and when he looked again whatever had been there had vanished.

He climbed the stairs with an old man's gait and stopped to rest at the top. Maybe he was too old for this job, he thought. He had retired from the railroad after forty-five years of service and then gone to work again at this watchman's job. He had been here nearly six years and he was close to seventy-four years old.

The thing in the basement had him completely dumbfounded.

He thought it might be a ghost but he hadn't told anyone about it, afraid they might think he was going crazy. Previous to this night he had made up his mind that if it happened once more he was going to quit this job and never go into that basement again.

The old man sat down in a reclining chair and pushed it all the way back, finally coming to terms with himself and making up his mind. This would be his last night on the job.

****

Howie had been waiting for the time when the old man went to sleep in the reclining chair. He had worked out his plan carefully. After school he had walked through the furniture store while it had been open for business and carefully studied the recliners. Essentially they were all about the same size and shape. He had brought a piece of cord with him and he wrapped it around the back of a chair. He extended it slightly to allow for the size of the person who would be seated in the chair. Howie added about six inches to the length and tied it off at that point. He then had a loop of cord about seven feet around. He took this loop home along with a strong piece of clothesline rope he had cut down and stolen from a neighbor's yard and made a rope loop the same size as the cord. This, along with his stick, was all he needed to take care of the old man.

Howie had dressed all in black and stood in the middle of the basement while the old man went to the time clock and returned. When he saw him hang his head and then shake it, Howie had stepped back into the darkest part of the basement. It had become apparent that the old man was not impressed with the ghost that lurked in the underground. Further action must be taken and tonight was the night.

Howie changed back into his own clothing and headed for the furniture store. He moved through the dark like a shadow, never making the slightest sound. The carpeted floor of the furniture store aided him as he crawled on hands and knees to the area of the reclining chairs. As he expected the old man was asleep in one of the recliners. Howie went to the bedroom section of the store and found a large feather pillow that would suit his needs. The rope was in his pocket and his stick in his other hand.

Howie stood at the rear of the chair and looked down at the sleeping man. He felt such a sense of power he had a hard time controlling his emotions. It would be so easy to WHACK-WHACK-WHACK but he knew he couldn't do it this time. He spread the rope on the floor and put the pillow inside the circle. Then he looped the rope around the back of the reclining chair while holding the pillow above the sleeping man's face. He placed his stick parallel to the back of the chair inside the rope. In one swift movement he dropped the pillow on the old man's face and started twisting the stick, tightening the rope.

The watchman tried to struggle but he never had a chance of escaping. Howie twisted the stick as tight as it would go and then stood behind the chair, watching the struggle. He was surprised at how quickly the old man died. He noticed the odor as the man's bowels and bladder let go but continued to keep tension on the rope until he was sure the old man was dead. After about five minutes he released the tension and unwound his stick from the rope. Howie lifted the pillow from the man's face and peered down while illuminating the watchman with the flashlight that had been on the table beside him. The man's eyes and mouth were wide open and, if Howie had been able to look closely enough he would have seen that the blood vessels in his eyes had ruptured exactly as they would have done if the man had suffered a massive stroke.

Howie examined the pillow he had used and found it had been torn where the old man had clawed at it. A few feathers were falling out so he picked them up while holding the pillow with the torn side up. Putting the flashlight back on the stand, he left the store and entered the underground carrying the pillow, the rope and his stick. He left the basement through a restaurant stairwell and on the way out shoved the pillow into a garbage can and poured garbage from a

second can on top of it. His night's work was complete.
****

The police were called the following morning to examine the dead body. A uniformed patrolman was the first on the scene and he, in turn, called the detectives.

The first detective, upon viewing the body, asked the uniformed officer, "What did you call us for? It's obvious the old man just had a heart attack or somethin'. There's nothing for us to do. Notify the coroner and do whatever he wants. He'll probably tell you to send the body to a funeral home."

The second detective was checking the price tag on the chair where the body was resting. He was thinking he might be able to buy it pretty cheap since someone had died in it. He wandered off to find the store manager so he could try and get a deal.

"Look here," the patrol officer said pointing to the old man's open mouth.

"Yeah, I see it," the detective answered. "A couple of feathers in the man's mouth. So what! Maybe the old man choked on them. Just make the call like I told you to do. We got a lot more important thing to worry about than a couple of feathers."

"Okay, Lieutenant, whatever you say," the patrolman answered.

At the funeral home they actually found several more feathers in the old man's mouth and throat but nobody paid any attention to this anomaly.
****

Martin had finally arrived for his promised visit and now he and Howie sat across from each other at the kitchen table. Martin had flown in earlier that afternoon and now with dinner over they sat alone talking. To be more accurate, Martin was doing most of the talking and Howie was looking curiously at their guest and wondering where this conversation was going to lead.

"Your mother tells me you're not happy with school," Martin was saying. "I want to offer you a deal. You're only in the seventh grade so there is a lot of time for you to get ready for what I'm going to suggest. If you get your grades up to average or better, when you graduate from high school I'll send you to any college you wish to attend. You won't need to work at anything but your schooling and I'll give you fifty dollars a week for spending money. You can major in any subject you like. How does that sound to you?"

Howie listened intently all the time trying to understand what the underlying reasons for this offer could be. "Why do you want to do this?" he asked.

"I have my reasons and those are not important now," Martin said. "I don't have any other relatives anywhere and it is something I'd like to do for you. In time I'll tell you more but for now, tell me what you think about the offer."

Howie sat stone still while thinking about what Martin had said. He stared at the older man, squinting his eyes and wondered if he was going to continue talking. The man looked back, saying nothing and waited for Howie to continue the conversation. He patiently out-waited the boy.

The man was an absolute enigma to Howie. Martin's face gave nothing away and Howie realized that he would have to be the one to speak next and he was baffled about what to say. The man made him very uneasy and Howie resented this feeling. Some type of answer was expected but Howie didn't know what to say so he finally answered, "Do I have to decide right this minute?"

"Of course not," Martin said. "Besides, there is nothing really to decide. If you want to go along with the proposition all you need to do is finish school with grades that are good enough for you to get into college. The offer will always stand. Any college in the United States will be yours for the asking, no strings attached. Maybe you will feel more comfortable after you talk to your mother."

"Does she know about this?" Howie asked.

"No," Martin answered, "I told her I was going to offer you a deal. She trusts me enough not to ask a bunch of questions. It's up to you what you want to tell her. That decision should be yours alone."

Martin had thought about the offer for a long time and felt that with both he and Cornelia confronting the boy it would increase the pressure.

"So far I don't like school very much," Howie replied, "so this is something I'm really going to have to think about." When he saw Martin brighten at this answer Howie knew he was on the right track. "It sounds like a pretty good deal but I'm just not sure."

"That's good enough for now," Martin said as he stood up from the table and reached across to pat Howie on the shoulder. "Now let's go in the room and see if we can talk your mother into going to the movie tonight. Marilyn Monroe is in a movie called 'Gentlemen Prefer Blondes' and we would like to have you go with us."

Howie had already watched it from backstage at the theater. He and Jess had stood behind the screen where Jess had made quite a fuss over the fact
that, from this angle, he could watch breasts that were more than six feet tall. Howie had not been that impressed.

"Okay, I'd like to go," Howie said hoping this smidgen of cooperation would keep this guy from pressuring him.

CHAPTER EIGHTEEN

Jess knew he had about as much chance of being successful at such an action as a dog had of following a cat up a tree. He also knew the consequences. Howie was nearly supernatural in the dark and if he saw what Jess was up to…Heaven help him because no one else would be able too.

Jess got back into bed and pulled the covers up to his chin. He tried to imagine what it would be like spending the next week at his friend's house. One thing was for sure, by the end of the week he should have a pretty good idea of Howie's frame of mind. That would be soon enough to decide what to do.

****

Howie and Jess had taken Cornelia to the airport in Columbus at six-thirty in the morning, dropped her off and were now driving back to Newton. The weather was clear and cold with snow on the ground. The highways themselves were clear. Howie was driving the Mercury since they needed the extra room for luggage and their passenger. They had asked Rosey to ride along but she had refused, not wanting to leave the house unattended.

The boys stopped for breakfast at a small restaurant a few miles West of Newton. Trips of this kind were less exciting than they had been in the past when they were younger and were exploring new country. For breakfast they ordered hot cakes, eggs, bacon and coffee to drink. They both would have preferred milk but didn't want to order a childish drink.

Jess had been watching Howie closely ever since they had started that morning and he could detect nothing untoward in his attitude or behavior.

It was Monday, the twenty-eighth of November and they had to make the return trip to the airport to pick up Cornelia on the following Saturday. She had arranged it this way so the boys wouldn't need to miss any school on her account.

As they walked out of the restaurant, Howie said, "You wann'a skip school today? All we'd have to do is put the car back in the garage and keep on going. Rosey would never notice which way we went."

"Naw, we better not," Jess replied. "We got a history test this morning and a math test this afternoon. If we miss we'll have to stay over a couple of times this week and make them up."

"Yeah, you're probably right," Howie answered. "We'll hold off for a while but if the weather is okay Friday, I'm gonna' skip whether you do or not."

"Sounds good to me," Jess said.

They were soon back at the garage and Jess got out to open the doors while Howie backed the car inside. They locked the door and saw Rosey looking out the kitchen window at them so they waved and headed up the alley for the school. It was nearly eight o'clock and they had to hurry to make it to their seats by eight-fifteen. Even though they were near to being late, they walked through the poolroom, in the front and out the back. It was a custom that could not be ignored.

The students were starting into the building when they arrived, the girls walking with the girls and the boys with the boys. Howie and Jess didn't join any group and walked straight into the school, ignoring everyone else. Another school day started, another day of hideous boredom for Howie.

The week continued to be uneventful and the boys spent their time in normal pursuits; television, movies, poolroom and various restaurants.

Howie never suggested leaving the house after Rosey had gone to bed and Jess didn't broach the subject. Every night, long after Jess had gone to sleep, Howie had lay on his bed reading. Occasionally he would walk to the window and stare into the darkness, yearning to disappear into its' embrace.

Friday they skipped school as they had planned. They went to the Mainline and slipped into the balcony where they sat through the movie 'Guys and Dolls' twice. After going home for supper they spent the rest of the evening back down town playing pool.

Now it was Saturday and they had to pick up Cornelia at the airport. Howie and Jess talked Rosey into riding with them and at two o'clock in the afternoon the three of them were in the terminal awaiting the arrival of her plane.

The previous afternoon two men from the railroad had carried yet another portmanteau into the house from the freight depot across the tracks. The boys had snuck a peek inside only to find that all the contents were neatly wrapped with cards indicating the recipient fastened to the packages.

Cornelia's plane arrived on time and she was happy to see Rosey with the boys. They pulled from the airport and headed to the nearest 'White Castle'. Now with a big sack of hamburgers in the front seat between Howie and Jess, they headed for home.

Cornelia was talking a mile a minute as she described the trip to Rosey. The boys paid little attention to her chatter until they heard, "and Martin will be getting here on Saturday, the twenty-fourth, and be staying through until New Years."

Howie mulled this statement over in his mind all the rest of the way home and wondered how Martin's presence would effect his coming and going in the night. By the time they pulled the car into the garage he had made up his mind he didn't care for the intrusion but there was not much he could do about it.

****

Howie stood backstage at the Mainline Theater and looked into the tangle over his head. It was four o'clock in the morning and the theater had been closed for hours. He had done everything there was to do and now that his preparations were complete his mind was no longer in a turmoil.

It was two weeks before Christmas, a Sunday night, and he had spent the previous evening helping his mother set up the Christmas tree and putting the gifts in place under the branches. Jess and Rosey had also helped. They all had a good time shaking and handling each gift trying to figure out what was inside. Jess had left to go home about ten-thirty and Cornelia had retired right after the eleven o'clock news. Howie had gone to sleep around midnight but had awakened a couple of hours later and slipped out the window and walked towards the downtown. For about an hour he had wandered over rooftops and through buildings and basements, finally ending up in the theater. He carried a flashlight and he used it as he went backstage and into the basement. With his earlier preparations completed, he was relieved. Everything would be finished at exactly ten minutes after nine tomorrow night. Howie knew he was going to miss Jess but this was something that just had to be.

****

Howie came home that Monday night the same as always, about ten thirty and sat down in the kitchen with some cookies and milk in front of him. Cornelia joined him at the table and asked what he had been up to.

"Oh, nothing much," he answered. "Me and Jess went to see that cowboy show, 'Vera Cruz' at the Mainline and then we just came home. Jess said he was kinda' tired and he went home along the short cut."

Cornelia answered exactly as Howie knew she would by saying, "You know I don't like for Jess to walk home that way. It's dangerous crossing that railroad bridge in the dark and there's always trains going up and down through there."

"Aw, heck," Howie answered, "me an' Jess know that way so good we could walk it blindfolded. There ain't nothing to worry about."

Cornelia, being a mother and a woman, was bound to have the last word and said, "I wish you'd promise me not to go that way anymore and I want you to tell Jess the same thing."

"Okay, Mom, if that's what you want, I won't go that way after dark an' I'll tell Jess what you said."

They both went into the front room to watch the news and soon after it was over they went to bed.

It was shortly after midnight when the phone rang, waking Cornelia. Howie had been in his bed reading but before the first ring was complete, his light was out and he was under the covers. He listened to his mother's side of the conversation.

"No, I don't think so. Howie came in around ten-thirty and said that Jess had gone on home," Cornelia said into the phone.

After a pause, she said, "Just a minute, let me check for sure."

Howie could hear his mother's footsteps approaching his room and then the door opened. "Howie, are you awake? Jess's mother is on the phone. She says he didn't come home and wanted to know if he was staying here with you tonight?"

Howie rubbed his eyes with his knuckles as he answered, "No, he's not here." I haven't seen him since he headed home after the movie. Is something wrong?"

"Just wait a minute," Cornelia said. "Jess's mother is still on the phone," and she left Howie's room.

Once again Howie could hear his Mother's side of the phone conversation. She repeated what Howie had told her and then added, "I don't know what to say but if it was me, I'd call them. It's not like him to not let you know where he's at." After another pause, "Well, be sure to let me know what you find out." Another pause and then, "Goodnight."

By this time Howie was standing in the doorway to his room. He said, "Is something wrong?"

"Just what I told you," Cornelia said. "Jess never went home tonight. Do you have any idea where he might have gone? Does he have a girlfriend he might have gone to see?"

"Not that I know of," Howie replied. "He told me he was goin' on home. I think I better get dressed and walk the tracks between here and his house."

"No, you better wait a few minutes," she said. "Jess's mom is going to call the police and maybe you should stay here until we find out what might be going on. Besides, they'll probably want to talk to you."

Howie looked at his mother with eyes large and piercing as he said, "You don't think something might have happened to Jess, do you?"

"I wouldn't think so, Baby. There could be a lot of reasons for him being so late getting home." But in her mind Cornelia could not think of a single one.

The police finally got in touch with Cornelia and Howie about one-thirty in the morning and Howie told the police the same story he had told his mother.

Howie asked the officers if they would like for him to check out the route along the tracks between the two homes. The officer, being wise in the ways of teen-age boys said, "Yeah, that's a pretty good idea, and if you find him, tell him to get his ass home where it belongs. He's got his mother half scared to death."

As Howie prepared to leave, one of the officers asked if he would like for someone to accompany him on the search. Howie declined saying he could cover the ground a lot quicker if he was alone. Howie did consent to take a flashlight with him, but it would be of little help in the expanse of the railroad yards.

****

After daylight the next morning a police officer rode with the engine crew and searched in the area of where Jess had vanished. Trainmen walked the cars looking inside, under and over every piece of equipment in the area. Every building was inspected from top to bottom and an airplane was used to fly over the area searching rooftops and the surrounding fields. It was all to no avail, Jess had disappeared.

After a few more days all except Jess's parents and Howie, who was constantly seen walking in the area, abandoned the search. Nothing more was found and there were no clues to Jess's disappearance.

****

It was Saturday, the twenty fourth, and Martin's plane was due to arrive at noon. Cornelia had been ready to leave for the airport since nine-thirty but Howie had managed to slow her down, not wanting to spend time just sitting in the terminal waiting room. They finally left shortly after eleven o'clock and arrived an hour later.

Cornelia had talked to Martin on the phone and told him about Jess's disappearance. That situation had thrown a blanket of gloom over the holidays but Cornelia was still excited about Martin's visit.

She had told him the police didn't have the first clue about what might have happened to Jess. They had even traced all of the railroad cars that had been in the yards on the night of the disappearance. Boats had used grappling hooks to drag the waters of the river downstream from the railroad bridge. The riverbank had been searched several times but nothing was found. Jess's father was seen wandering through the railroad yards, his head down, hoping against hope that something would turn up.

Howie also walked the area and would stand on the bridge looking down at the river. It nearly broke Cornelia's heart to watch her son grieve after his friend.

Rosey was also deeply disturbed. She had loved Jess like the son she never had and often stood on the porch looking in the direction Jess was last seen.

When Martin came into the terminal the first words out of his mouth were, "Any news about Jess?"

Howie just looked at the floor and shook his head.

Cornelia answered, "Nothing. He's gone like the ground opened up and swallowed him."

They left the airport and drove straight back to Newton. They couldn't bring themselves to stop for hamburgers without Jess being along. Howie was driving and the two adults were talking, Martin swiveling his body around in the front seat to talk with Cornelia who was in the back.

"The police hope something will turn up," Cornelia said. "Up to now they've done everything they could."

"It certainly is a terrible thing to have happen," Martin replied shaking his head, "especially this time of the year. I would imagine not knowing is the worst part for his parents. As bad as we feel, think how hard it must be on them."

"I talk to his mother every day or two," Cornelia said, "and Howie sees Jess's dad every once in a while. They're still praying something will turn up."

Howie just drove, listening to the conversation. Deep inside him was the satisfaction that he knew something nobody else knew. He could have taken them to see Jess but they wouldn't have liked what they saw. Actually, he was somewhat surprised that he missed Jess as much as he did. Howie had no other friends and no immediate prospects of making any. Being alone didn't bother him a lot because he was happy with solitude. Reading a book or prowling at night, he was happy.

That day being Christmas Eve, all of the business places were closing early. Howie knew there would be little for him to do if he did go out that evening so he had planned on just staying home and watching television or going to his room to read.

After they had carried Martin's suitcases inside, they all sat down at the kitchen table. Martin was tired from the trip and Rosey fussed over him with a big strudel, fresh from the oven, and coffee. Howie sat for a few minutes before becoming bored with the conversation and wandered into the front room.

Back at the table, Martin said, "I brought a couple of small gifts for Jess but now I'm not sure what to do with them."

"We're having the same problem," Cornelia replied. "It doesn't seem appropriate to give them to his family because of the pain it would cause them."

"How is Howie doing?" Martin asked.

"It's been hard on him but he's getting by," Cornelia said. "Every day he walks from here to Jess's house like he's lost. I believe that Jess was the only friend he had."

"Howie is sixteen now," Martin said, "so before long you will probably have a different set of problems on your hands. He'll meet a girl and then things will really change, isn't that right Rosey?" he added when Rosey set next to him at the table.

"Lordy, Mister Martin, you outta' know a lot more about that than I do," she said.

"Why I'll have you ladies know that when I was sixteen I chased girls the same as the rest of the boys my age. It was only when I got older that I changed my quarry," Martin said. They all three laughed long and loud, the first laughter that had been heard in this house for several days.

Martin went on, "I can say there has only been one woman in my life and there will never be another," and he reached across the table and squeezed Cornelia's hand.

Howie had only been half listening to the conversation in the kitchen but when Martin said this last, Howie caught the underlying meaning. That old guy is a fag, he thought. He had wondered for a long time what the reasons for Martin's visit might have been and never reached any clear conclusions. Now he accepted and welcomed the fact that their relationship was only a matter of friendship, nothing more. This put his mind more at ease in that respect and he went back to watching the movie 'The African Queen' on television.

Martin had taken over Howie's room for the time he would be staying and Howie would be sleeping on the front room couch. This would curtail any chance of nocturnal excursions. If Howie left the house for any extended period of time he would probably be missed and have to answer a lot of questions about his whereabouts. This would be a bad time for that so he had gone to the library and taken out a stack of books. By midnight the adults were all in bed and Howie was sitting at the front window, looking outside and thinking it was going to be a long week.

The next morning everyone was up bright and early to exchange his or her Christmas gifts. Martin had given Howie a complete set of Indian head pennies including the three rare coins, 1864 L on ribbon, 1869 over 1868 and the 1873 double liberty. These three coins alone were worth the price of a new home and then some.

Rosey had received the same gift from both Martin and Cornelia. By coincidence they had both given her an envelope with a thousand-dollar bill in it.

Dinner that day would have served forty people instead of the four who were in attendance. Rosey had fixed a ham for Cornelia, Howie and herself and a whole roasted chicken for Martin. They all shared the many and varied side dishes of scalloped, mashed and sweet potatoes, green beans, baked beans, corn, apple sauce, waldorf salad, cole slaw, oyster dressing and four kinds of pie.

Full of food, they settled down in front of the television to watch a football game. They sipped coffee during the game and the adults discussed the actions of Martin Luther King, a black minister who was leading a boycott of the Montgomery, Alabama bus system. Martin felt that this would lead to important political changes, not only in the South but also in the whole United States.

Cornelia was more interested in the news from the entertainment trade papers, notably the story about RKO Pictures selling all of their old movies to television. She was anxiously awaiting the arrival of Ginger Rogers and Fred Astaire movies to the local TV stations.

"Can't I get you to take anything seriously?" Martin asked her.

She looked at him closely to see if he was really upset and then answered, "There are a lot of things I take seriously. It's just that these racial things you're talking about don't mean much here in Newton. If I would ever leave here and go back to living in the real world, I'm sure I would be much more interested."

Howie, hearing this last statement spoke up and said, "Don't you like living here in Newton, Mama?"

Cornelia hesitated before answering. "I like it here but I have always liked the big city better. There's a lot more to do there but this place has its' advantages also. I can't really compare the two since they are so different."

Howie tried to digest her answer before asking, "Are you thinking about leaving here and going back to New York?"

"No," she said, "I've never even thought of doing that. Until this thing with Jess I've always felt this was the perfect place to live. There are just so many dangers in the city and that was the reason we came here. I wanted you to have a safe and quiet place to grow up."

Martin joined the conversation by saying, "How would you like to come to the city and visit me some time, Howie? You could stay during your summer vacation for as long as you like. I'd show you around New York and that way you could learn what a big city is really like so you could see the differences between here and there."

"I don't know," Howie answered. "Maybe. I'll have to think about it. But if I did come, it would only be for a visit. I like living here pretty good."

As Martin and Cornelia went on talking, Howie tuned them out. He could not really imagine living in a town where he would be the prey instead of the predator. He was certain he would never want to leave Newton.

****

The week rushed by for Cornelia and Martin as they reveled in their friendship. They went out every night, most often to Columbus where they dined and danced at all of the best spots. A couple of times they had asked Howie to accompany them and he did go along to eat at the Jai-Lai Restaurant and then to see a movie. The weather was cold but had been free of snow so travel was not a problem.

****

Almost before they knew it New Years Day had arrived and Martin had to start preparing to go home. They watched on television as Michigan State beat UCLA in the Rose Bowl. Rosey fixed them up with pie and coffee for a late snack and Martin and

Cornelia sat at the kitchen table, sad and happy at the same time. Howie had gone out for the evening and Rosey had gone discreetly to bed after serving up the snack.

"Do you remember what we were talking about earlier in the week?" Martin asked. "About living here compared to New York."

"Of course," Cornelia answered. "Why do you ask?"

"You know it won't be long until Howie is grown and out on his own. When this happens you will be pretty much free to do as you please. If you wanted to come back to the city you could move in with me. You know you'd be more than welcome."

"Oh God, that sounds wonderful," she answered. "But having me there would cramp your style, wouldn't it?" She smiled politely as she said this last, not wanting it to sound derogatory.

"Not at all," he said. "I do want to ask you about one thing, though. Earlier in the week we talked about the civil rights movement that is going on around the country. I believe it is going to lead to trouble in the ghetto areas of the cities. The area around the apartment house has become a rather depressed neighborhood and I'm thinking of moving my shop to one of the new shopping centers away from the center of town. If I do, I'd probably make my residence somewhere near my new store. If there was a chance you might come to stay, I'll get a house. Otherwise I'll hunt for an apartment that would be sufficient for my needs."

Cornelia tapped the ashes from her cigarette into an ashtray and said, "Let me think about it for a while. We still have a lot of good years ahead of us."

"I know we do," he replied, "but there is one more thing I wanted to ask you about. If I decide to move, what do you want to do with the apartment building? I know it's in my name but I've always felt as though I was just keeping it for you in case you ever wanted to come back."

"Like most places" she said, "it has good and bad memories." Then she said what had never been mentioned before. "It is where our son was born. For that reason I'd like to keep it. If money becomes a problem, I would be glad to help out in any way you wanted."

Martin patted her hand as he said, "Thanks, I'm doing fine. Just so you don't worry, I recently sold off some gold coins I bought during the thirties for over a million and a half. That was only about ten percent of my good stuff. I'm in good shape as far as money is concerned."

"Well, let's plan on keeping the old place when you move, even if it's only for sentimental reasons," Cornelia said.

He smiled and said," You're nothing but an old softy at heart, you know that?"

They just sat and looked at each other for a few seconds before she got up and walked around behind Martin and leaned forward, kissing him on the top of his head. "Yeah, I guess I am," she said.

CHAPTER NINTEEN

It was the end of the first week back in school after the Christmas holidays and Howie stood at his locker as he got ready to leave for the day. Someone tapped him on the shoulder and he turned to see one of his classmates, a girl he knew only slightly standing there.

"I sure like your jacket," she said. "Did you get it for Christmas?"

Howie looked at her gravely and answered, "Yeah, my mother got it for me."

He was wearing a gray suede leather coat, waist length with knit cuffs. He liked it because it was both warm and stylish.

Howie stood looking at her and did not offer to carry the conversation any further so she said, "I heard that your friend disappeared and I'm sorry. I saw you two riding around last summer when you drove past the swimming pool. What do you suppose happened to him?"

"I don't know," he said not offering to help with the verbal exchange.

"Some of the kids said he was the only one besides you who ever got to go for a ride in your car. Is that right?"

"I suppose it is," he answered. "Why do you want to know?"

"I thought you might take me for a ride in your car sometime," she said around a large wad of chewing gum she had in her mouth.

Howie looked at her curiously. He knew her name was Sally Nichols and she was in his history class. He had heard talk that she was somewhat promiscuous but this meant little to him. He could see she was flattered by his close scrutiny, not realizing he was admiring her use of make-up and not her personal charms.

"Why would you wanna' ride in my car?" he asked.

"It's a really neat car," she said, "and besides some of the girls dared me to ask you, so I'm askin'. If you let me take a ride I might show you some of the new clothes I got for Christmas."

"What's that," he asked falling into the trap.

"This stuff right here," she said as she pulled down the neck of her

sweater to reveal the top of a lacy bra. "New underwear. If you wanna'
see, let me know," and she turned and walked away trying her best to
wiggle and catch his interest.

Howie watched her go, slightly intrigued by her raucous
mannerisms but not sexually captivated. Aside from his friend in the
mirror he was asexual and this..this..trollop, was the word that flashed
into his mind, only interested him in so far as her clothing and make-
up. The underwear did intrigue him slightly but not because of what
it covered. He was more curious to find out if he would look as good
in it as she did. He would think about her and see if he could come up
with a plan.

****

Sally Nichols was really a pretty good girl, free spirited and fun
loving. She laughed and talked with all the boys and gave them the
impression that she was very worldly while, in fact, all she did was talk
a good game. She had managed to fend off all of the semi-determined
advances made on her virtue but had done so with such good nature
that nobody was offended. The boys still liked being with her and she,
in turn, enjoyed their company much more than spending time with a
bunch of simpering females. She was an individual who enjoyed life at
the top of her voice. The boys would have labeled her a teaser if they
had been willing to admit they had never had any success with their
sexual forays.

****

The winter months had dragged by for Howie. There had been
more snow than usual so that had curtailed the use of his automobile.
If he left the house at night to wander around he left tracks in the
snow and this was like drawing a map for a suspicious person to follow.
Many a night he set looking out the window at the dark and wishing
for spring.

It was the middle of March when Howie noticed something
different at the train station. He could see it very clearly from his
window and was familiar with the daily operation that went on there.

Mike McConnell was sitting in the depot obviously now working for the railroad. Apparently he had quit college and was now working as a telegraph operator. His mother had told him that the woman who had previously worked at night had moved out of their house a week ago and had taken a station job up around Lake Erie. Cornelia had been sorry to lose such a good tenant.

As he watched the railroaders, Howie was thinking about Sally Nichols. He had not entirely made up his mind but he believed he kind of liked her. She was loud and flamboyant in manner, quite the opposite from the way he behaved. So far he had not taken her for a ride in his car but he did stop and talk with her whenever they met. Not that he sought her company but neither did he avoid her. He had about decided that when the weather was nice and the roads were clear he would take her someplace, maybe over to Columbus for some White Castles.

The weather cooperated with the old adage, in like a lion and out like a lamb. The days towards the end of March were beautiful with high blue skies and warm breezes from the South. It was on such a Saturday that Howie was walking towards the poolroom when he ran into Sally on the street.

Sally wasted little time on the preliminaries. "Is this a nice enough day for you to get your car out? You said when the weather was nice we could go for a ride."

Howie looked at her for a few seconds as he made up his mind. Sally was with another girl that Howie didn't know so he said, "My car's only got two seats so I couldn't take both of you."

"That's okay," Sally retorted. "My friend Judy was going shopping. Oh, Judy, this is Howie. Howie, this is Judy. Anyway, she's got a lot of other things to do, right Judy?" Sally accompanied this last statement with an elbow to Judy's arm.

"Yeah, that's right. I got things to do," Judy said. "See you later, Sally. Nice meeting you, Howie." She smiled at both of them and winked at Sally as she turned and walked briskly down the street.

"Well, I guess we're going for a ride," Howie said. "I'll have to go get the car and come back for you."

"Where's your car?" Sally asked.

"At home in the garage. I never let it set outside if I can help it," Howie explained.

"You mean at your house?" Sally said. "Why don't I walk there with you?"

"I guess that would be okay," Howie answered. "It's this way."

As they turned and started walking, Howie had his fingers stuck in the pockets of his Levi's so Sally put her hand through the crook of his elbow. It would have looked very formal to anyone who happened to notice.

A slow, fifteen minute walk brought them to the garage and Howie fished a key from his pocket and opened the padlock, letting the doors swing open. The T-Bird was as spotless as the first day he had seen it. Howie stood for a few seconds admiring his car.

****

In the house, across the alley unbeknownst to the young people, Rosey was dashing from the kitchen into the front room. "Oh Miz Cornelia, come quick and look out back here!"

Cornelia hurried into the kitchen and saw Howie at the garage with an attractive girl about his own age. She watched as Howie went into the garage, started the car and pulled it outside. The girl got in the passenger's side, laughing and talking all at the same time. They sat there for a minute or two and then Howie got out and put the top down on the car. He opened the trunk, removed the white cover used to hide the reclining top from sight and snapped it into place. Next they drove slowly up the alley and out of sight.

"Well how about that?" Cornelia said. "He really is starting to grow up. I wonder who the girl is. Rosey, have you ever heard him mention anything about who she might be?"

"No ma'am, I ain't never heard him say a word about any young ladies."

"I'm sure we'll find out soon enough," Cornelia said with a wide smile of approval on her face.

****

Howie drove carefully with both of his hands on the wheel and listened to Sally's chatter. By the time they had reached the edge of town they agreed that putting the top down had been a bit premature. In spite of the warm sunshine there was still a chill in the air so they pulled over to the side of the road and put it back up.

Sally never asked where they might be going, she was just happy to be doing something a little different this afternoon. When they passed a sign denoting the Columbus City limits she mentioned that she seldom got out of town and this trip was a real treat for her.

"My mom and dad got a divorce a few years back and I don't see much of him. He lives here in Columbus but he's got a new wife and I don't like her much, ya' know." she said.

Howie didn't answer so she went on, "How come you never drive your car to school? An' how come you never let anyone else ride with you? Am I the only one besides Jess who ever got a ride?"

She was talking so fast that Howie had no chance to answer any of her questions. He nodded, shook his head and shrugged whatever seemed appropriate and finally decided she was not really looking for any answers.

She continued to talk. "You know I was just kidding about my underwear that day in the hall, don't you?" Sometimes I say things and do things just for the fun of it, don't you? Like now, I jus' keep talking when I really don't have anything to say, ya' know? You really do make me kinda' nervous, ya' know?"

"Why would I do that?" he asked.

"You never say much. The other boys are always talking and acting up but you're real quiet. I can never tell what you might be thinking, ya' know?"

"I know that you say 'you know' an awful lot."

She looked at him to see if he was joking and saw by the expression on his face that he was. She also thought as she looked at him that he was the most beautiful boy she had ever seen. Not sissy like but way beyond just handsome. If he had been a girl he would have been a beauty queen.

When they got to the White Castle they went inside and sat on the hard plastic chairs and ate their hamburgers and fries and washed them down with Pepsi-Cola.

On the way back to Newton the talk turned serious when she asked, "Do you miss Jess a lot?"

"Yeah, I guess so," he answered slowly. "He was about my only real friend."

"Heck, I'll be your friend if that's okay," she said. "I'll even promise not to get your car dirty and if it does get messed up, I'll help you clean it."

"Jess used to help me keep my car clean," Howie said with a big sigh.

"I might not be able to do as good a job as he did but I'll try if you let me," she answered. "Maybe I'll end up being just like him."

Howie looked at her and squinted his eyes as he said, "Anything's possible."

After Howie got home that evening and put his car in the garage, he found Cornelia and Rosey waiting for him at the kitchen table

"Hi, Baby," Cornelia said as he came in the back door. "What have you been doing today?"

"I wish you'd quit calling me that," he answered. "I went for a ride. It was a nice day to get the car out. Why?"

"We saw you when you left," his mother said. "We were wondering about the young lady we saw you with."

"That was just some girl I know from school," Howie said with no hint of reticence. "Her name is Sally Nichols."

"That's the first time we ever saw you take anyone in your car except me or Jess," Cornelia said. "Is she someone special?"

"Not really, Mom. She's just a friend, that's all."

Cornelia decided to push just a wee bit more and said, "Well you know what they say, 'In the spring a young man's fancy,' and so on."

"Not in this case," he replied. "She's just a casual friend."

"Where did you go?" Cornelia asked.

"Just over to Columbus for White Castles."

"Well the next time she's here, bring her in so I can meet her," Cornelia said. "You know how I would like to meet your friends."

"Sure, Mom, if there is a next time I'll have her come in," Howie answered. "Now if you're done with your twenty questions I'm gonna' watch TV for a while." He said this last with a chuckle so she would know he wasn't bothered by her curiosity.

"Sure, Ba… honey, go ahead."

Howie stretched out on the couch and thought back over the afternoon. It had been pleasant enough and when he had dropped Sally off at her home she had said, "Thanks for a really great afternoon," and had trotted quickly into the house and out of sight. He drove away immediately and came straight home.

That was the longest time he had ever spent in the company of a female other than his Mom or Rosey so he was not sure if he had done things right or wrong. She seemed to enjoy herself, laughing and talking all the time they were together. One thing was certain, the girl was not a tramp in spite of some of the talk he had heard. Sexually she didn't interest him at all but as a friend to spend time with, she had possibilities.

****

With the return of good weather he had gone back to prowling the downtown. Nothing had changed in the basement of the many stores and the watchman had not been replaced thus he was free to roam at will. He enjoyed dressing up and meeting his friend in the mirror, discussing the problems of existence. They ate ice cream and drank colas together and reminisced about Jess and the good times they had shared. One night he had even gone to see Jess but that had been a mistake. Jess wasn't up to having company.

CHAPTER TWENTY

It was the first week of April and had been unusually warm for this time of year. The movie 'Around the World in Eighty Days' was playing at the Mainline Theater and there was a packed house at each showing. At the seven o'clock feature on Tuesday it was so warm inside that the management had to turn on the cooling apparatus for the first time that year. Everything was automatic requiring the flip of a switch in the projectionist's booth to set it in motion. The camera operator was a good judge of the temperature since his booth was high in the back of the top balcony. He had called the manager earlier and told him it was getting warm and the manager had told him to use his own discretion. Forrest Fletcher, the cameraman, had noticed the odor that he recognized as a dead rat. He had become accustomed to the smell having worked in theaters all of his life. Rodents and movie theaters went hand in hand.

At seven-fifteen he flipped the switch and the trouble started. The smell flooded through the audience like an emanation from the bowels of hell. People ran choking and gagging for all the exits, literally pouring out of the fire doors. Within ten minutes the movie was playing to an empty house with even the cameraman abandoning his post.

The police were summoned and the first officer on the scene, Patrolman Johnson, the downtown beat cop, told the manager what he smelled. "There's a dead body in here somewhere. I've smelled enough of them to recognize that odor anywhere."

The two-man cruiser that worked the downtown area arrived a couple of minutes later and the three officers met outside with the manager. They were told that the smell had exploded when the cooling system had been activated so they went there first. The manager had shut down the movie and turned on all the house lights so they had little trouble finding their way into the basement and locating the cooling apparatus. The officers turned on a light switch at the bottom of the stairs and found the source of the smell.

A body was floating in the pool of shallow water in front of the huge cooling fan. It was face down and, as bodies in water tend to do, it had swollen up to three times its' normal size. The head was as big as a gymnasium medicine ball and the entire body was as black as coal.

Seeing what was there, the uniformed officers retreated to the fresh air outside the theater and called for the detectives. It may or may not be a homicide but they took no chances. Besides it smelled so bad they took the first opportunity to pass the buck.

It was nearly two hours before the detectives and the coroner finished up at the theater and removed the corpse. By then they had tentatively decided that they had finally located the missing boy from last Christmas time. Now all they had to do was figure out how he got there.

The detectives were immediately suspicious of Howie's story about Jess going home by himself. They had checked with witnesses who remembered seeing the boys at the movie on the night of the disappearance and now they thought there was a good chance that Jess had never left the theater. If this was true then Howie was lying. He had suddenly become a suspect in a murder case.

While they waited for the results of the autopsy, the detectives went to Cornelia's home and talked with her and Howie. Howie stuck to his original story that he had told them on the night that Jess had vanished.

Howie was adamant, insisting he and Jess had parted company after leaving the theater. The detectives didn't believe him but they had no proof to contradict the story.

A week after the discovery of the body the police received the results of the autopsy. Jess had died from massive head injuries ascribed to some type of blunt instrument, possibly a baseball bat or some similar weapon. Shortly before the time of death the victim had eaten popcorn and corn kernels were found in his stomach. Due to the extreme state of decomposition of the body, little else could be determined.

One thing the detectives noted was the lack of defensive injuries, such as to the hands or arms. Broken bones were often present where the victim had tried to ward of blows to his body. A meeting was called in the Chief's office in the station house to go over what evidence they had and to decide how to proceed. Nobody remembered to invite the prosecuting attorney although his legal advice would have been most helpful. At the meeting the Chief decided he would personally interview Howie and his mother. When the meeting ended he had his secretary call Cornelia and ask her to come to the station to see him as soon as Howie got home from school that day.

From the evidence available, the Chief could not bring himself to think that Howie was a suspect in his friend's murder. He felt he could handle the situation as well as any of the Detectives. After all, he was the Chief of Police.

At three-thirty that afternoon Cornelia and Howie were ushered into the Chief's office. His first impression was that no woman this beautiful could have a killer for a son. Mother and son sat in chairs in front of his desk. When Cornelia sat down and crossed her legs she gave the Chief a good look at her charm, well aware of what she was doing. Then she demurely adjusted her skirt down over her knees. She said nothing, waiting for him to begin the conversation.

He stood behind the desk and said, "Mrs. Lawson, I'm Chief Moore. This young lad with you must be Howard. I'm pleased to meet you."

Cornelia rose and offered her hand across the desk, meeting him much as a man would have done. Howie also rose and shook hands and looked the Chief right in the eye without any waver to his stare.

The Chief sat down slightly confused by the direct approach of the woman and boy and said, "Hum..a..yes.. a.. well we're in the midst of an investigation into the death of the little colored boy, the friend of your son and I..we..wanted to ask you a few more questions."

"So I understand," Cornelia answered. "The boy's name was Jess and we would be glad to help in any way we can. We were both very fond of the…how did you put it…little colored boy."

The Chief immediately caught the tone of disapproval in Cornelia's voice and tried to make amends by saying, "Now don't misunderstand, his being colored has no bearing on the case whatsoever. We'd work just as hard if it was a white person who got hisself killed."

At this point the Chief had lost total control of the interview.

"How may we be of assistance?" Cornelia asked.

"Well, the problem seems to be the fact that your son and the… deceased.

were at the movie together and then your son claims they left the theater and the col…deceased went home by himself. The problem we're having is trying to figure out how the deceased got back to the theater."

"I'm afraid I don't understand what you're trying to say, Chief," Cornelia said. "Are you insinuating that my son might be lying about what happened that because if you are I……."

"Not at all, Mrs. Lawson, not at all," the Chief answered obviously trying to placate Cornelia. "It's just that ..well..we.. can't figure out how the deceased ended up back where he started."

"Do you know how Jess was killed?" she asked bluntly

"Yes we do, ma'am," the Chief said. "He was struck over the head by some type of heavy object, like a ball bat or something similar."

"It seems to me like you would be a lot better off trying to find the killer than worrying about how poor Jess got back into the basement of the theater," Cornelia said brusquely.

"Yes ma'am, we are trying to find the killer, the Chief answered, talking faster with every word out of his mouth. "How the victim ended up in the theater is also an important part of the case. I'm sure you understand that."

"Yes, I do," Cornelia said as she stood up abruptly. "If you make any progress on solving this mess I hope you will let me know. Now, if there is nothing else…." and she let the words hang in the air.

"No, no, that will be all for now and I want to thank you and the boy for coming in," he said. "You've been most helpful."

It was only after they had left his office that Chief Moore realized Howie had never said a word. But the Chief relied heavily on his intuition and that told him that Cornelia was a good woman with an equally good child. He would pass on the word to the detectives to forget Howard Lawson as a suspect. The Chief knew that no woman as good looking as Cornelia Lawson could be related to a murderer.

****

Howie expected to hear more from the police but after a week went by they had still not been back to talk with him. He wasn't worried because they couldn't prove he was lying and whatever they suspected didn't mean that much without any evidence.

Jess's family was particularly distraught over the discovery of the body as was Rosey. They had all been hoping that Jess would eventually turn up but now all hope had been taken away and they faced the reality of murder.

As the police continued to search for any possible motive for the killing they discovered that Jess didn't have an enemy in the world. Eventually they ran out of leads to check and other activities began to steal time away from the murder investigation. The detectives still believed that the Lawson boy knew a lot more than he was saying but the Chief had decided the boy was innocent and had forbidden them to talk with him further. They finally admitted it would never be solved unless something very bizarre happened.

CHAPTER TWENTY-ONE

April turned into May and school was out for the summer. Howie passed to the next grade. He was indifferent to schooling but as a result of his constant reading, was as well taught as most of his classmates. In history, english, spelling and geography he was a whiz. As far as the sciences, math and civics were concerned, he could care less. He discovered the writings of Ayn Rand and practiced her teachings, to thine own self be true. He was true to what he wanted to do and nothing else.

Howie had not taken Sally for any more rides although he continued to be cordial whenever they happened to meet. He had decided he didn't want a close relationship with her. He had been close with Jess and that had caused all kinds of problems and he never wanted to go through anything like that again. Life had become boring and he needed to find something new to occupy his time.

During the summer months he often stayed out late and when he drove his car, Cornelia waited up until he got home. When he was afoot, she would go to bed and not worry about him.

It was a rainy June night when he left the poolroom about eleven-thirty and started home. It occurred to him that nobody would be awake so he thought he might check out the basement on his way. As he started up the alley he saw a figure ahead of him silhouetted against the street light at the other end of the block. He stepped into the shadows and advanced cautiously, wanting to see without being seen. When he got close enough he saw it was Patrolman Johnson, the beat cop.

Howie began following Johnson but the fun didn't last long. It was getting close to midnight and Johnson was headed for quitting time at the station house. When Johnson left the street, Howie headed back for the basement. He needed to talk with his friend in the mirror.

****

During the summer it didn't get dark until after nine o'clock so Howie was limited to the amount of time he could spend following the beat cop. It wasn't fun to follow him in the daylight and Howie was already getting bored with following him after dark. Johnson never actually DID anything. except wander aimlessly around the downtown. He went in and out of theaters and coffee shops with no discernible pattern. Only one thing was a constant and that was going to a call box every hour and reporting in to the station.

Howie saw only one way to have fun. When he left home that evening he wore a black sweater with his Levi's and put a black stocking cap in his pocket. He waited in an alley near where he knew Johnson would make his ten o'clock call. As Johnson walked away from the telephone that was in a metal box on the side of a lamp pole, Howie ran to the phone, and took the receiver off the hook and let it hang from the cord. Howie had checked out all of the call boxes in the downtown and knew they were nothing more than a direct line into the police station, a telephone with no dial. Howie ran back to the shadows and waited to see what would happen.

Within five minutes a cruiser pulled up and the driver got out and hung up the phone. Howie could see where this game could be fun. He knew the location of the ten different call boxes and that none of them were locked.

He ran through an alley to the next closest call box and again left the receiver hanging from the cord. Howie climbed to a rooftop and watched as a different cruiser arrived to put the phone back on the hook. He next went to a spot where the boxes were only a block apart and removed both receivers in quick succession. This time he didn't wait for the cruiser to arrive, instead running back to the first location, removed the receiver and then ducked into the back door of the big poolroom and sat in a chair, laughing to himself.

At about quarter of twelve Officer Johnson came in the front door of the poolroom and stopped to talk with the owner. Johnson pointed out the front window as he talked and Howie could see the owner shaking his head. Johnson walked on through the place and out the back door. Howie followed him at a discreet distance to make sure Johnson went to the station house. He planned on spending some time in the basement and stores and he wanted to make sure Johnson was going off duty so he didn't pop up unexpectedly.

Howie went up a fire escape, across the roof and up a ladder to the roof of the furniture store. He entered an unlocked stairway that led down into the store. Walking through, he stopped every three or four steps to listen. It was dark but he moved surefootedly among the displays and headed for the steps that led to the basement. From there he went up into one of the two beauty shops that had access to the underground. Wearing the dark clothing with his hair concealed, he moved like a shadow to his destination.

At the beauty shop he gathered up the cosmetics he would need and went into a booth and closed the door before turning on the row of light bulbs surrounding the mirror. Howie applied his make-up and then leaned back in the chair.

"What did you think of that game tonight?" he asked the woman in the mirror.

"It was okay but there's got to be something we could do to make it more fun."

"What did you have in mind?"

"That beat cop, Johnson, is kinda' old and fat. Do you think he could catch us if he saw us doing something?"

"You mean like tonight? Chasing us on foot?"

"Yeah, like that. We could let him see us and then we could run. We might even give him a surprise in a dark alley."

"I never liked him much," said the woman in the mirror, "and neither did Jess."

"I don't want to talk about Jess. He almost got us in a lot of trouble."

"Do you want to talk about Sally?"

"You can if you want to but it won't mean nothing."

"What do you mean by that?"

"Well, she could get nosy like Jess an' then we'd have'ta do somethin' about her. It would be better for everyone if we would just stay away from her as much as possible."

Howie had arrived at this decision in a very roundabout manner. He was doing the kindest thing he could do for the girl without realizing it.

Howie turned off the lights around the mirror and went out into the business area and selected a red wig. He came back into the dressing room, closed the door and put on the wig. He turned the lights back on and, after careful scrutiny decided he still didn't care for redheads.

****

There was a very narrow access alley that was used for delivery to some of the stores on Main Street. It was also close to one of the call boxes that Johnson used for his ten o'clock pull. In this alley were two telephone poles on opposite sides of the alley directly across from each other.

On his way downtown Howie had walked through a few yards until he found a clothesline and cut a piece out of it about twenty feet long. In the access alley he stretched it between the two telephone poles about eighteen inches off the ground. He next took a cardboard box and put it in the center of the alley under the rope. If everything went as planned he would be able to see the box in the dark alley and know when to jump to avoid the rope. Now all he had to do was get Johnson to chase him. That shouldn't be very difficult.

****

Johnson looked at his watch and saw that it was nearly ten o'clock and time for his pull. He had been keeping a close watch on the call boxes because someone was taking the phones off the hook and just letting them hang. They would automatically buzz into the station until they were put back on the hook. Johnson had been the butt of several jokes because the harassment seemed to be directed towards him personally.

As he approached the box he was going to call from he saw a figure, either a large boy or a small man, step up to the box and open it. The figure removed the receiver from the inside and dropped it, letting it hang from the cord.

"HEY YOU," he yelled, "STOP RIGHT WHERE YOU ARE!" He started running towards the figure only to see it turn and start running away from him. Johnson had his nightstick in his left hand and used his right hand to keep his gun from flapping around. Then he yelled something that sounded funny even to him as it came out of his mouth, "STOP IN THE NAME OF THE LAW!" Oh God, he thought, I can't believe I really said that.

Johnson continued to lumber up the street, running as best his age and condition would permit. He saw the figure was not about to stop. The figure went down one alley and turned left into a second alley and Johnson
saw him jump over a cardboard box. Johnson ran around the right side of the box when suddenly his feet came to a stop but his body kept moving. He saw the ground rushing towards his face and then everything went black. He imagined he could hear laughter echoing around him as he passed out.

****

In a manner of speaking, the trapping of Officer Johnson in the alley led Howie to a whole new form of entertainment. He liked to have the police chase him so he could show his superiority by getting away. He had such an intimate knowledge of the downtown that in the dark he proved to be untouchable. A rock or an egg thrown against a cruiser windshield or a broken window in a store with a burglar alarm was the two best ways to initiate a chase. He had even gone so far as to wear a ski mask over his head.

The police countered Howie's actions by putting two men on the downtown beat. He would walk through town dressed in a white tee shirt and blue jeans, his blond hair standing out whether it was daylight or dark. He kept a full change of clothes hidden in the underground and he had so many ways in and out that the police patrols offered no problem. He would walk the streets scouting the walking officers until it got dark. To them he was just another kid loitering on the street corners. One thing that had become routine for the beat men were periodic trips through the poolroom to try and get a clue to the identity of the villainous prankster.

The police had tried using unmarked cars for the patrol of the downtown but this was a waste of time. Whenever the unmarked cars were not in use they were parked in front of the station house for everyone to see. Howie, of course, saw everything.

The police had become reluctant to enter into a foot chase after what happened to Johnson and two other patrolmen. One officer, watching the ground for a trip wire found a rope that had been left chest high. He had been unable to talk for a week and needed more than twenty stitches to the back of his head. Another beat man had discovered a pane of glass hanging from a rope. It had been suspended head high from the ground by using wire and duct tape. Luckily he had not been running when he made contact.

By the end of August when school was ready to take up again, Howie tired of the game. All of the call boxes had newly installed locks and the police had never come close to catching him. The police would continue their search for months to come but the attacks had stopped as mysteriously as they had started.

CHAPTER TWENTY-TWO

Howie turned eighteen years old while he was still in the eleventh grade. A small dinner was planned at home and, of course, Martin was invited. Cornelia had offered to replace Howie's two-year-old car with a new 1957 T-Bird but he declined. He was well satisfied with the car he had.

Martin and Cornelia had been encouraged with Howie's progress in school. He had been holding a B minus to a C plus average so Martin had decided to talk to him a little more about college on this trip. Martin also had something else to tell him now that he was eighteen years old and an adult.

It was a Saturday night and after dinner was over an unusual thing happened. Cornelia and Rosey announced they were leaving the house to go grocery shopping leaving Howie and Martin home alone.

Shortly after the women left, Howie picked up his coat and announced to Martin, "I think I'll go down town for a while."

"Wait a bit," Martin said. "I want to ask you about a couple of things. How about sitting down at the table so we can talk for a few minutes."

Howie caught on and realized the women had left so that he and Martin would be alone to talk. It made him uneasy. He was going to be asked to make a commitment of some sort and he resented Martin pressuring him. What right did the old guy have to do this, anyway?

But Howie answered in the affirmative and said, "Yeah, okay, I'm not in any big hurry to go anywhere," and he sat down at the table, fidgeting and holding his jacket as he looked out the back door and not at Martin.

"The first thing I want to ask you about," Martin said, "is what you have probably guessed. That is college. You're grades wouldn't get you into Harvard or Yale but they are quite adequate for any state university or most private schools."

"One more thing you should know before we go on talking

about college," Martin continued. "Your mother and I want you to know that whatever you decide you will never need to get a job and work for a living. Money will never be a problem for you if you use common sense."

"What do you mean about money?" Howie asked.

"Your mother and I have set up a trust fund for you in one of the banks here in Newton. We each deposited a half a million dollars and it will be yours, free and clear plus all the accrued interest when you turn twenty-one years old, absolutely no strings attached."

"Why would you want to give me that kind of money?" Howie asked. He had moved around in his chair and was now looking at Martin instead of out the back door. Howie's eyes were squinted about half shut, a look Jess would have recognized had he been there.

"This is something Cornelia and I put off telling you until you turned eighteen years old," Martin said softly.

"Yeah, well what is it?" Howie asked.

"Howie, I am your real father."

Howie sat back in his chair, stunned by what Martin had said. Then he shouted, "NO YOU AIN'T!! My father was killed in the war, my mother told me. You're saying my Mama is a LIAR and that ain't so!"

"Now calm down, son, and let me explain…"

"Don't you call me that, you old..fag. That's what you are, just an old queer. I heard you talking and you said it yourself."

Howie bounced to his feet, his face turning purple with rage as he shouted, "YOU'RE LYING! I KNOW YOU ARE!"

****

Martin was completely taken aback by Howie's violent reaction and tried to calm him by saying, "Listen to me. This doesn't mean your mother doesn't love you. She just wanted to wait until the right time to tell you all the circumstances of your birth. We both love you, Howie."

Howie stood up from the table and looked at Martin with terrible eyes, a look similar to what Martin had seen years before. It had scared him then and it scared him now.

Howie turned and walked away from Martin and into his room, slamming the door behind him.

Martin sat at the table in shock, the minutes seeming to drag by. He had convinced Cornelia to let him handle the situation and now he saw he had made a horrible mistake. Martin raised his eyes to the back porch and saw Cornelia standing just outside the screen door. She was looking into the kitchen, directly into Martin's eyes. Now he hoped things would get straightened out. He trusted she would come up with the proper things to say. He smiled at her, glad for the years they had shared and thinking of all the time they had ahead of them. Funny, he hadn't heard the car pull in.

****

When Howie had gone to his room and slammed the door, he had gone directly to his closet for his materials. He laid his gray pants suit and white blouse on the bed and began applying his make-up. His blonde wig came next followed by his underwear and clothing. He jumped out of the window and, with keys in hand, went to the garage. He had to get to the trunk of his T-Bird. Once there he removed his long white stick that had served him so well over the years. Now he walked to the house and stood on the back porch. It was starting to get dark and the lights in the kitchen made it easier for him to see inside than for someone inside to see out into the dark.

He had been looking at Martin through the back door for two or three minutes when Martin looked up and saw him. Howie opened the door and started inside.

Martin was surprised to see Cornelia all alone and he wondered where Rosey might be. He was also slightly taken aback to see that she was carrying a long white cane. What possible purpose could that serve? He didn't have to wait long to find out.

Howie raised the stick and swung it down at Martin's head. Martin threw up his left arm to ward off the blow and as a result his left arm was broken between the wrist and the elbow. The force of the blow accompanied by the pain drove him down to one knee. As he attempted to rise he saw another blow coming and threw up his right arm to protect his head only to have the stick turn and come crashing against his ribs.

"WHACK!" Howie said, "WHACK, WHACK, WHACK."

Only then did Martin realize that this was not Cornelia. "Howie!" he screamed, "NO!…NO!…Please don't…"

****

Howie struck again, this time to the side of Martin's knee, turning his foot to an impossible angle. Martin went to the floor and Howie struck again, this time to Martin's exposed head. Martin's scalp split from over his right eye to over his right ear and blood poured from the wound. Martin was nearly unconscious as the next strike hit him directly on top of the head leaving a furrow like a thumbnail through a cake of soft soap.

Howie continued to swing his stick at Martin's face and head until he was just too tired to go on. Howie collapsed onto a chair, completely exhausted.

Howie had no idea how long he sat there. As he started to come back to his senses, he was amazed at the amount of blood. It was everywhere. The floor was a giant pool, six feet across as it spread away from what had been Martin's head. While flailing away with his weapon, blood and other things normally covered by skin and bone had been scattered to the walls, ceiling, furniture…everything.

Howie's coat and pants were soaked as well as his underwear and the skin beneath. "Whack, Whack," he said in a near whisper as he looked at what previously had been Martin lying on the floor. "Whack—Whack, Whack—Whack."

****

Rosey, who was the first one in the door with a sack of groceries in her arms took one look at the room and fainted dead away.

Cornelia stood just inside the doorway. "Oh, dear God," she said, "Howie, what have you done? Dear Lord God, Baby, what HAVE you done?"

Cornelia walked slowly to where Howie was sitting at the table, his stick still in his hands. He looked up at her and said, "I asked you not to call me that any more, Mama. I'm not a baby anymore."

Cornelia stood behind his chair and took his obscenely filthy head in her arms and pulled it tight against her breast. She cried for a long time, even after the police had arrived and taken Howie away.

****

CHAPTER TWENTY-THREE

It was Friday, June 2nd of 1967 when Howie came home, ten years, two weeks and one day from the time Martin Fields had been murdered. The trial had been a mere formality, lasting a day and a half. Howie had been sentenced to serve twenty years to life in prison.

For most of the first two years he had been in the psychiatric ward of the prison. While there he had finished his high school education and graduated with perfect grades while he was in the prison school. The psychologists and psychiatrists who worked with Howie were impressed by his intelligence but not fooled by his mild manners. They had been exposed to numerous abnormal personalities in their work and when discussing Howie, found they could not completely agree as to whether he was, or was not, still dangerous. As far as they knew this was the only incident of violence in his history. They knew that ninety-eight percent of all people who kill, it would be their first and last crime. In most cases it was a matter of temporary passion that would never be triggered the second time.

The main thing that concerned the doctors was Howie's lack of remorse. Whenever they tried to get him to talk about the murder he would only shake his head and say he couldn't remember anything about it. Some of them accepted his denial and others thought it was all an act to cover his feelings.

After nearly two years of study the doctors agreed that they couldn't agree and Howie was taken from the hospital and placed in the general population of the prison. His activities were more closely monitored than the other prisoners due to the fact that some of the doctors felt he could still be dangerous.

All of this information was kept in his file and, prisons being what they are, word soon got around of the doctor's findings. Most of the prisoners, having had experience with violence, recognized the mild, young man for what he was, a person who would invariably have the last word, one way or the other.

When his first parole hearing came up ten years into his sentence, he had done all he could do to make a case for himself. He walked into the room and did not sit until told to do so. He looked every member of the panel straight in the eye and never flinched from their obvious curiosity.

They, in turn, saw a smallish man, five foot eight inches tall with blond hair the color of fresh cream. His blue eyes were captivating and proclaimed his sincerity. Two of the panel members were women and they sided with him immediately.

The panel asked him a number of questions and he gave all of the right answers. When they asked him about the crime he had committed, Howie stuck with the story of not being able to remember. He had been preparing for this hearing for the last ten years and had read every book about the process he could get his hands on.

Within a week he was being processed out, free but on parole.

****

During the time he was incarcerated, his mother had visited him at every opportunity making the drive from Newton to the new state facility at Lucasville in Southern Ohio. Every other Tuesday, as regular as clockwork, she would be shown into the visitor's room and Howie would quickly join her. By the third visit she would arrive with a box of two dozen White Castle hamburgers and Howie would eat every one of them while they talked. Cornelia would never eat, just sit and smoke her cigarettes.

By the third month she was bringing more and more of the greasy sandwiches with her for some of the other prisoners. By the sixth month two guards were needed to help her bring all of the boxes into the visitor's hall.

The guards were always ready to help any attractive woman and were captivated by Cornelia. The fact that she always left several cartons of cigarettes in the guardhouse didn't hurt her popularity.

Towards the end of his fifth year Cornelia started losing weight and looked a bit haggard. Not even the best make-up job could hide the fact that she was ill. Her heavy smoking over the last twenty years had taken its' toll. Cornelia admitted to Howie that she had cancer. Six months later the big C had claimed another victim. Two guards accompanied him to the funeral.

****

The bank where Cornelia had always done business handled the arrangements. Howie, by phone and mail, hired a local attorney to take care of the legal requirements.

After the death of his mother, other prisoners near Howie's cell could hear him talking quietly in the night. They were sure that the death of his mother had taken a greater toll on him than the faculty believed.

From the date of her burial, Howie had brought his mother into his cell and every night he would sit and visit with her in a mirror.

Cornelia had given the apartment house to Rosey. Everything else was placed in a savings account for Howie. Mr. Wilson, at the bank, was holding the bankbooks until Howie was released. Howie had never thought about money because it had always been there for the asking. Now he was a very wealthy man. All of Martin's money had gone to Cornelia and subsequently to Howie. He knew it was a lot but he had never asked exactly how much. Under the circumstances it wasn't very important.

Now Howard Lawson was out of prison. He stepped off the bus at the depot right across from the bank where he would make his first stop.

Entering the bank, Howie asked at the information booth for Mr. Wilson.

"Who shall I say is here?" the woman asked.

"Tell him Howard Lawson. Cornelia Lawson's son," Howie said.

She picked up the phone and dialed two numbers, spoke briefly and looked up at Howie, saying, "He'll be right with you."

Within seconds Mr. Wilson was standing at the desk introducing himself. "Please come this way, Mr. Lawson," Wilson said as he led Howie to an office in the front of the bank.

As soon as they were seated Wilson came right to the point. "I have your bank book right here in my private safe. You have quite a bit of money in your account. As you requested, your attorney has access to the interest you have been receiving so the taxes could be kept up to date. I have an itemized statement current to the last month of all expenses."

Wilson handed the bankbook and file folder across the desk to Howie who opened the folder and glanced briefly at the totals in the bankbook and said, "I'd like to get some money today. I'm going to need a car, some clothes and a few other things. I prefer to pay cash."

"Whatever you want is fine with us here at the bank," Wilson said. "We'd be glad to open a checking account for you if you like but if you want cash, just tell me what you'd like to have and I'll get it for you."

"I'm sure things are more expensive than they were ten years ago," Howie said with a smile. "I think I'd like fifty thousand dollars. That amount should last me for a good while."

"What denomination bills would you like, Mr. Lawson?"

"Give me five thousand in twenties and the rest in hundreds." Howie said, "and possibly something to carry the money in."

Wilson nodded and picked up the phone, dialing two numbers and telling the person at the other end of the line what he wanted. When he finished talking he picked up a black attaché case next to the desk and removed the contents.

"Hey, you don't need to do that," Howie said. "Just put it in a bank bag of some kind."

"Mr. Lawson, you're the second biggest investor we have in this bank," Wilson said. "I assure you I will be reimbursed for the price of this case."

After ten minutes a girl came into the office with a gray bank bag containing Howie's money. She stacked it on Mr. Wilson's desk and left the room without a word.

"Would you like to count your money, Mr. Lawson?" Wilson asked.

"Of course not. If I was still at my most recent residence I would, but not here," Howie said getting the appropriate chuckle from Mr. Wilson.

Howie left the bank carrying the attaché case in one hand and a small gym bag in the other. After receiving his money he had extracted ten of the twenty-dollar bills, putting nine in the pocket of his Levi's and getting change for the other one.

He walked three blocks to the Ford dealer and went inside to find a salesman. The vehicle he wanted was in stock so one hour later he was on his way again. His next stop was the attorney who had been taking care of his business. Howie had phoned ahead from the car dealer's office to make sure the man was available.

When he arrived he was ushered right into the lawyer's office and pleasantries were exchanged. Howie came directly to the point and said, "Mr. Berry, I have a list of things I would like for you to do for me."

Howie removed a sheet of paper from his pocket and handed it to the attorney as he said," Would you look it over and tell me what the charge will be and I'll pay you now."

Mr. Berry looked over the sheet and said, "This seems fairly simple. Drawing up a will with these provisions and tracking down the address of one person shouldn't be complicated. One fifty should cover it."

"That's fine," Howie said. He opened the attaché case and handed the lawyer two one hundred dollar bills. "Keep the rest and when you get it all together I'd like for it to be delivered to Mr. Wilson at the People's National Bank."

****

The men rose and shook hands across the desk and Howie left the office. He was no sooner out the door that Berry's secretary came rushing in, wanting to know, "Who was that gorgeous man who just left?"

"Terri, he's not for you," Berry said. "He just got out of prison for beating a man to death with a club. It happened ten years ago right here in Newton. His mother died while he was in prison and he inherited her money. I've been handling the estate for the last several years. It wouldn't be right for me to tell you the exact figures but I can tell you that he is indubitable the richest man you will ever see."

"He's not married, is he?" she asked. Being twenty years old and not far out of high school she was still judging people strictly by their looks. "He's got dreamy blue eyes."

"You get back to work," Berry said, "and I promise that the next time he comes in I'll introduce you to him. Who knows, maybe you'll get lucky."

****

Howie was sitting in a restaurant eating his second cheeseburger and drinking his second milkshake. It was a meal he had been wanting for the last ten years. Just to be able to have whatever he wanted was marvelous. He took his time eating, looking out the window onto Main Street and enjoying the view. Car styles had changed a good bit in the last ten years and he could not easily distinguish the different makes without checking the name on the front or back. Of all the cars he had seen he liked the little Ford Mustang the best. It reminded him of his T-Bird. It was a shame he couldn't go and get the Thunderbird out of the garage and driven it but that would have attracted too much attention. The big white van he had just purchased was much better suited for what he had in mind.

Howie left the restaurant and headed back to the Ford dealer. They should have his vehicle ready by now. The salesman that he had dealt with met him at the door. The van was parked in one of the diagonal parking places in front of the dealership. "All ready to go,

Mr. Lawson," the salesman said. "It's been fully serviced and filled with gas. The boys just got done putting the license plates on. All you need to do is get in and drive away."

Howie walked to the van, opened the passenger door and placed his two small bags on the passenger's seat. He walked around the van to the driver's door where the salesman was waiting with the keys in his hand. "Now remember, Mr. Lawson, if you have any problem just get in touch with me and we'll take good care of you. Service is our middle name."

"Thanks," Howie said as he got into the van, "but I'm sure everything will be just fine."

Howie backed from the parking space and drove two blocks back to the center of town and parked. Before getting out he opened the attaché case and removed a packet of twenty-dollar bills. Closing the case but keeping it in his hand for safety reasons, Howie got out and locked the van.

His first stop was a store he had often frequented years ago, a beauty parlor. He stood at the glass counter in the front until a middle-aged woman who was working on a hair-do at the rear of the store noticed him. She came to meet him and asked if she could be of assistance.

"I'm looking for a gift for my girlfriend," he answered. "I'd like to get her a wig. Her hair is light so I think a blond one would be best. Do you have something I could look at?"

"We surely do," the lady said as she pulled open a large drawer under the counter where they stood. She set two Styrofoam heads in front of Howie, both with blonde wigs. One was styled long and the other was cut to a shorter length.

"I think this one would be okay," Howie said picking the shorter cut.

"Good choice," the woman said. "Will this be cash or credit card?"

"Cash," said Howie noting the price on the attached ticket.

Howie left the store with the wig still on the head, carrying it in a large hatbox. He placed his purchase in the van and started to drive.

In less than an hour he was at a shopping center on the east side of Columbus. There were numerous stores that sold ladies clothes and he went to each of them buying more gifts for the fictitious girl friend. Next he visited a drug store where he finished up with the cosmetics.

That night Howie stayed at a motel on old route 40, east of Columbus and the next morning headed back to the shopping center to buy a set of luggage to hold all of his recent purchases. When he had everything packed, it was time to outfit the van.

At a store specializing in camping equipment he purchased blankets, sleeping bags and an air mattresses. At a second store he bought battery-powered lanterns and a large stainless steel mirror. Then on to a hardware store to purchase an electric drill, drill bits, fifty-foot extension cord, screws and a screwdriver. He also bought a Stanley cutting tool, Model 10-099 with a retractable blade.

At a gas station he stretched the extension cord and used the drill to make holes to fasten the mirror to the inside wall of the van. When the job was completed he drove off leaving the cord, drill, drill bits and screwdriver laying in the parking lot.

Howie stopped for lunch on the way back to Newton at the same place where he and Jess has stopped so many years before. Again he ate cheeseburgers and this time had Pepsi, his favorite drink with lunch. Not once did he think back to the past. He was considering the refinements he was making to one of his favorite games. He was older and smarter and he had everything worked out to perfection.

Howie spent the rest of the afternoon driving slowly around the town. There was no nostalgia in him as he viewed his old haunts. Instead he was looking for any changes that had occurred while he had been gone. Essentially everything was pretty much as he had left it except there were more one-way streets and automobile traffic was more congested.

He drove carefully as he had always done but now he didn't have a driver's license. It had expired long ago and he had no intention of getting it replaced.

About eight o'clock that night he stopped at a small motel on the South side of town and checked in for the night, paying cash. He carried one large suitcase in with him and tossed it on the bed. In it was the clothes, make-up and wig he would be wearing when he left the next morning. He opened the case and set all of his cosmetics he would need on a dresser in front of a large wall mirror. Next he pulled up a chair and got to work.

Thirty minutes later he was satisfied with the results. The wig and make-up took care of his head and face and for the rest of his facade it was a matter of style and color. Pink and white low cut tennis shoes for his feet, semi-tight Levi's and a pink and white blouse with short sleeves made a perfect summer outfit.

It had been a long time since he had been able to indulge himself and dress this way. Now, as he stretched out on the bed, he was reluctant to change back. He did take off the shoes, pants, and blouse before going to bed so they wouldn't get wrinkled. He left on the underwear and removed a bulky terry cloth robe from the suitcase and slipped it on.

Howie looked in the mirror and Cornelia looked back at him. "Hi, Mama," he said. "Did you miss me?"

"Of course I did, Baby," the mirror answered.

"I wish you wouldn't call me that," Howie said. "How are things going with you?"

"Much better now that we're back together. I'm glad we finally got out of that place."

"It wasn't so bad," Howie answered her. "Nobody bothered us much and I did pretty much as I pleased. Those doctors were a nuisance for a time with all of their questions but they finally gave up. I was more willing to take my time than they were because I had a lot more of it. It's much nicer to be here where we can talk as much as we want. I really like that."

"I do too, honey. What are you going to do now that you're free?"

"There's this game I like to play…it's kinda' hard to explain but I'll try. I do things and get the police to chase me and try to find me. You see, policemen are all alike. They make trouble for people and push them around. The jail guards were like that, always tellin' everyone what to do."

"Isn't that a dangerous game to play?" the mirror asked.

"No, it's okay. I'm just gonna' do little things, just enough to make them know somebody's around. They'll never know it's me."

"All right, you know best, Baby."

"Mama, I wish you wouldn't call me that. How are things with you"

Early the next morning a tall, good looking woman with blonde hair left Howie's room carrying a suitcase which she tossed in the side door of the van. She drove out of the parking lot and headed north looking for a good place to get breakfast. A Perkin's Pancake House caught her eye and she pulled in and parked, locked the van and went inside.

The woman ordered breakfast in a low, husky voice and sat sipping her coffee as she waited for her food. She attracted little attention except for a couple of young men at the counter who noticed her trim figure and captivating blue eyes. She finished her breakfast, eating with obvious pleasure and, after paying her bill with money taken from a shoulder bag, went back to her van.

Howie was elated. Everything had gone perfectly and no one had given him a second glance. Now he was ready for the next step.

He drove to the 'Y', took a room for the next month and paid cash in advance. Even if things didn't work out he could move on and not be out very much. On his first trip to his room he carried one large suitcase and a small cosmetics case. He would bring any additional bags in one at a time so as not to appear over burdened. His room was on the second floor and quite adequate to his needs.

There was a dressing table along the wall on the right as you entered and the bed was on the left. At the far end of the room by a window were two easy chairs and a five-drawer dresser. A large closet with sliding doors was off to one side. A full-length mirror covered the back of the entrance door. Two small stands, a bookcase and a table that could hold a television completed the furnishings. There were two pictures on the wall, one a seascape and the other a street scene of what might have been Paris. The walls were concrete block, painted white. Howie thought the room was perfect.

He unpacked and put his belongings where they should go and, after undressing put on his robe and slippers and headed for the shower room. This was the final test. Inside he found things as he had hoped they would be. There were individual shower stalls with opaque glass doors. The toilet stalls also has doors. Howie walked back to his room and lay down on the bed. He immediately realized he had failed to purchase an alarm clock. He would remedy that as soon as possible. While he was at it he would get a small TV for the room. Now he locked the door and took a nap. He was so happy with being able to do as he pleased.

CHAPTER TWENTY-FOUR

Johnson came to work that day the same as he had been doing for the last twenty-one years. He was operating at his usual efficiency, thirty seconds behind the rest of the world. Johnson was not really inept so much as it just took him a little longer to comprehend everyday life. Because of this he held the perfect job. His seniority allowed him to hold the four to midnight shift and the job of downtown beat man, the same job he had started at all those many years ago on the police department. Andy Johnson was as satisfied with his life as he could possibly be.

He drove to work from the same house, by the same route and to the same parking place every day. He parked in a space that was marked off for one of the judges in municipal court but that judge had always left for the day by the time Johnson arrived at work. Because of his years on the department, supervision turned a blind eye to this minor transgression. He got out of his old Ford, not locking it because he would rather have a thief open the door to find there was nothing worth stealing than break a window for the same result. Besides the car was parked on his beat and he could, more or less, keep an eye on it.

Johnson entered the station through the back parking garage and went into the muster room. It was exactly fifteen minutes before his shift started and the other nine offices were already there. The Sergeant was at the front of the room sitting at a large table with a stack of reports in front of him that he was scanning and sorting into two separate piles. He noted Johnson's arrival by looking up, nodding and starting the daily briefing.

"You all know about the asshole that has been running around the downtown area cutting people. We've received information about the knife he's been using and it could be helpful. When he cut the first one last month, the cuts weren't very bad. The person was cut three times and the injuries were treated with antiseptic and Band-Aids.

The second attack was treated about the same way but the third, forth and fifth needed stitches. The two last weeks were much more serious and one lady needed thirty stitches in her arm and twenty more in her face. That was the first person he's attacked in the face and apparently this guy's getting more out of control. Anyway, the coroner has gone back and talked with several of the victims and he has come up with a theory. He thinks the guy is using one of these knives with a retractable blade like they use in grocery stores to cut the tops off boxes. This way he can carry it in his pocket without hurting himself. Doc Williams also said when the guy first started doing this he only pushed the blade out a little ways but now he has it all the way out and he's going to kill someone. Doc's sure it will only be a matter of time."

"Listen up now," the Sergeant went on, "five of the people who got cut had been to the movies and were either walking home or going to their cars when they were attacked. You all have what little description that is available. All the people who have been cut claim it happens so quick, and the guy runs so fast, they haven't got a very good look at him. Male, white, about five- eight, fairly young and runs like a goddamn rabbit. That's not much to go on but that's all we got. Any questions?"

The first question was the one the Sergeant expected and it came from Patrolman Fred Carter, a three-year veteran who was starting to shed his rookie status. "Can we shoot the little son-of-a-bitch if we get a chance?"

This time the question that had been asked so many times in jest actually amounted to something and the Sergeant held up his hands for quiet before he answered and said, "We discussed this in staff meeting earlier today and this is going to be our policy on the situation. We want this guy and, as of now, you will bring him in by any legal means at your disposal. You all carry loaded guns with the thought in the back of your mind that you may need to use extreme force. If you get a chance at this guy, don't let him get away.

Keep in mind that if you do need to shoot it will probably be in the downtown area so be careful. There are about fifty thousand people living in Newton and we don't want any of them hit by a stray bullet. Also we have two K-9 units patrolling the downtown so if we get into a foot chase let's give the dogs a chance to chew on this guy's ass."

After making that statement the Sergeant held up his hands again and asked for one more thing. "You know this asshole is dangerous so don't do anything foolish and get yourselves hurt. Our job is to catch him, not kill him but I'll back you on whatever move you make."

The officers glanced at each other as they picked up the deadly tone and realized what the sergeant was telling them without actually saying it. He wanted this guy really bad and if you got a chance, punch his ticket for good and certain.

The men also heard another thing that they appreciated and that was when Sergeant McConnell has said he would 'back you on whatever move you make'. All of the street patrolman knew that any other supervisor would have qualified the statement by adding, 'I'll back you up as long as you're right'. Hell's fire, you didn't need backing as long as you were one hundred percent right. You need backing and help when you had to go out on the edge and make the split second decisions. They were glad to be working for Sergeant McConnell; he might be young but they knew they could count on him.

As the men left the assembly room McConnell called to Johnson, asking him to wait a minute. When everyone else had left, McConnell said, "Andy, come up front to the office for a minute. There's something I want to talk to you about."

The two men walked to a small office in the front of the station house and the Sergeant thumped down into a seat behind a desk. Johnson took a seat across from him in an orange fiberglass chair and waited for the Sarge to start the conversation.

McConnell took a deep breath and blew it out between his lips.

He said, "Andy, we're having a hell of a time with this guy cutting people. You heard what I said in the back. Nobody's ever seen anything like it. He just appears and disappears like some kind of goddam ghost. Every time it's happened it's been on the four-to-twelve shift. On every one but the first one I've been working. This thing is making me crazy."

Johnson didn't know what to say so he kept still.

"Andy," the Sergeant asked, "I want you to do something for me, okay?"

"Sure, Sarge, you know I'll do anything I can"

McConnell had his forearms resting on the desk and was leaning forward as though he had a heavy weight on the back of his neck. He took another deep breath and said, "Andy, I've known you since I was a kid growing up and you've always had the downtown beat. Just what do you think about this guy?"

"I don't know, Sarge. The only thing I ever seen like this was that summer we had a guy runnin' around trying to get us to chase him. He'd set traps and get the guys to run into them. I chased him down an alley one night and ended up with two teeth knocked out and a broken nose. That's been more than ten years ago and that guy just quit. Do you suppose there's any chance this guy might just quit?"

"It don't look like it," the Sergeant answered. "Andy, I want you to keep a special watch on the theaters. Look real close at the people going in and out. This guy has got to be there but we keep missing him for some reason. And be careful. This guy would cut you or me as quick as anyone else, quicker maybe."

"Okay, Sarge, I'll keep my eyes open." Johnson stood up to leave as he said, "Is there anything else?"

"No," McConnell replied, "just remember what I said about being careful."

****

McConnell watched Johnson go out the door and knew he had probably been wasting his time but right now he was willing to try anything. He was well aware of the limitations of Johnson as a policeman and tried to allow for them but now he was desperate.

McConnell had gone on the police department in 1959 when he was twenty-three years old. He had made Sergeant four years later. He was probably the youngest Sergeant they ever had but there was no way of being certain. Now he was at his wit's end. When he had to appeal to Johnson for help things were really bad.

****

Johnson left the Sergeant's office and headed for the street. In his mind he was going over what he had been told and sorting out the useable information. He particularly remembered he was supposed to check the theaters and this suited him fine. He touched his back pocket to make sure his paper bag was there and started to walk.

Johnson carried an old-fashioned wooden nightstick on a leather strap and not one of those plastic potato mashers that had no style. While he walked he played with the stick constantly, spinning it like a yo-yo or bouncing it from the sidewalk, into the air and back to his hand. Whenever he was moving the stick would be in motion. People who knew Andy Johnson recognized this trademark and strangers, seeing it for the first time, were fascinated. He was never vain about the display, it was instead an unconscious act on his part that had gone on for all of his years on the beat.

Johnson went casually around the business area as he stopped and talked to everyone he knew. He was heading slowly but inexorably towards his first stop, George's Coffee Shop. Andy had been stopping at George's every day he worked since the first day he had spent on the beat. His training officer had taken him there and Andy had discovered the coffee was free.

The restaurant owner undoubtedly had a last name but Andy didn't know or care what it might be. Andy did know that George had come over from the old country because he had heard George say so. Which old country was hard to say but Andy suspected it might have been Greece. Somewhere along the way George had been told that he should never charge policemen for their coffee and he had always complied.

As Andy entered the front door of the restaurant, George looked up and said by way of greeting, "So Officer, what's new?" George called all of the policemen who came in his shop by one name, Officer, except for the important ones with the three stripes on their sleeves—these men he called Sergeant. Two Lieutenants, two Captains and the Chief stopped in his establishment but they were called Officer the same as Andy Johnson. In George's way of thinking the Sergeants were the only policemen who knew what was going on in the world and they made things happen.

The big, black-rimmed clock on the wall showed four-thirty and Johnson knew he had plenty of time before his five o'clock pull at the call box on Main Street.

There were sixteen bars, two poolrooms and five restaurants on the downtown beat. The rest of the businesses were retail stores that closed about five o'clock and could be ignored until after dark when Andy would make his rounds and check all of the doors and windows.

Johnson sat down at the counter and rested his feet on the adjoining seat, his white socks accenting the space between the top of his high black shoes and the bottom of his shiny blue pants. The owner and Andy talked about the weather and baseball for a few minutes as the policeman drank two cups of coffee and then Andy moved on. He walked slowly along the street, nodding and speaking to the passing community until he arrived at the call box. Lifting the receiver, he waited as the phone automatically rang into the station. The desk officer answered by saying, "Hey Andy, why don't you catch a bad guy tonight and surprise everybody."

"Bullshit!" Andy said as he hung up the phone and went on about his business, ignoring the sarcasm. He had his rounds to make and he headed out. In the cab company office there was a continual penny-ante poker game going on and Johnson kibitzed there a while

before moving on to the lobby
of the biggest downtown hotel. The desk clerk was an old school
buddy and Johnson visited with him about all the local gossip.
Now it was time for Johnson's six o'clock pull—there were no jokes
from the deskman because he was too busy to do any more than
acknowledge the call. With dinnertime approaching, Johnson went
in the back door of Tony's Pizza.

Andy always ate his dinner in the kitchen of whatever restaurant
he visited. Long ago he had discovered that when he ate out front
with the regular customers that someone was always interrupting his
meal with questions or complaints and this was annoying. He sat
down at one of the pizza making tables and ordered up a medium
pepperoni with mushrooms along with two cans of Pepsi. While
he ate he talked to the bakers and delivery boys who were rushing
around the kitchen. In the process he only added one stain to the
accumulation on his necktie.

Tony wasn't there but Andy knew the help had been told to only
charge him half price. He paid one of the bakers what he owed and
Andy thought the boy would probably stick the money in his own
pocket--he did--and Andy headed back to his beat.

It was getting close to his seven o'clock pull and he had not yet
inspected the theaters. He patted his back pocket to make sure he
had not lost his paper bag and started to do what he really lived for,
checking the movie theaters.

****

Earlier, Johnson had no sooner left the station house than the
Prosecuting Attorney had walked in the door. He talked with a
couple of the officers in the record's room before knocking on the
door to the Sergeant's office. He didn't wait for a response before
walking in.

"Mike, you look like somebody who could use a friend, " he said
to the Sergeant.

McConnell was glad to see him in more ways than one. Bob

Bailey had been elected Prosecutor the year before and they had worked on several cases together since then. Many years ago they had imagined this scenario could develop and now it had happened.

"Yeah, I sure could use some help on this cutter we got running around town. You wouldn't believe what I just did. Thirty minutes ago I asked Andy Johnson for help. Not that he isn't a good guy but….is that desperate or what?" McConnell said.

That's the reason I stopped by," Bailey said. "Have you got anything to go on?" He emphasized the word 'anything.'

"Not a goddamn thing," McConnell said with vehemence. "Everyone thinks this has got to be a stranger in town so the detectives have been checking out all the newcomers. They've been to every hotel, motel and rooming house for twenty miles in every direction. Two uniformed men have been calling every real estate dealer who handles rental property. They've also checked out everyone who has purchased a new house in the last six months. Every apartment complex has been checked to see who has moved in recently. They even went back over the rental ads in the newspapers for the last three months and checked on all of them. Hell, we even contacted Welcome Wagon."

"Have you got any better description?" Bailey asked.

"Only what you already know," McConnell answered." "Dark clothes with a toboggan on his head, slender build, fairly young and runs like a rabbit."

"I wish I had some ideas," Bailey said. "but I don't. When I was at the range last Wednesday it was all the men were talking about." Bailey, as Prosecuting Attorney, often accompanied the men on the street and he always carried a gun. He had no illusions about the officers protecting him. Most times it was all they could do to protect themselves.

McConnell brought up a subject only a very close friend could broach when he asked, "How are things at home?"

"About as bad as they get. Jan's going through with the divorce.

She says she can't stand the hypocrisy of politics. The campaign last year was pretty tough on her. She never realized what all it took to win an election and now that it's over it seems that I'm always away from home for one reason or the other. Maybe if we had kids it would help, I don't know. At least without children involved the divorce won't be all that messy."

"If there's anything I can do…," McConnell said, letting the offer hang in the air.

"I appreciate it," Bailey replied, "especially since I know you really mean it, but I guess all we can do now is let things run their course."

The conversation was interrupted by a knock on the door of the office and one of the K-9 handlers entered the room. "Sarge," he said, "I got an idea and I wanted to check with you before I went ahead," and he glanced over at Bailey and added, "Hi Bob, how's it going?"

Bailey nodded to the patrolman as McConnell said, "What have you got in mind?"

"How about me patrolling in a plain car tonight? You know Fullen that runs that car lot on Mercer Street? Anyhow, he's a friend of mine and he said we could use one of his old clunkers if we wanted. I thought it might give us an edge. God knows we can use one."

"I wouldn't think there would be any problem," McConnell said looking over at Bailey for confirmation.

"That's perfectly legal as long as you don't try and make any traffic arrests," the Prosecutor said looking at the K-9 officer. "I hope you do get lucky. Mike and I were just talking about this guy and if he doesn't get caught soon we're going to have murder cases to work on."

"Okay guys, and thanks," the patrolman said. "I'll keep you posted on what's going on,' and he went out of the office.

Alone again, McConnell asked Bailey, "You got any plans for this evening?"

"Nothing special," Bailey said. "I was going to grab a bite to eat and then go back to the office and catch up on some paper work. There's not much sense in me going home."

"Then come on and go with me," the Sergeant said. "As soon as everything's running smooth we'll get a sandwich and I can drop you off at the courthouse."

Bailey nodded and McConnell started to gather up his gear.

As they left the office and headed for the cruiser parking area, Bailey said, "Do you remember that Lawson kid they sent up for murder about ten years ago. Anyway, I was talking to a parole officer over in court today and it seems they let him out of prison. That was a little over a month ago and nobody has seen hide or hair of him since."

"I remember that kid," McConnell said as they started to get in the car. "He used to hang around the poolroom. Quiet, nice looking kid with real blond hair. I was still working on the railroad when that happened but I've heard some of the older guys talking about it. They say it was a real mess."

McConnell backed the cruiser out and started to drive.

****

Howie walked down the hallway of the 'Y'. It was brown and white tile, spotlessly clean with white walls and overhead recessed lights every ten or twelve feet. He passed some of the other residents and they smiled and spoke to each other. Howie went out the front door and down the sidewalk past where his van was parked and headed downtown, three blocks away. He passed two marked police cars during his walk but the men inside paid no particular attention to the young woman with blond hair striding briskly down the sidewalk. It was just past six-thirty when he passed the old beat cop, Johnson, coming out of an alley beside a pizza shop.

****

Johnson saw only a thin girl wearing jeans and a sweater, paying her no real attention. He was patting his back pocket when he passed Howie.

There were two first-run theaters in the downtown. One was the Mainline and it was showing a James Bond thriller, 'You Only Live Twice".

The other big theater was the Audition and a John Wayne movie, 'El Dorado' was playing there.

As he walked, Howie thought back over the preparations he had made for his nightly excursion. That afternoon he had gone jogging on the bike path and had run his usual distance of four miles. He had timed himself at twenty-two minutes and twenty seconds, the fastest time he had ever run. When he had returned to his room he had showered and then rested on the bed for a couple of hours.

When he awoke he had powdered his lower body and slipped into a pair of skin tight Levi's. Next came the pink and white tennis shoes and then a short sleeved dark blue sweater. He had already done his make-up so the only thing left was the short cut blond wig.

Howie was carrying a rather large shoulder bag and he checked the contents one more time. There were two pairs of surgical gloves, his Stanley Model 10-099 cutting knife with a new blade and a medium sized screwdriver. He knew there were three new blades stored in the handle of the knife and the screwdriver was there in case he needed to change blades. He also had money, a comb and cosmetics in case he needed to fix his face.

There was a black nylon jacket and a black toboggan rolled into a ball and shoved in one end.

****

The K-9 officer left the car lot driving an old 1958 Ford. The body was an absolute mess and the interior was none to clean. This didn't hurt a thing due to the fact that his dog kept jumping from the front seat to the back and making a mess of his own. In the cruisers that were assigned to the K-9 units there was a screen between the front and back that prevented this and the dog was enjoying the change. The driver soon found that in spite of its' looks the car ran fine and was equipped with a big 390 V-8 engine. The officer drove around the edge of town so no one would spot the car before he began his search after it got dark.

****

That same night at the Senior Citizen Center, two blocks from the center of town, there was some excitement. Two of the residents were going out again and everyone there knew what that meant.

Linus Peters was a retired railroad engineer who had been living at the center for only a short time. He was seventy-one years old, had lost his wife and had moved to the center to be with people his own age. Soon after he moved in he had become acquainted with one of the women who lived on the floor below him. Her name was Amelia Markham.

Amelia had been living there for nearly three years. When Linus had first moved in she made a point to see him in the halls as often as possible. When he finally got around to noticing her she delivered a plate of fresh baked brownies to his room and one thing led to another and he asked her out to lunch. Amelia was seventy and her banker/husband had left her, as they say, pretty well fixed when he had passed on.

The luncheon had amounted to no more than an afternoon walk to Wendy's for sandwiches and frosties. All the other residents were happy for both of them as things progressed to evening outings together. A couple of weeks ago they had gone to see the movie 'Bambi', had returned to the building and, looking up, they saw smiling faces looking down at them from almost every window.

Tonight they were going to see James Bond fight the evil villain, Blofeld. Linus had read the book and wanted to see the movie. Amelia, on the other hand, didn't know James Bond from a sack of horse chestnuts but she wasn't about to turn down a night out on the town. Because it was such a lovely evening they were going to walk down to see the nine-thirty feature.

****

Officer Johnson had the timing pretty well set on the movies.

He knew he could watch all of "El Dorado' at the Audition and then scurry to the Mainline and catch the end of the James Bond movie. He stood in front of the Audition and watched the people buy tickets, remembering what the Sergeant had said. He didn't see anyone who looked suspicious. The crowd gathered mostly in pairs with a few family groups mixed in. The few men he saw who were alone nowhere near matched the description he had been given. He hardly looked at the women. Johnson walked into the lobby and took a look around. Going back outside Johnson checked his watch and saw it was almost seven o'clock so he went to the call box on the corner and checked in, patting his back pocket as he so often did. Now back to the lobby. Soon it emptied out and now he approached the concession stand.

The high school boy working at the counter knew Johnson well. The policeman had been a fixture around the theater since before the boy had been born and he was well aware of what the officer wanted.

"Hi there, Mr. Johnson," the boy said.

"Evening, son," Johnson said as he reached in his back pocket and pulled out a folded bag, handing it to the boy.

The usual ritual was completed as the boy filled the sack to the top with hot popcorn and handed it back to the policeman. Johnson knew that the theater counted popcorn boxes and not popcorn. He smiled at the boy and walked to the chest high partition that separated the lobby from the seating area. When the scenes were bright Johnson scanned the audience, but as the movie progressed he forgot about that and watched only the movie. He had seen it many times before but that didn't matter. He loved westerns, especially if they had John Wayne in the cast.

****

Howie had seen Johnson standing in front of the theater when he had bought his ticket and had surreptitiously watched him for any reaction. There had been none. Now Howie sat in the theater watching the movie for the second time this week. He had been looking over the patrons for anyone who would fit his need but had not spotted anything promising. He wasn't in any hurry. Last night he hadn't found a quarry and there was a chance that tonight would also prove to be fruitless. Howie had the patience to wait and see what developed.

Halfway through the movie Howie walked to the concession stand, bought a box of popcorn and returned to a different seat where he could scan the other half of the crowd.

****

Johnson left the theater to make his eight o'clock pull and while he was at the call box the Sergeant went by and waved. He saw the prosecutor riding in the Sergeant's car. Johnson ducked back into the theater to watch the second half of the western.

****

It was only eight-thirty and not yet dark when the old Ford parked behind a church on the north edge of the business district. For some reason both the driver and the dog were kind of antsy. They stayed a few blocks north of Main Street so he wouldn't ruin their cover.

****

It was nine o'clock when Linus and Amelia walked out the front door of the Seniors Building and began their stroll towards the theater. The sun had just gone down and it was a beautiful time of day. Linus pointed out the first star in the sky and the old couple smiled at each other. She took his arm in the manner of a close relationship and he reached over to cover her hand with his own. They were still in sight of the Seniors Building and if they could have heard there were many a sigh behind them.

As they passed along Main Street they window-shopped and watched the people coming out of one of the other theaters. A police officer standing on the corner absently was spinning his nightstick like it was a toy on a string. A tall, blond girl stopped next to them to look in a store window and they both noticed her startling blue eyes. They went on to their movie.

****

Because of the Sergeant and the Prosecutor riding around the downtown Johnson had stood on the street corner after his nine o'clock pull. He just watched the people, occasionally speaking to some of them. He noticed an old couple stop and look in a jewelry store window. A tall blond girl was also looking in the window. Nothing suspicious there, he thought. Another cruiser went by and waved. Johnson wished to hell they would hurry up and catch this cutter. There hadn't been this many cruisers on Main Street at this time of night in a long time. The cops didn't like to fight the traffic any better than the civilians. Damned inconvenient, Johnson thought, to have to change his schedule because of this cutter guy.

****

Howie walked behind the old couple that had been looking in the window. There was not much he could do right here with people all around. He wondered where they were going.

****

As it got darker, the old Ford crept into the downtown and started going up and down the alleys, peeking and peering, as the driver liked to think of it. He continued to drive slowly, back and forth, up and down. He was a good cop and had learned patience.

****

Howie followed the old couple to the theater and watched them go inside. He was mildly amused that they would be going to see a James Bond movie. He thought their taste would have been to the something more mundane. After they had been inside for a couple of minutes he bought a ticket and followed them. Howie bought another box of popcorn and started looking around. He saw them seated about halfway down on the right and slipped into a seat three rows behind them.

Howie was now back in the Mainline Theater, a place that had played such a prominent place in his life. He remembered how Moosie and his buddies had chased him and Jess in the back door.

How the two of them had stood behind the screen and watched the people in their seats without them knowing it.

Also he remembered how he had told Jess to take the flashlight and go ahead of him down the steps and then picking up his stick he had hidden nearby and swinging one crashing blow to the back of Jess's head. He had used some rope to tie Jess's hands and feet together and held him under the water in the pool until the bubbles quit coming up. Howie had removed the rope and thrown it in a trash dumpster.

Now he sat and looked at the couple in front of him, making up his mind about what he was about to do, or rather how he was going to do it. He had already made up his mind about what was going to happen; he just wasn't sure exactly where. He had never tried to do two at one time but these feeble old people should be a piece of cake. It would certainly be worth the effort because with as many cops that were running around, when he pulled it off all the police would look really stupid

****

McConnell dropped the prosecutor off at the courthouse and continued to patrol the downtown area. The first time he saw the old Ford with one headlight he wasn't aware that it was his K-9 units. He swung in behind it as it came out of an alley and was just getting ready to turn on his flashing lights when he saw the dog in the back seat. The driver slowed and McConnell pulled up beside it.

"Hey Sarge," the driver called, "I told you I was gonna' be using a plain car and this was the plainest one we could find on the whole lot."

"It sure is," the Sergeant called back. "Did you know you got a headlight out?"

"Yeah, I noticed after it got dark," the K-9 Officer said. "I'm gonna' leave it like that. It helps my disguise."

"Okay with me," McConnell said. "It's ten-thirty now so the next couple of hours should tell the tale for tonight. Good luck."

"You too, Sarge," the dog handler called back.

****

Johnson stood at the rear of the theater and watched Sean Connery make one miraculous escape after the other. He had finished his last sack of popcorn and had the bag folded and safely tucked away in his back pocket. The concession stands were all closed now and the movie would be over shortly after eleven-thirty. He decided to skip the last scene. He liked the show but not as well as he liked westerns. Standing on the corner in front of the Mainline, he watched as the audience started to spill out onto the sidewalk. He saw the old couple he had noticed earlier as they walked away from the movie house, the woman holding onto the man's arm. The weather was perfect for this time of year and they were obviously enjoying it.

****

Howie came out of the theater and stood watching the old couple for a minute to see which way they were headed. They were strolling back the way they had come at a leisurely pace. Officer Johnson was standing on the corner playing with his nightstick. Howie walked around the corner at a normal pace and as soon as he was out of Johnson's sight he cut through an alley and started to jog. As he ran he pulled off his sweater and used it to wipe his face clean of make-up. He jerked off his wig and stuffed it into his shoulder bag along with the sweater. The black toboggan went on his head to cover his blond hair and he slipped into the black nylon windbreaker. Now his clothing was what he wanted.

Howie paused at the corner and looked down the street. He could still see the old couple but now he was ahead of them and they were walking towards him. He pulled the surgical gloves over his hands and slipped his Stanley knife from the inside compartment of his purse. He slid the blade in and out a few times to make sure it operated freely. Howie dashed quickly across the street when no cars were coming; he wanted to stay a block or so in front of the old couple until he found the perfect spot. He was almost across when an old car with one headlight came around the corner a block and a half away. It didn't concern him because he doubted if the driver would have been able to see him. He knew anyone who drove a car like that would not be something to worry about.

Howie made an educated guess that the old man and woman were headed for the Senior Building just up the street a ways. He ran to the end of the next block and waited to see if they were still coming. In a couple of minutes his suspicions were confirmed.

****

The dog handler was not sure there had been anything to see. It was as though the shadows had shifted. You're trying to hard, he told himself. Relax and keep going. He turned his walkie-talkie up a bit so he could hear the conversations between the other cruisers. Up until now he had kept the volume low so the noise wouldn't give him away but now, as it neared midnight, he was ready to call it a night and get out of this junk automobile. I'll give it another thirty minutes, he told himself, and that's all.

****

Amelia had held Linus's arm until they turned the corner off Main Street and their building came into sight. At that point she took his hand in hers' and from a distance they looked like a couple of infatuated teenagers.

The trees and shrubs around the front of the building cast many long shadows because of the well-lit foyer. Linus thought stepping into the shadows for a goodnight kiss might be nice never realizing that Amelia was thinking the same thing. There were so many prying eyes in the building it would be nearly impossible once they went inside. It was as Linus scanned the bushes looking for an appropriate spot that he detected a movement.

****

Howie stepped a little closer to the sidewalk knowing he was invisible to the aged couple's vision. He slid the blade of his knife all the way out and was waiting the final few seconds for them to come within range. No other people were in sight and only one car, three blocks away with one headlight.

Howie stepped out of the bushes and slashed at the woman's face. For a reason he would never understand the old man moved quicker than he would have thought possible. The man swung his arm up and deflected the blow while at the same time suffering a severe cut across the palm of his right hand. The woman stumbled as she fell back, crashing to the ground and letting out an agonizing scream. Howie tried to step around the old man to get at the woman but found the man blocking his path. He swung the knife a second time, this time his target was the man's face.

Linus suffered a terrible wound across his left eye and nose, blood pouring from the gash. Howie struck for the third time, now for the neck and as he did so the woman screamed louder than ever. It was then that Howie became aware of another noise, the old car with one headlight was less than a block away, its' engine roaring. Howie turned and started to run.

****

At the sound of the first scream the officer tried to figure out where it might be coming from. He knew that the echoes around the buildings could be deceiving. Then, three blocks ahead, he saw people on the corner and realized they were struggling. He slammed the gas pedal to the floor, throwing the dog against the back seat as the big V-8 did its' job. The driver was within half a block when he saw a figure dressed in black break away and start running in the opposite direction. The other two figures were both down on the sidewalk. He slid to a stop and jumped from the car to pull the back door open, pointed his finger at the fleeing figure and gave the dog the command, "GET HIM!!, GET HIM!!"

The policeman looked at the people on the ground and saw that residents were running from the building to come to their aid. Leaving them, he ran off in pursuit of his dog.

****

Sergeant McConnell was four blocks away when the radio sprang to life. "K-9 One in pursuit of subject in the area of Senior Center. Subject dressed in black and last seen headed west. K-9 Thunder is loose and also in pursuit." He added this last so the other officers would be aware of the attack dog. They would know better than to get out of their cars and in the dog's path.

****

Johnson was halfway between the theater and the station house, oblivious to what was developing. He had wrapped the strap of his nightstick around his handcuff case and was preparing to draw his pistol. For years he had watched the fast draw of the cowboys in the movies and tonight, alone and bored on a deserted street, he was going to practice for a few minutes.

****

As Howie started to run he retracted the blade of his knife and slid it into the back pocket of his jeans. He stripped off the rubber gloves and shoved them into his shoulder bag and threw the bag onto a garage roof as he ran by. Howie made two left turns and was now headed back downtown and toward his many sanctuaries. Behind him he could hear the dog barking and he knew he had to find a place to hide pretty quick. He was back downtown when he realized he still had the knife in his back pocket. As he came to a corner he threw the knife to his right as far as he could throw it and saw it fall through a grate in the sidewalk. There was a figure in the shadows near where he threw the knife but it was looking the other way. He increased his speed as he heard more and more sirens start to sound.

****

McConnell made an educated guess and slowed his cruiser thinking that the suspect would circle around and head back downtown. He was right but as he went west on Main Street, Howie ran east one block to the north of him on a parallel street. They passed in the middle of the block and the Sergeant didn't see him.

****

Neither did Johnson see Howie as he crouched with his hand over his gun. As he glanced behind him to make sure he was alone, a black clad figure ran across the street ahead of him. Neither did he see an object come flying through the air and disappear down a grate. Satisfied no one was watching, his hand slapped towards his Smith & Wesson, jerking it from his holster. To his horror the gun jumped from his hand and went skittering along the sidewalk and disappeared down a grate a few feet in front of him. Just as he reached the grate and looked down a huge dog galloped through the intersection ahead. He never saw it. The hole under the grate was only about a foot deep and by using his flashlight Johnson could see his gun. He started working the grate loose to retrieve his weapon. He was still working as the out of breath dog handler went pounding down the street fifty feet away.

****

At the end of the next block Howie's flight ended. The dog knew his job and he hit Howie in the lower legs, spilling him to the pavement and then fastening his teeth in the meaty part of Howie's thigh. Howie knew better than to fight and he sat still waiting to see what would happen next. Ironically he was only a few feet from the back fire door at the Mainline Theater that could have led to his possible escape. In less than a minute Howie had plenty of company.

****

McConnell drove past the arrest scene and saw that everything was under control so he headed back to where the chase had started. He drove slowly, looking for anything that might be helpful when he saw Johnson down on his hands and knees on the sidewalk. The Sergeant stopped immediately.

"Hey Andy, are you okay?" he called.

Johnson looked up to see that the Sergeant was almost on top of him. He had just managed to recover his gun and was in the process of putting the grate back into place.

"Yeah, Sarge," Johnson said, "I'm all right."

"What the hell are you doing down on the sidewalk looking in that hole?" McConnell asked.

"Well, it's like this," Johnson lied, "I thought I saw somebody throw something down in there and I was takin' a look to see what it was."

"Let me help ya'," the Sergeant said. "We just had a chase go down the street there and maybe he's the one who threw it. We think we caught that cutter that's been giving us so much trouble."

McConnell shined his light down into the hole and saw the knife off to one side. Johnson started to reach for it when the Sergeant jerked his arm back.

They could both see there was blood on the knife and the Sergeant said, "Good God Gussie, I think you just recovered the weapon. It looks like the guy must have thrown it here when he ran by. Good work, Andy, good work!"

McConnell found a couple of popsickle sticks in the hole and used them to pick up the knife. "You got anything on you we can put this in?" he asked Johnson.

"Uh..no..wait..yeah," Johnson answered remembering the sack in his back pocket. He fished it out and the Sergeant dropped the knife inside.

McConnell handed the bag to Johnson and told him to hang onto it and said something about chain of evidence that Andy didn't understand.

Both men got into the Sergeant's car and headed for the station. When they arrived they were informed that Linus Peters was dead, his throat cut, and Amelia Markham had suffered a broken hip and had been taken to the hospital. Another old resident had suffered a heart attack and died after viewing Peters lying in a pool of blood.

CHAPTER TWENTY-FIVE

At eight o'clock the next morning Howie sat alone in an interrogation room. He had been fed a breakfast of cornflakes, milk and black coffee.

Last night they had taken all of his clothes and issued him a set of blue coveralls and a pair of cotton slippers. Howie sat patiently waiting to see what would happen next.

When the officers had taken his clothes the night before there had been a few remarks over Howie's underwear but he had been oblivious to the comments. He had known why they were taking his clothes. They were searching for evidence that would connect him to the murder of the old man. To the naked eye he had not seen any stains on his clothing so now he continued to wait.

When Bob Bailey came into the room and introduced himself Howie was slightly taken aback. He had not known that Bailey was the prosecuting Attorney until right then. Bailey was dressed smartly in a three-piece suit and appeared to be very much at ease. He looked to Howie like a man waiting to play his trump card at just the right moment.

"Well Howard," Bailey said, "it's been a long time. I think I was still in college when you…a…left town, shall we say."

"When I was sent to prison, you mean," Howie corrected.

"Exactly," Bailey answered. "Just the other day I was talking with your parole officer and he was concerned about you. He said he hadn't heard from you since your release. Just for the record you're now being held for parole violation but I want to talk to you about something else. Do you mind?"

"Not at all," Howie said. "It's always nice to talk with old friends."

"Good," Bailey answered. "Let's get right to it then. These are Miranda forms," and he picked up two sheets of paper from the table between them and handed one to Howie. "We'll just read them together and then I'll ask you to sign yours."

The procedure was quickly formalized and Bailey went to work. "What can you tell me about the old man who got his throat cut last night? I suppose you know he died?"

"Yeah, the uniformed cops told me. They seemed to think I might have done it."

Bailey sat back in his chair, steepled his fingers under his chin and said, "Anytime something like this happens there is always the unexpected to contend with and that has a big influence on the outcome. Luck, or whatever you want to call it has a lot to do with every case. Sometimes we are fortunate and occasionally it goes the other way. This time we got lucky."

Howie listened with rapt attention. They were discussing what could be a matter of life and death for him. He looked at the Prosecutor and waited for him to continue.

Bailey did not. He sat looking at Howie and gave the appearance of being very much in control of the situation. Howie waited for as long as he could before weakening and asking, "What do you mean?"

Bob Bailey smiled knowingly when Howie broke the silence and asked the question.

"Let me tell you what happened," Bailey said. "You hid in front of the Senior's Building and waited for those two old people to walk right up to you. Next you jumped from the bushes and tried to attack the woman but the man got in your way. The woman was knocked to the ground in the struggle and broke her hip. Linus Peters continued to fight and you cut his throat. When you saw a car coming you ran away with the Police K-9 chasing you and along the way you threw your weapon down a grate before the dog caught up. I'll grant you that, you can really run. This is where we got lucky and you messed up."

"Just what are you getting at?" Howie asked, impatient with Bailey's superior attitude.

"When you threw the knife away you almost hit an Officer with it. The downtown beat cop, Andy Johnson saw you throw the knife and recovered it from where it landed. When the lab men examined it, all they looked for at first were blood and fingerprints. The blood matched the deceased, Mr. Peters. The only fingerprint was a partial we got from one of the spare blades found in the handle. There were smudges in the blood but no real prints. We think you were wearing gloves when you handled the knife. Then we got our second piece of luck. On the pants you were wearing we found lots of popcorn residue. We also found the same thing on the knife and the lab men tell me that even in things as mundane as popcorn and salt there are different characteristics. We got a perfect match."

Howie sat still looking down at the table. He went back over everything in his mind but couldn't figure out how popcorn or salt could have got on his knife. He had carried it in his purse separate from everything else. He had removed the knife only after he had donned the surgical gloves.

"Tell me more," Howie said.

"Nothing more to say," Bailey answered. "We have enough evidence to get a conviction, I'm sure of that. Now do you want to tell me a few things?"

"Maybe," Howie said. "First tell me what the charges are going to be?"

"I'm speaking for the Prosecutor's office when I tell you we won't make any kind of deal. If you come clean and tell me everything all I can do is let the judge know you were cooperative. I will agree not to seek the death penalty."

"Suppose I tell you about other things that don't have anything to do with last night?" Howie asked. "Would you agree not to charge me with any of that stuff?"

Howie endured the prosecutor's scrutiny for several seconds as the proposition was mulled over by Bailey. He answered and said, "Okay, Howard, I can live with that. You will not be charged with any crime other than the Peters murder. Now what do you want to tell me?"

An hour later Bailey stopped Howie's oration by saying, "How about we take a break and have a cup of coffee?"

"Sure," Howie said, "and I need to use the bathroom."

Bailey pressed a button to summon a jailer to take Howie to the toilet and then he walked out into the lobby of the station house. Sergeant McConnell was waiting for him there.

"Have you been listening to what this Lawson guy's been saying?" Bailey asked.

"Yeah, I sure have," McConnell, said shaking his head. "How many has he admitted to killing so far?"

"Eleven so far, counting the one last night and the one he went to jail for. If you add the one that died from the heart attack last night, it makes twelve. Good God, I don't know how much more of this I can take."

Bailey was pale as a ghost. He had heard Howie speak with absolutely no remorse about anything he had done. Bailey turned suddenly and rushed into the restroom. McConnell followed discreetly and heard the Prosecutor in one of the stalls retching his guts out. The Sergeant waited until Bailey appeared and handed him a paper cup full of water.

"Are you going back in there?" McConnell asked.

"Yeah, let's get it over with. Make sure you get it all recorded so we won't need to do it again."

"We're getting it," McConnell answered. "The part about him staying at the YWCA caught us all by surprise. You can be certain that every sound in that room will be on tape."

"They still got coffee in the lab?" Bailey asked.

"Cum'mon," the Sergeant answered. "I'll buy."

Bailey returned to the room to find Howie waiting calmly in the same chair. His hair and eyes made him look like an angel while in reality he was a monster. Bailey felt as though he was losing control as he sat across from this killer and was starting to feel as cold towards Howie as Howie had been to his victims. That the man was insane there was no doubt. Bailey knew with the information they had gathered that Howie would never go to prison. He would end up in a psychiatric hospital. It was possible he could even be free at some time in the future. God help the people if he ever got back on the street. Bailey handed a cup of coffee to Howie and waited for him to continue.

"Are you ready to go on?" Howie asked as he sipped his coffee.

"Do you mean you've got more to tell me about?" Bailey answered.

"I surely do," Howie said leaning forward on the table, resting his forearms and looking right into Bailey's eyes. "I wanna' tell you how I killed your MAMA!!!" Howie screamed out this last word.

CHAPTER TWENTY-SIX

The jury filed back into the crowded courtroom and took the seats that they had occupied for the last several days. As soon as they had reached their assigned places the bailiff stood and said loudly, "All rise. Court is now in session, the honorable Judge Stepleton presiding."

The judge entered the courtroom in his black robe and went up the five steps to his ornate mahogany desk. As he sat down the bailiff called out "Be seated."

The judge looked over at the jury seated in the enclosure on his right and said, "Ladies and gentlemen of the jury, have you reached a verdict?"

The jury foreman rose and said, "We have, your Honor."

The judge spoke again, following the ritualized format by saying, "Bailiff, please bring me the verdict."

The black shirted deputy walked to the foreman and took a folded piece of paper from his hand and returned to the judge's bench. When the judge took the paper from the deputy's hand he studied it for more than a minute. He then handed the paper back to the deputy who returned it to the jury foreman.

From his seated position behind his bench the judge began to speak. "There has been considerable interest in this trial from the very start. The courtroom has been filled to standing room only since the first day and now it is about over and I'm going to take an unusual action. I am going to order the courtroom cleared of all spectators. Only the press may stay along with the attorneys for both sides. Bailiff, see that my orders are carried out."

There were murmurs of protest as the bailiff ushered the many spectators into the hallway. He pulled the two large swinging doors shut and stood with his back to them and facing the judge across the large courtroom. With the crowd gone the press moved to take seats in the front row.

When everyone had settled, the judge looked at the foreman and said, "Mr. Foreman, would you please read your verdict."

"Yes, Your Honor," he said. "We, the jury, find the defendant NOT GUILTY."

The judge held up his hands for silence, quieting the press who had stirred noticeable at the pronouncement and said, "I thank the jury for handling this very difficult trial and bringing in the verdict. I am going to add my sentiment to theirs'."

The judge looked directly at Bob Bailey as he continued. "This trial and the events leading up to it have been bizarre to say the least. When we listened to the taped confession of Howard Martin Lawson, we never expected what came out at the very end. It was then we knew that justice had been served. The man who had done so many terrible things in this town did not deserve to live. As the jury has seen fit to say, Bob Bailey did not commit murder with that final gunshot that ended the taped confession. Instead he executed a monster that had preyed on this town for twenty years."

The judge had actual tears in his eyes as he said, "Mr. Bailey, you're free to leave the court. You and the jury have earned my deepest gratitude."

****

Sergeant Mike McConnell was standing in the doorway that led to the jury room and went immediately to Bailey's side, forcing his way through the throng of reporters. "This way, Bob," he said. "Let's get the hell out of here."

When McConnell had heard the sound of the gunshot on the morning of the confession he wasn't sure what had happened. He had rushed in to see Bailey placing his gun back in its' holster under his coat and Howard Lawson on the floor with a bullet in the head.

As he drove Bailey back to his apartment, McConnell was relieved that the jury had seen fit to acquit him. Bailey had lost his job as Prosecutor but under the circumstances that wasn't all bad. In fact he was the biggest hero in Newton and his law practice should benefit accordingly.

When they arrived at Bailey's place they were surprised to see Bailey's wife parked out front. She got out of her car as they pulled up and started walking towards them. Bailey jumped from McConnell's car and ran to meet her. They were embracing and talking a mile a minute as McConnell drove off.

It had been a fabulous day. First Andy Johnson got a medal of commendation and a front-page story complete with his picture for being instrumental in solving the murder by recovering the murder weapon.

The jury acquits Bob and saves his career and possibly his marriage.

When McConnell arrived home he walked into the house to find his wife, Sally, sitting in the couch and crying like a baby, the sobs and tears rolling out.

"What's wrong, honey," he asked. "Didn't you hear the good news about Bob? The jury found him not guilty."

"Yes, I heard it on a special news bulletin just a little while ago," Sally said, "but something else happened. An attorney named Berry was here and left these papers. That Howie Lawson, the one that Bob shot…well… he left a will. Years ago when we were still in school I went for a ride one day in his car. We went to Columbus and got some White Castles. Just that one time. I never saw him much after that. Well…well…" and she started to pour tears again.

Sally handed a fat white envelope to her husband and said, "He left everything he had to me, his whole estate." There were more huge sobs following her statement

"Here, let me take a look at the figures," her husband said as he started unfolding the papers. " He probably didn't have much but… JESUS CHRIST!" and he started laughing and crying right along with her.

<u>THE END</u>